Ghost
Tears

Ghost Tears

A Novel

Helen Lamberton Gates

Helen Lamberton Gates

SUNSTONE
PRESS

SANTA FE

Sunstone books may be purchased for educational, business, or sales promotional use. For information please write: Special Markets Department, Sunstone Press, P.O. Box 2321, Santa Fe, New Mexico 87504-2321.

Book and cover design › Vicki Ahl
Body typeface › Book Antiqua
Printed on acid-free paper
∞
eBook 978-1-61139-457-3

Library of Congress Cataloging-in-Publication Data

Names: Gates, Helen Lamberton, 1937- author.
Title: Ghost tears : a novel / by Helen Lamberton Gates.
Description: Santa Fe : Sunstone Press, [2016]
Identifiers: LCCN 2016001666 (print) | LCCN 2016013767 (ebook) | ISBN 9781632931160 (softcover : alk. paper) | ISBN 9781611394573
Subjects: LCSH: Female friendship--Fiction. | Haunted houses--Fiction. | Santa Fe (N.M.)--Fiction. | GSAFD: Mystery fiction.
Classification: LCC PS3607.A78853 G48 2016 (print) | LCC PS3607.A78853 (ebook) | DDC 813/.6--dc23
LC record available at http://lccn.loc.gov/2016001666

SUNSTONE PRESS IS COMMITTED TO MINIMIZING OUR ENVIRONMENTAL IMPACT ON THE PLANET. THE PAPER USED IN THIS BOOK IS FROM RESPONSIBLY MANAGED FORESTS. OUR PRINTER HAS RECEIVED CHAIN OF CUSTODY (COC) CERTIFICATION FROM: THE FOREST STEWARDSHIP COUNCIL™ (FSC®), PROGRAMME FOR THE ENDORSEMENT OF FOREST CERTIFICATION™ (PEFC™), AND THE SUSTAINABLE FORESTRY INITIATIVE® (SFI®). THE FSC® COUNCIL IS A NON-PROFIT ORGANIZATION, PROMOTING THE ENVIRONMENTALLY APPROPRIATE, SOCIALLY BENEFICIAL AND ECONOMICALLY VIABLE MANAGEMENT OF THE WORLD'S FORESTS. FSC® CERTIFICATION IS RECOGNIZED INTERNATIONALLY AS A RIGOROUS ENVIRONMENTAL AND SOCIAL STANDARD FOR RESPONSIBLE FOREST MANAGEMENT.

WWW.SUNSTONEPRESS.COM
SUNSTONE PRESS / POST OFFICE BOX 2321 / SANTA FE, NM 87504-2321 /USA
(505) 988-4418 / ORDERS ONLY (800) 243-5644 / FAX (505) 988-1025

Dedicated to
William, Anne and James

Acknowledgements

My profound thanks to my son, James Alley, for his endless and good natured tech support, to my daughter, Anne Lamberton Alley, for her encouragement and information concerning animal traits and law, and to my step-daughter, Amy Gates, for her knowledge and love of pueblo culture. Elizabeth Trupin-Pulli performed a meticulous editing job; Betty Baxter offered thematic ideas; and Susan Harrison Kelly provided artistic expertise.

I also appreciate the invaluable suggestions of those who read my manuscripts: Claudia Adams, Nan Bourne, Helen Brunet, Deborah Cornelius and Gertrude Wilmers.

Two helpful books were *Santa Fe Ghosts* by Susan Blumenthal and *Gifts of the Crow* by John Marzluff and Tony Angell.

Above all, I'm deeply grateful to my beloved husband, William Gates, for his brilliant assistance with each and every step in the evolution of this book.

Prologue

Each August, for the past twenty years, Pat, Louise and Carol left their families in Midland, Texas to attend Indian Market in Santa Fe, New Mexico. This was their special week together. They'd been sorority sisters in college, and the trip gave them a chance to deepen their friendship while adding to their Native American art and jewelry collections.

They always rented the same adobe house on Upper Canyon Road, from which, when Indian Market was over, they hiked the surrounding mountains. They started on the lower trails at Bandelier and Holy Ghost Canyon, then, as they grew accustomed to the altitude, progressed to Santa Barbara Canyon and the Winsor Trail. They marveled at the brilliant skies, the abundant wild flowers — especially the blue-purple gentians — and the tumbling streams. The aspens were beginning to think about turning their glorious, autumn gold. From time to time, the women found a fallen, saffron-colored leaf, and sometimes, a brilliant red one.

But this year there was trouble. Pat, who always made the arrangements for the rental and a daily maid, reported the Canyon Road house was no longer available. It had been sold and the agent had no other similar property in Santa Fe. After many calls and emails, Pat located an old adobe house, a few miles north, outside the village of Tesuque.

And this year Louise's emotional state presented a problem. Her husband had suffered a massive heart attack in April and died unexpectedly. Louise's initial devastation had become a chronic low-level anxiety. Her only child retreated to a summer job in New Hampshire, so it was up to friends to offer companionship, support, and comfort. The annual trip to Santa Fe seemed an ideal get-away, but Louise refused to go. "I'm a mess. You don't want jittery ol' me around. I'd be a drag. Please, please, go without me!"

But Pat and Carol insisted. If she didn't come, they wouldn't go either. Finally, Louise reluctantly relented.

They left early in the morning on the Thursday before Indian Market weekend, traveling in Carol's Mercedes SUV, which had plenty of space for transporting their expected art haul, as well as the ability to convey them safely to the trailheads. After stopping in Santa Fe to get keys and directions to the Tesuque rental, they arrived in good time to unpack, have a drink, and enjoy a picnic supper on the terrace.

The house was graceful and spacious. There were four West-facing bedrooms with baths. Carol and Pat insisted on Louise having the grandest. They had met the maid, Dolores Chavez, who was leaving as they arrived. Dolores would come each morning to straighten up, clean, and wash the dinner and breakfast dishes.

Indian Market didn't officially open to the public until Saturday, so they spent Friday getting in groceries and touring galleries in Santa Fe. Upon their return, they were disturbed to find the front door wide open, several chairs in the kitchen overturned, pictures crooked on their hooks, and sofa pillows on the living-room floor. Upon careful inspection, they concluded nothing was missing. The maid, Dolores, must have gone into a whirlwind cleaning, and hurriedly left, without straightening-up. The ladies agreed that thorough cleaning-people seldom possessed a curator's touch. "My Rosie leaves our house looking like the Titanic," Carol asserted. Nevertheless, it was agreed that Pat would speak to Dolores about leaving the house in a more civilized state.

No one slept well. It was probably the wind, and the cries of coyotes and owls, that disturbed them. Nevertheless, they were eager to get to Indian Market right after breakfast. Dolores arrived just as they were leaving. After recounting the previous day's chaos, Pat suggested to Dolores that she make a point of leaving the house in good order.

"You can count on that," Dolores exclaimed. "But you might as well know, this house is haunted. Nothing is ever taken, nothing broken, but when new people come, it upsets the ghost."

All four women were standing together in the patio as Dolores spoke. The friends glanced at each other and Carol laughed, but Louise looked terrified. Pat said to Dolores, matter-of-factly, "Well, we'd appreciate it if, in future, you'd smooth over the ghost's activities before our return."

As they drove into Santa Fe, Carol broke the stunned silence: "Well, that's the damnedest excuse for carelessness I've ever heard!"

"She's pretty creative, isn't she?" Pat replied.

"I thought it was kind of scary," Louise said.

"It'll be all right, honey," Pat reassured her.

Unfortunately, it wasn't. Though everyone had a terrific time at Saturday's Indian Market. Louise bought a magnificent black-on-white jar from an Acoma Pueblo potter, and Pat purchased a Zuni polychrome pot. Carol was delighted to find a pair of Hopi kachina dolls. She'd been searching for kachinas for her collection but hadn't dreamt she'd come across anything so fine and affordable. All three friends were ecstatic. Perhaps on Sunday, if their luck held, they'd find some marvelous jewelry.

Thunderheads built throughout the afternoon. Suddenly the clouds turned black, lightening flashed, and colossal winds threatened to blow down the Indians' stalls. Carol, Louise, and Pat raced for the car, clutching their treasures. They reached shelter just as a furious downpour of hail descended. Visibility was nil. They sat in the SUV almost twenty minutes before they could drive back to Tesuque.

They waited out the remainder of the storm inside the house, hoping it would clear, so they could grill steaks outside. Finally, the hail ceased, the sun broke out, and they were able to move to the terrace. The slanting sun imparted the magic of a lit stage. Off in the distance, they saw curtains of receding rain. Hail had beaten down the surrounding growth, releasing its pungent scent. The three friends stood together taking deep breaths of the damp, fragrant air.

"Oh, look!" cried Louise. "Look over there!" They turned and saw the largest, brightest, double rainbow ever, arched above the mountains. "That's a miracle..." Louise whispered.

Dinner was delicious and the three women happily reviewed the day and their expectations for Sunday. When the light waned, Louise confessed, "I shouldn't have had that second glass of wine. I'm really sleepy. And I'm feeling a little chilled. Would you all mind if I excused myself to take a warm bath? It's about beddy-bye time for me."

"Go right ahead, Sweetie," Carol said. When Louise was out of earshot, she said to Pat, "I think it's the first time she's been happy since Ronny's death."

"It was a wonderful day," Pat replied. "We were right to make her come with us."

After a few contemplative moments, while the landscape fell into shadow, and a myriad of stars appeared across the sky, Carol said, "This is such a beautiful spot. It's really nicer than the Canyon Road place, but you know, there's something creepy about it. Have you noticed that moaning sound? It was very faint yesterday, but it's louder now."

The two women stood listening. "Yes," Pat said, after a moment. "What could it be?"

The night was suddenly pierced by a terrible scream. "Louise!" they gasped in unison and ran into the house.

They found Louise struggling to get up from the bathroom floor, her eyes wide, her face deathly pale. In a terrified whisper, she said, "I slipped getting out of the bath. Something pushed me."

When Dolores arrived the next morning, she was not surprised to find that the tenants and their belongings had departed.

1

The room in which she stood was eerily out of keeping with its surroundings.

Delia Hager Duval, the well-known garden columnist, suspected her cousin had simply transplanted her family's Maryland guestroom in its entirety. But this was New Mexico and the effect was bizarre. Later, looking back, Delia thought the queerness of that moment anticipated the uncanny events to follow.

Alice Spencer's flat, stuccoed house stood in a small development off a winding road north of Albuquerque. The guest room had two metal-framed windows facing east, which overlooked a desolate wintry garden surrounded by a low wall. A vast straw-colored field of dark, grazing cattle stretched beyond. In the distance, triangular mountains dusted with snow rose abruptly from the dry, flat land. Delia remembered telling her new husband, Jean-Paul, as she navigated from their road atlas, that the mountains were called the Sandias.

Happy to have finally arrived after an eventful, first-time cross-country road trip, Delia, Jean-Paul, and their two Bassets, Rumpus and Hark, had sprung from the car at the end of Alice Spencer's drive. Delia hadn't seen her cousin since Alice was twenty and Delia a girl of ten. Their mothers had been sisters and Alice, like Delia, had had a Maryland childhood. But because of their age difference and subsequent geographic separation—Alice had studied anthropology at the University of New Mexico, married a scientist and remained in Albuquerque—their paths seldom crossed.

Alice, followed by a small, excited terrier, had emerged from her open garage, spreading her arms in a gesture of welcome. Rumpus and Hark immediately raced off with the terrier, appropriately named Zippy. Alice came first to Delia, hugged her, and then turned to shake hands with Jean-Paul. Delia noted her husband intently studying Alice's face as she welcomed them. Delia, too, had wondered how Alice would look. Would she still see the face she'd known as a child, or would age have changed her cousin beyond recognition?

As if reading her mind, Alice proclaimed, "Delia, dear little Delia, I'd have known you anywhere. You've hardly changed at all—except you've grown up! Your hair's a little darker—lucky you, it hasn't started to gray—and you've still got Granny's brilliant green eyes." Alice held her affectionately by each arm and Delia laughingly studied Alice in return. Alice had changed a great deal and Delia doubted she would have recognized her except for a particular family look: broad brow, long, sharpish nose, and, like Delia's, a small mouth that turned up at the corners in repose. A happy mouth, her father used to call it. Delia noticed, too, that Alice's hands, like her own, were vital and exceptionally beautiful, with long tapered fingers and dainty wrists. Delia took great care of her hands and now, since she'd been away from her garden for several weeks, noted with satisfaction that the nails had grown and were easy to keep shaped and polished. However, Alice's hands of almost identical proportions were rough and callused. Obviously, she worked hard with her hands and lacked, Delia surmised, her own vanity. From the corner of her eye Delia saw Jean-Paul reach back into the car for the camera and within minutes he began snapping pictures of this long over-due reunion.

Alice was more than half a head taller than Delia, almost as tall as the lean and sinewy Jean-Paul. Her long gray hair was pulled back in a ponytail, held by a silver barrette. She wore a plaid flannel shirt, a man's watch with a big face, jeans and running shoes. Unlike Delia's, her face was weather-beaten and deeply lined. Delia noticed Alice moved stiffly, due to the arthritis in her hips. (She had written Delia that she was considering hip replacements.) But the crow's feet around her eyes suggested that she—like Delia—was blessed with a happy nature. Although close to retirement, age had not diminished Alice's spirit. Clearly, she remained a vigorous, dependable, no-nonsense sort of woman with an active body and an enquiring mind.

Jean-Paul had begun to remove a few things from the car. They didn't need much as they planned to stay only one night before going on to Santa Fe.

"Here, let me help you." Alice picked up two bags and strode back into the garage. Delia and Jean-Paul, hands full, followed, smiling secret smiles. They each knew the other was thinking how funny it was to greet guests and lead them in through a garage. They sidled between a large four-wheel drive vehicle and a muddy red pick-up truck, an assortment of tools, skis, a wheel barrow and several pick-axes, before arriving at what in Maryland would be referred to as a mud room where parkas, jackets, boots, wide-brimmed hats and dog equipment completed the décor. Continuing to follow their hostess through a similarly crowded kitchen where something fragrant cooked in the oven — a pork roast, Delia correctly surmised, they reached a dining room that segued into a cluttered but not unattractive living room with a large stone fireplace and sliding glass doors leading to the walled, wintry, patio. Flanking the fireplace were two elderly, comfortable-looking couches, a large low table covered with books and magazines of the western variety, and against the far wall an upright piano piled with stacks of music. A cello leaned precariously in the corner. Delia hoped her Bassets wouldn't bump against it during their playful attentions to Zippy.

"Just this way, m'dears," said their guide as they turned into a hall. The front door was directly before them and again the guests turned to each other amused. Delia and Jean-Paul were intensely visual and rather formal people. Their Maryland life was fairly traditional and their European life was decidedly so. This front door looked unused. Then, immediately beyond the living room, the first door off the hall was the peculiar guestroom. Well, not peculiar exactly — just out of place.

"We'll have dinner in about an hour. When you're settled, come out for a drink. It's chilly, isn't it? Jean-Paul, would you light the fire in the living room while I finish fixing supper? Matches on the coffee table."

Off he went, giving his wife's shoulder a squeeze. She could tell he liked her cousin. She did, too. It was a case of instant rapport.

Delia went to the window and saw the three dogs tearing through the field beyond, free from the car, working off pent-up energy. She was glad to see their racing path avoided the cattle. Rumpus and Hark had enough experience not to tangle with large creatures of doubtful disposition. Since Delia had sold her Baltimore house and moved to Jean-Paul's country place, the Bassets had lost their city ways and become canny rural animals.

As she continued gazing out the window, she was struck by the extraordinary brilliance of the late afternoon light and the contrasting depth of shadows. The sun would soon set, but fluffy little clouds tinged with gold still cast their dark shapes upon the earth. Delia loved the mirrored patterns of nature: plots of melting snow echoing the shape of clouds above or over-hanging branches with leaves arranged like the stones in water below.

Now, this abundance of cloud shadows sharpened the dramatic articulation of the harsh mountain shapes. Delia had never seen anything like it, except, perhaps, in the south of France. Here the light offered a clarity that her native Maryland countryside seldom achieved: the ancient time-smoothed Blue Ridge Mountains were usually a hazy, subtle, gentle blue. But these young, impetuous Sandias, poking up in aggressive geometric shapes, offered a study in contrasts.

Turning back to the room, Delia experienced a sense of dislocation. She'd expected knobby fabrics, casual furniture and brilliant colors to stand against the strong New Mexico light. But no, the room was furnished in faded pale silks, Georgian mahogany furniture, a fifties-style kidney-shaped dressing table with frilly skirt and a mirrored top beneath a three-paneled standing mirror reflecting tiny porcelain boxes and silver-framed family pictures. Small, worn, Oriental rugs covered the beige wall-to-wall carpet. There were twin canopied mahogany beds, matching antique dressers covered with more silver relics, and an antique chaise longue with several limp satin pillows.

Like many guestrooms, this one did not anticipate guests. It was complete unto itself with no space for the belongings of visitors. Their overnight bags stood on the floor without a place to alight except the silken bedspreads or the chaise longue. Delia opened the closet door hoping to find luggage racks, but the closet was full of clothing, precariously piled boxes, and, on the floor, boots, shoes, and a sprawling vacuum cleaner. Luckily there were four free wire hangers, slightly askew, looking forlorn but useful.

But Delia couldn't keep from glancing out the window: it was such an odd and seductive landscape. A flock of crows now roosted along the adjacent patio wall and in several nearby trees. The dogs were nowhere to be seen; they'd probably returned to the house. She needn't worry. Alice and Jean-Paul would take action should anything be amiss. It was nice having a sensible husband. Her first husband, Arthur, who had died several years before, had also been a responsible, kindly man — not fascinating or as sexually enthralling as Jean-Paul, but a dependable person. For the most part, Delia considered herself a woman of immense good fortune, though at the moment, she glanced toward the twin beds with disappointment. Sleeping with her lover — now, her husband — was one of the joys of her life.

After the long drive, she decided to freshen up in a quick shower. The adjoining bathroom, though small, was well equipped with fluffy towels, sweet-smelling soap and bath salts. An odd scratching sound made her look up. Menacing dark forms hovered above the skylight, their shadows falling across the tile floor. She had to laugh. They were two very large crows, slipping and sliding over the plastic dome of the skylight as they attempted to climb to the top, only to slide back down. It was a game. Delia supposed the thick plastic of the skylight was held by metal screws which attracted the crows' attention in the increasingly intense cantaloupe light. The birds looked formidable, their heavy dark beaks pecking as they slid. She shivered and shed her clothes. Standing below and looking up was not a comfortable viewpoint.

After her shower, her small compact body wrapped in a towel, Delia went back into the bedroom where she'd laid out some clothes. Her fresh underclothes smelled faintly of the lavender sachet she'd packed with them. She pulled on well-cut gray corduroy pants and a gold angora sweater with a low V-neck. Jean-Paul was fond of this sweater, probably because it revealed her ample cleavage, she mused to herself. She decided to put her makeup on at the dressing table; there was too little space for her cosmetics bag in the bathroom and the light wasn't very good in there. The two frilly lamps enhanced the rosy glow of her complexion. Delia took good care of herself and looked younger than she was. Most people guessed she was still in her forties. But here in New Mexico she sensed the dryness of the air and patted on extra moisturizer before adding makeup and lip-gloss.

While brushing out her short wavy hair, Delia noticed a silver-framed photograph of a woman holding two infants dressed in flowing christening dresses — one child cradled in each arm. The woman smiling into the camera was, Delia knew, her own mother. She picked up the oval frame and examined it. The initials at the bottom of the frame were her aunt's, Alice's mother. The photograph might have been hand-tinted: the color was delicate and faded. The babies were only a few months old — twins obviously — and one, she thought, was herself. But who was the other? She had grown up an only child and there was never any mention of a sibling. So who was this other baby? Delia experienced a knot in her stomach. The pretty photograph made no sense. Something felt amiss. It occurred to her it might be a joke. Somehow, the photographer had doubled the image, like a Rorschach test. But that would not have been in keeping with her parents' conservative natures. They would never have permitted such deception.

Delia's hand shook as she continued to examine the picture. She'd just have to ask Alice about it. But not yet. They first needed to get reacquainted. It occurred to her that she was actually afraid of the answer. She despised deception, and though of a gentle nature, strove to be realistic and honest. Yet she was not so innocent as to believe the world was without riddles and mysteries, some profoundly disturbing. At the moment, she had a distressing premonition.

2

elia stood for a moment at the living room entrance. Jean-Paul and Alice sat side-by-side facing the big east window, watching the last reflection of the setting sun on the craggy mountain. The snowy mountaintop shone gold and a cloudbank had crept along its base. From the kitchen came the delectable fragrance of dinner. A fire blazed in the fireplace; both Jean-Paul and Alice had their legs stretched out in front of them, their feet on the table. Jean-Paul held a glass of red wine, Alice a bottle of beer.

Jean-Paul must have come into the bedroom while Delia showered; she'd noticed his bag was open. He now wore the blue cable-knit sweater she'd made for his birthday, trim jeans and polished loafers. Alice had changed her running shoes for beaded moccasins and had added a turquoise necklace. The three dogs were stretched out asleep, Zippy on the opposite sofa, Rumpus and Hark, who were never allowed on the furniture, in front of the fire as if they were long accustomed to this place. The cross-country trip had made them flexible. After several weeks on the road, stopping off to stay with various friends and at motels, they took their changing surroundings in stride. They had even become accustomed to sleeping in the car at night, when required.

Delia regarded the peaceful scene, her hands resting lightly on the sofa back: it was as if she had awakened from an unpleasant dream to the reassurance of benign reality. The harmony of what she saw assuaged her confusion about the photograph. Her discomfort diminished.

Jean-Paul's good looks earned him a lot of attention, wherever he went. His hair was short, very dark but flecked with gray. Luminous dark eyes dominated his bony face, which at the moment was turned from her.

His features and body were chiseled, spare and strong. Delia had never met a man so sympathetic. Emanating a vital masculinity, he was particularly attractive to women, perhaps because he also possessed an answering feminine aspect within his masculine essence, which, Delia surmised, was not often the case with American men imbued with a macho ethos.

Falling in love with him had been an unexpected adventure. As a widow, she had managed to create a satisfying life for herself, full of fond friends and the contentment of her garden and garden writing which had culminated into a best seller of essays and a syndicated newspaper column. But Jean-Paul, a Frenchman, had opened a new world to her. They now lived part of each year in France and she, who was childless, had become profoundly attached to his daughter, son-in-law and their little twin girls. Jean-Paul's previous wife had drowned when she was still in her twenties. Delia and Arthur were introduced to Jean-Paul at a dinner party years before Arthur's death. Jean-Paul had surprised Delia by confessing that he'd been in love with her for decades, but because her marriage was clearly satisfying, he'd given up hope. Now their intense happiness was a surprise to them both.

Delia could see that Alice, too, found him charming. Already they appeared to have established a comfortable rapport. They were chatting away like old friends.

Sensing Delia's presence, the hounds opened sleepy eyes and slowly wagged their tails, which alerted the humans. Jean-Paul turned and rose to greet her, and Alice swiveled about, chuckled and said, "Well, did you survive the guestroom?"

Delia hadn't expected so direct a question and wasn't quite sure how to answer. She gripped the sofa back a little more tightly. Was Alice referring to the picture? Had she deliberately set it in her path to throw her off balance? After a moment of consideration, Delia thought not.

Jean-Paul came around the couch, leaned down and kissed Delia's neck. "What to drink, my treasure? Your cousin has the cupboard well stocked."

"Maybe... only water for now. I'm feeling light-headed." She probably shouldn't have said that. She immediately saw the concern in

Jean-Paul's face. The christening photograph had not only been a puzzle but a shock. Her chest felt constricted and she experienced a distinct shortness of breath. But she certainly didn't want to alarm Jean-Paul and Alice, especially since she wasn't yet ready to speak of her confusion.

Alice put her arm along the sofa back and patted Delia's hand. "It's the altitude, Delia. We're at six thousand feet above sea level. Good idea to limit your alcohol until you get used to it. You need to stay hydrated."

"And Santa Fe? Is it not even more high?" asked Jean-Paul.

"Another thousand feet. I'll get some sparkling water for you, Delia." She rose and padded toward the kitchen in her beaded moccasins.

Jean-Paul leaned down and studied Delia's face. She liked the tiny mole on his left cheekbone. "You are well?' he asked in French.

She made herself smile. "A little tired, perhaps."

Alice returned with an amber-colored Mexican glass and a plate of guacamole and chips garnished with cilantro, which she placed, somewhat precariously, atop a pile of archeological journals.

"To answer your question," said Delia, bending down and dipping a chip in the guacamole, "about the guest room... I think I remember an almost identical room at your mother's house." Delia's strong, curvy little body wasn't long enough to allow her to prop up her feet as the others had, so she snuggled at the end of the opposite couch beside the fire, careful not to disturb Zippy, dozing at the other end. Hark, showing some jealousy, got up with an audible sigh and positioned himself in front of Delia so that she might caress his long Basset ears.

"You got that right, Delia," replied Alice. "It is Mother's guestroom! Ever since her death I'd stored her furniture. But when Miles — my husband — retired from the Lab, we sold our big house by the Rio and bought this small one. We decided to have a massive clear-out of what we'd been using — and finally get the Maryland stuff out of storage. I know it's terrifically out of context, but it reminds me of my childhood, and now that Miles is dead, it's comforting. Objects have magical properties, don't you think? They resonate and are imbued with symbolic value. Even the Ancients knew this."

Delia felt this was an appropriate opening for asking about the photograph, but she hesitated, recognizing that she wasn't ready for an answer. Confusion trumped curiosity. She also sensed it was important to first get reacquainted with Alice, to form a liaison upon which a more intimate conversation could rest. Delia was a sensitive, orderly person, not given to impetuous actions. She was relieved that Alice, who had resumed her place beside Jean-Paul, seemed not to notice her hesitation.

"I'm still teaching two classes at the university, and this house is much closer than our old one," Alice said. "Only a fifteen-minute commute—a big time savings for me. People kid me about that room, but it was either use the stuff or get rid of it. Somehow, I couldn't let go. Until you showed up—happily—it was almost my only remaining connection with my childhood.

"You know, I haven't been back East for decades. There's always so much to do here in the Southwest. And I've done quite a few digs in Mexico and South America. That's the direction I face. As a matter of fact, I'm setting off for a dig next week. For a month. I'm pleased I'll be back before the two of you leave.

"But that little bit of Maryland—the room, I mean—offers me a sense of my roots. I guess I'm trying to suggest it's not quite as nutty as it seems." Alice took a hearty swig of her beer and smiled warmly at her guests.

"But Jean-Paul tells me you'll be staying in Guillaume Duthuit's house outside Santa Fe for several months."

"You know him?" Delia asked, dipping three more guacamole chips, taking one for herself, then pushing the platter across the coffee table to the others. She was really feeling hungry and the fragrance from the kitchen was sharpening her appetite.

"Oh, yes. I was just telling Jean-Paul. Both Miles and I were on the Santa Fe Opera Board. We're extremely fond of music. Miles sang in a choir for years and was a fine pianist. I play the cello. We met a lot of the performers over the years and Guillaume is one of the most interesting. He has a magnificent bass voice! Have you heard him perform?"

Jean-Paul replied, "*Non*, we have never met him, even though we all have property in France. M'sieur Duthuit is the client of my son-in-law,

André. We were told there is a problem with his house. Whenever he wish to rent it—we understand he is never here but for part of the year—the tenants... they depart."

Alice laughed, shifting her feet back down to the rug with a muffled thud. "Yes, there's an absurd story about that. The locals say the house is haunted." Alice leaned forward and fixed more chips and offered them around. Hark indicated he'd like one, but Delia shook her head.

"We heard that, too," replied Delia. "That's part of the reason we've been offered the house. We're not paying rent. M'sieur Duthuit hopes we'll figure out the problem for him. His tenants won't stay and the management company says they have no idea what the problem is. When they check the house, they find nothing wrong. They did, however, disconnect the burglar alarm because it kept going off. After a certain amount of false alarms, apparently you get fined in larger and larger amounts. We were assured that nothing has ever been stolen."

"It's odd. The house contains some good art," said Alice, looking around at her own house with its rather ordinary décor. "I suppose unless you're a special fine-arts thief," she laughed at the title she'd inadvertently invented, "you usually don't know what's art and what's not. Thieves seem to look for quick-sale items—or at least here in New Mexico they do. They usually need drug money."

"*Eh, bien*... Delia and I, we hope this haunting will not be a problem for us. In the past year we had several adventures and changes of significance, *n'est-ce pas*, my treasure?" He glanced fondly at Delia, then turned back to Alice beside him. "My daughter, Claire, and her family are unable to visit us this year for Christmas, as they usually do. So we decide, Delia and I, to change the er, er, pattern of our life and come to the West for an American holiday."

"You see," explained Delia, "we're planning a new home for ourselves in Maryland—on the site of the original eighteenth-century farm house on Jean-Paul's property..."

"And now your property, too, Délie," Jean-Paul broke in. They were still not used to being married and thinking of themselves as a couple.

Delia acknowledged his statement with a smile. She was constantly struck not only by Jean-Paul's generous spirit but by his charm. Charm, that magic component, is hard to pinpoint. It wasn't just his good looks and quirky English pronunciation. She remembered her first husband, who had known Jean-Paul well, describing him as "a prince among fellows". That was true, but it wasn't the whole story.

Delia refocused on the conversation. Nodding, she added, "We need a change before we begin the next project." She paused for a sip of water and then continued, "Actually it's quite exciting. We've found an eighteenth-century house and are moving it from its present location in southern Maryland. It'll be a tremendous challenge for Jean-Paul and his crew. They have to dismantle the entire house—which is almost, though not quite, a ruin—then number each part, haul it on a flatbed truck, and rebuild it on our property, where a great deal of additional work will be needed."

Jean-Paul's dark eyes sparkled as they always did when contemplating a new project. His endemic enthusiasm affected everyone around him.

"And," continued Delia, sitting up a little straighter, forgetting the bothersome photograph for the moment, "I've been involved in selling my Baltimore house. I do sympathize with your guestroom furniture dilemma. Stuff Management is a consuming job involving various different levels of decisions. Frankly, I don't know how I accumulated so many things. I'm not a collector. I've always preferred less rather than more.

"And Jean-Paul has been embroiled in unraveling the intricacies of his uncle's estate in France and dealing with the French courts and his uncle's extensive and ancient property. There lies a tale without end!" Delia laughed. She relaxed as she talked of the life she knew.

"Oh, yes," said Alice. She got up and moved off to the kitchen for a moment to check the oven and then returned with the wine bottle and another beer for herself. "I heard you inherited a title and you're now count and countess. Very chic to have titled cousins." She smiled with benevolent satisfaction.

Delia and Jean-Paul exchanged looks. Embarrassed, Delia studied the bubbles in her glass. "We've been hoping to keep that quiet. It causes comments and misunderstandings on this side of the Atlantic. People have peculiar ideas about what it means."

"Hmm, yes, I can see they might. I suppose it's because we just aren't used to it. Well, don't worry, I won't say anything. I think I heard it from someone in Maryland anyway, one of our other cousins, I suspect, so it's probably not general knowledge here in the West."

Jean-Paul poured himself more wine and looked toward Delia's glass to see if she needed a refill.

"Thanks," she said, "I'm fine. But, Alice, do please tell us about the Duthuit ghost."

Zippy had slipped across the couch and was attempting to climb into Delia's lap. Delia was a favorite of animals and children. She liked them; they liked her.

"Zippy, no! Get down," commanded Alice. Zippy jumped to the floor, slipped under the table and up into Alice's lap. Alice caressed the little dog and continued. "Oh, yes. The silly ghost. Sure, I'll tell you, but first, before we forget... Back up a little and tell me...why are you going to so much trouble to move the Maryland house? Isn't it a tremendous expense, and couldn't you build a similar one—if you like it so much?" She tilted her head and looked from one to the other.

"*Ah, oui.* You, Alice, are correct. The expense is great. Others also ask why we move the old house. It has not been lived in for thirty years." He sipped his wine. "We move it because it is very, very beautiful and also, as you would remark, a structure of great excellence."

He drew a deep breath, and from the expression on his face it was clear he was imagining each detail of the old house with the attention only an architect could muster. "The materials—they are very fine."

"You see, Alice..." Hark's tail began to wag as he sensed the excitement in Delia's voice, "the floor boards are virgin wood—wonderfully wide—there is nothing like them on the market today. The house was put together with enormous care and totally by hand."

"Yes, they are tongue and groove, with hardware most wonderful... And, of course, the old materials are non-toxic. This is not a structure to sink into the earth. It is the example of an age most marvelous. We desire to save it and use it. Besides, to tear down old structures is more waste in the land-fill." Jean-Paul, in his excitement, was sitting straight up, hands on knees. Even Rumpus and Zippy had come to attention.

"I see. I see. I definitely get it!" Alice's hands flew into the air. Luckily, her beer was nearly empty. "You've both got great passion for this structure. You've convinced me of its value and beauty. Now I've got to see it with my own eyes!" She slapped her knee. "I think after all these years away, this might be the project to bring me back home." Then lowering her voice to a confidential level, she said, "I'm rather partial to old things, you know, especially now that I'm becoming one myself. It's one of the reasons I like my Maryland guestroom. Let's just say your house piques my archeological interests."

"How sympathetic, you are!" Delia said happily as she grasped Hark's big Basset head with both hands to give him a hug.

"And you will be most welcome," Jean-Paul confirmed. "You will be our first guest upon completion of the project." He raised his glass in a toast to her and gazed at her with expectation. "But now, Madame Alice, please tell us more about the haunted house we are about to inhabit."

Alice laughed and looked down into her empty beer bottle. She glanced first at Delia then Jean-Paul. "Well, of course, the whole thing is crazy, but it has economic consequences for Guillaume. He bought the property not only to give himself a nice place to stay when he's performing, but as an investment. It's part of an original Spanish land grant. You, with your passion for old structures, will appreciate it. It's one of those lovely coincidences in life: a wonderful old property being occupied by connoisseurs. The house and outbuildings are adobe and built in the old style. And the property has a glorious view. It's just north of Santa Fe, as I suppose you know, in the Sangre de Cristo foothills, facing southwest. And surrounded by ancient cottonwoods and fruit trees, which is unusual at that altitude, but the place has had water for years—fed by a ditch, or *acequia*, as we call it. Anyway, it's wonderful. You do have a four-wheel drive car, don't you? I didn't notice when you drove in—I was so excited to see you. But, you'll probably need four-wheel drive to get up the road in the snow."

"We bought the Subaru before we left for this trip. Yes, it has four-wheel drive. My Peugeot, it had become ancient. Is there always much snow in Santa Fe?"

"There used to be—before global warming set in. Unfortunately, we've had very dry winters recently. But, at least so far, this year has been more like the winters of the past. We've had lots of snow, which is a blessing. We're dependent on the snow for our water supply."

"I see. Our weather in the East has also been unusual. But tell us, Alice, this haunting, what form does it take?"

"I'm not sure, Jean-Paul. You might talk more with the management company or even the police. I also have friends, Ethan and Molly Ridgeley, who live nearby—on the same road, in fact. You'll like them. I've let them know you're coming and they can give you more information. I'm sure they've heard the rumors."

"Molly Ridgeley... That's a familiar name. Does she write cook-books?" Delia asked, moving the guacamole plate a little closer to the center of the table, further from Hark's sneaky mouth.

"Oh, yes. Like you, she's justly famous. I mentioned to her that you and Jean-Paul would be staying in Guillaume's house. She and Ethan—he's a retired doctor—are looking forward to meeting you. She says she keeps your garden book beside her bed."

"Ah, but surely," said Jean-Paul, who as a landscape architect was profoundly knowledgeable about plant life, "she is unable to garden as we do. Is not the altitude and climate unsuitable?"

"You have a point, Jean-Paul—of course. But lots of people read your wife's work for the delight of it."

"As well they might. *Moi aussi.*"

Alice looked at her oversized watch and stood up. "Well, it's time... everything should be ready. Remind me, before you leave, to give you some tips for high-altitude cooking. Stuff cooks too fast and burns on the outside while remaining raw on the inside. Not what you want with pork. Extra liquid is the key. And three-minute boiled eggs take five minutes to cook, because water boils at a low temperature. Molly will help you. She knows everything."

They moved to the dining area, leaving the dogs snoozing by the fire. Delia was enjoying herself, though she knew she was going to have to clear up the mystery of the identical child before they left the next day. Perhaps it was an easily explained situation and wouldn't signify anything at all disturbing.

3

Jean-Paul pulled off the pillow from the second bed, lifted Delia's covers and slipped in beside her. Feeling his body snug against hers brought her both peace and excitement. But tonight, arousal was dampened by confusion and dread.

"Délie, my treasure, you are not happy. Is it the thought of the haunting which disconcerts you?"

Though married for less than a year and lovers for only some months longer, Delia and Jean-Paul had already survived several taxing situations which had deepened their rapport and sensitivity to one another's moods. They intuited each other's emotions and never shied away from dealing with problems head-on.

"Could it be that now, in the twenty-first century, a ghost causes the disturbance in a house? It is unlikely, *n'est-ce pas*? Although, *oui*, there are people in Europe who will tell you the problem continues. The house with the reputation of haunting, it will not sell. People... people they not wish to buy trouble." Jean-Paul pulled his wife close, cupping her breasts in his hands.

Delia drew strength from him. His arms secured her as she moved against him as close as she could. "Oh, darling, I don't know what to think. Perhaps there's a local grudge. Folks are sometimes suspicious of foreigners. Or Duthuit did something to offend them. Who knows? I suspect if we find there's a real problem, we'll be able to sort it out."

"But, then, my precious, what is it that troubles you? Most surely you enjoy your cousin..."

"Oh, yes. Indeed I do. She's awfully welcoming and nice. And interesting." Delia paused. She caressed his hands. "Do you think you can reach the bedside light? There's something I want to show you."

He turned, felt around on the bedside table before managing to turn on the light. He had taken off his pajamas when he'd gotten into her bed and now his nakedness was so enticing Delia was tempted to forget the whole discussion. But having decided to tell him her worry, she slid from bed and walked across the old soft, layered rugs to the dressing table. There was just enough light to see her reflection in the mirror. Without makeup her face looked tired—she definitely needed sleep. But she also needed to know what she'd walked into.

Returning to bed and helping Jean-Paul prop up the rather too thick pillows against the headboard, she handed him the silver-framed photograph, feeling worried and a little silly. Whatever the explanation for the second baby, could it really matter? Perhaps it wasn't her mother and herself after all. Perhaps she was deceived by the style of the times.

He took the picture from her hand, deliberately brushing his fingertips against hers in a gentle caress, tipped the photo toward the light and studied it. Delia watched as his frown deepened. It was some moments before he spoke. "The infants, they are identical, are they not, Délie? Of course, I did not know your mother, but from the portrait in your study, I think this is she. And you, too. Precious baby—you." He suddenly turned to her and grinned. "Always so charming—so adorable. You are."

She laughed. Whatever his thoughts, he was attempting to lighten her mood by injecting nonsense. And she was grateful.

Then, becoming serious, he asked, "Do you not know the second child? Is this not another baby, a cousin, perhaps, who was christened the same day? No? I see you are mystified. You are disturbed. The infants, they are very similar. May we not enquire of Alice? She is the elder. And is it not her picture? Certainly she will know and then this little mystery, it will be solved. And you, my treasure, will no longer fret." Carefully, he laid the picture on the table and turned out the light.

They awoke with a start. "*Mon dieu*! Délie, awaken! It is nine-thirty in the morning!"

"What? Oh, how could we have slept so late? What about the dogs?"

"Your cousin—is she not the lover of animals? She must have seen to them." They were both struggling toward consciousness. Rumpus and Hark never permitted sloth. Getting out into the day was their primary objective. But last night, Jean-Paul had put the hounds' beds in the mudroom with Zippy's. Thus, the uninterrupted sleep for the hounds' owners.

Quickly readying themselves, Delia and Jean-Paul emerged from the guestroom dressed for the drive to Santa Fe and an appointment with the rental agent in charge of Duthuit's property. They found a note in the kitchen telling them Alice and the three dogs were out walking and that there was a bowl of mixed chile and eggs in the fridge. Also juice, toast and coffee. Jean-Paul soon found milk, heated it and stirred it into strong coffee in the French manner.

Delia and Jean-Paul were seated side-by-side at the kitchen counter, enjoying breakfast, when Alice and the three dogs came in through the garage, the animals' collars jingling and Rumpus and Hark skidding toward their owners as if to tell of their recent adventures. Delia and Jean-Paul naturally made a fuss while Zippy, in her excitement, ran around the living room in circles. Alice greeted the sleepyheads, as she called them, and filled the dogs' bowls with fresh water. The Bassets immediately commenced their slurping routine, which is why, at home, their bowls stood not in the kitchen but in the mudroom with the stone floor.

Delia had brought the mysterious picture from the bedroom and perched it on the counter beside the electric clock, which now read ten-thirty. "Never in our American life," announced Jean-Paul with his slightly crooked grin, "did we sleep through the morning. *Les chiens*, they do not allow it."

"That's what they told me. But when they saw Zippy's leash, they forgot about you, if you can bear to hear that, and were all for joining our walk. They had a glorious time. Just like regular western dogs." Then, picking up the picture, Alice examined it with a smile. "Adorable, isn't it? Perhaps you'd like to have it, Delia..."

Delia took a deep breath and hesitated. Jean-Paul laid his hand on her arm as she asked, "Alice, is that me?"

Alice continued to study the picture as though she hadn't seen it for years. "Of course, dear, and your mother—such a lovely woman, wasn't she?—and precious little Dorothy." Still looking down at the picture. "So awfully sad about Dorothy. Mother said it broke everyone's heart."

There was silence.

"Dorothy?" asked Delia. "Who is Dorothy?" Jean-Paul had not removed his hand from her arm.

Alice looked up for the first time and saw Delia's face. "Why, your twin sister. Dorothy Davis. Who had the bad heart..." She put her hand to her mouth. "Oh, don't tell me you didn't know..."

There was now a profound stillness in the kitchen. Even the animals had grown silent, as if they, too, comprehended the gravity of the moment. "No, I know nothing... nothing about this, about Dorothy. Alice, please tell me." There was a note of desperation in Delia's voice.

"Oh, my dear, I had no idea. I just assumed... How stupid of me. Jean-Paul, could I have some of that *café au lait*? Of course, Delia. Of course, I'll tell you. I assumed you knew..." Alice was clearly upset. Delia clung to the side of the counter as if she might fall off her stool. Jean-Paul set a mug in front of Alice and resumed his seat beside Delia.

"Your mother gave birth to twins. I remember it well—I was about nine or ten. Everyone had been worried because it had been a difficult pregnancy. Of course, I didn't understand what was going on. People didn't explain much to children in those days. I just knew there was a lot of tension and my mother was worried." She sipped her coffee with a far-away look in her eyes.

"There was tremendous relief when Aunt Ellen came through the delivery and you were strong and healthy. Dorothy was weak, something

29

about her heart, but at first she seemed to thrive, as you did, and then, well, I guess it must have been a few months after the christening—after this picture was taken—she suddenly died." She shifted her gaze and looked directly at Delia, her expression filled with sadness.

"It was quite unexpected, but then again, it wasn't. Mother never talked much about it. And you were such a winning little thing, as they said in those days. Did no one ever tell you, Delia?"

Delia was stunned. "No one," she murmured. Jean-Paul looked at her, his face full of compassion, but he no longer touched her. "Why? Why did no one ever tell me? I don't remember anything. I don't remember—I don't remember my sister." Delia felt the tears welling up behind her eyes, but they were held in place by a sudden fury. "What the hell were they thinking? Why should they keep this from me? Something so important as the death of—of—my twin sister!"

Clearly, Alice, too, was trying to figure it out. "Perhaps they were sparing themselves. Maybe they just couldn't bring themselves to talk about it. I suppose," Alice moved toward the window, looked out at the abrupt mountain range, "I suppose there never was the perfect time to tell you, and then somehow, it was too late. I don't remember anyone saying, 'Now, don't tell little Delia about Dorothy. It'll just upset her.' No, I don't think anything like that happened..."

The room was quiet again, except for the distant sound of a tiny silver plane leaving an increasingly fuzzy contrail across the sapphire sky, outside the large kitchen window.

Finally Jean-Paul spoke. "Claire—she is my daughter, Alice—often said after learning that her half-sister had drowned with her mother when she was a child... Claire, she said she experienced guilt for being the one to survive. She was too young to sail on the little boat that day. She slept in her cot at home. Claire told me she worried she was not good enough to be the one to live. That it was her older sister who should have survived. Not her. That thought, it upset her many years."

"Maybe," said Alice, looking directly at Delia for the first time, "your parents feared you might feel something like that and attempted to spare you. Do you suppose?"

"Oh, hell," said Delia, sliding down from the stool and slowing pacing the length of the kitchen in a daze. "I don't know what to think. You say her name was Dorothy?"

Abruptly Delia stopped pacing, looked about as if she wasn't sure where she was and rumpled her hair with both hands. Her voice trembled, "I wonder where she's buried. I never noticed a little gravestone in our cemetery. Dorothy. I can't get used to the idea. I had a sister... I'm not an only child. Crazy, isn't it? I'm a mature woman and suddenly I feel as if I'm a five-year-old, not knowing who I am."

"I suspect," murmured Alice, thinking aloud, "hearing this alters your sense of identity—like finding out you're adopted."

"Or..." Jean-Paul handed Delia her mug. "Like people who grow up Catholic, suddenly finding they are Jewish. You are no longer quite who you thought you were."

"Something like that," agreed Delia, wrapping her hands around the warm mug and trying to get a grip on herself. "In any case, I was betrayed. Everyone knew something important about my life except me. It was kept from me. Well, maybe not deliberately, but I was set-up to live a lie. Me, the joyful only child. The apple of my parents' eyes. When all the time I was reminding them of their unspeakable—literally unspeakable—loss. Oh, oh my god, this really is awful. Betrayed. I was betrayed..." She carefully set her mug on the counter beside the clock, walked into Jean-Paul's arms and began to cry very quietly.

4

After hugs and a promise to set up a time for Alice to visit, Delia, Jean-Paul and the hounds headed down the driveway toward "The Big I", as Alice called the interstate to Santa Fe. They'd wanted to stay with

Alice through lunch and talk more about Dorothy, but Kimber Garcia, the management person, could see them only at one o'clock and they needed to get the keys to Guillaume Duthuit's house.

Alice had drawn a map to the Garcia Agency on Old Pecos Trail and indicated a nearby grocery store. It all seemed simple and straightforward.

Despite their affection for Alice, they were relieved to move on, as if the disturbing revelation could be left behind. But Alice had given the troublesome photograph to Delia, who continued to feel caught in unsettling ambivalence — grateful to have discovered a missing piece of her life, distressed by the sense of betrayal. Her parents, whom she adored, had, in effect, lied to her. It would take some time to rearrange the pieces of her past in her mind. She even wondered if her first husband, who was considerably older than she, had known of the tragedy. Certainly, Arthur had never hinted at it. But people whom she'd trusted were now proving treacherous. Delia's past life, which had always seemed simple, was now a tangle. Steady ground had shifted beneath her feet.

They must have made a wrong turn for it took some back-tracking to find the entrance to the interstate. "Is it not surprising," commented Jean-Paul as they entered the on ramp, "there is so much traffic at the middle of the day? After all, this is not Paris."

"I suppose we're still within the limits of Albuquerque."

Jean-Paul swooped onto the highway directly behind an ancient, rusting pick-up truck loaded with firewood. The speed limit was fifty-five, but the traffic was going faster, except for the truck, which weaved from one side of its lane to the other, moving between forty and fifty, depending on the road grade.

Office buildings and billboards stood helter-skelter on both sides of the highway. From the office designs — Delia couldn't bring herself to think of them as 'architecture' — there had obviously been little thought to placement or style. It was the usual case of soul-killing urban sprawl ringing an American city.

Their cross-country trip had been an education. Neither Delia nor Jean-Paul had ever visited inland America. They knew only the East

Coast, although Delia, as a teenager, had once flown with her family to a wedding in San Francisco. America's natural beauty was amazing, but what humans had done to their environs dismayed them. They were startled by the poverty they encountered, both economic and cultural. They spent parts of their lives in Europe, where pockets of poverty still existed. But they were shocked to drive through the richest country in the world and encounter people who lacked the bare minimum—good health, for instance. Many were grotesquely obese. While on the road, Delia and Jean-Paul, who admittedly were gourmands, found themselves living off the nuts and fruit they carried in the car. They simply couldn't find edible food in the restaurants along the highways. Jean-Paul developed the theory that highway and chain-restaurant food was so devoid of nutrition that people were actually starving. They ate gross amounts simply to get a minimum level of nutrients, and then, if allowed, went back to the buffet table for more.

As they continued behind the wobbly truck, traffic whizzed past in the left lane. Delia noted that the sun was directly overhead and there was only one small puffy cloud in the sky. "Partly cloudy," Delia muttered to herself as she dug into her purse for her sunglasses.

New Mexico was so bright! Alice had given them each wide-brimmed, brown leather hats that certainly diminished the glare. Jean-Paul's had belonged to Alice's husband. Delia thought it gave Jean-Paul an appealing Latin look. She pulled down the window visor to look at herself in the mirror. She thought she looked foolish. Her skin was so light and the hat fell too low around her ears—obviously, Alice's head was bigger than hers. But she was grateful to have it. She suspected that even in December, her fair skin could burn.

They drove in companionable silence until Delia asked, "Don't you feel that where we come from—it's all about earth and plants? But New Mexico is about sky and light? I'm looking in a different direction—mostly up—up and up into an infinite sky."

"Ah, oui, that is so. This world is altogether different." Although Jean-Paul's English was fluent, Delia could hear the French syntax in his English, and when he was excited or very relaxed, he sometimes lapsed into noticeably imperfect English. He'd been taught English by French people and his accent reflected that. Delia, on the other hand, was not so fluent in French, although their now-frequent trips to France allowed her to improve rapidly. She had a good ear, and her French teachers had been French, so her accent was remarkably authentic. By unconscious agreement, they found themselves conversing in English in the United States and in French while in France. Except, of course, when they intended their conversation to be private; then they'd automatically reverse the habit.

Delia turned in her seat to talk to the hounds sitting up behind her. They preferred English; although she sometimes overheard Jean-Paul offering them a little French conversation. Bassets were originally a French breed, so that made sense, she thought. She did not, however, know Rumpus and Hark's assessment of the linguistic situation.

There was a wire barrier between the backseat and luggage space, behind which the dogs could ride; but it was easier to pack the luggage directly from the back. Rumpus and Hark, therefore, usually rode in the back seat behind their owners. Animals and humans enjoyed one another's proximity.

The highway climbed higher. Jean-Paul had moved into the left lane; the overloaded old pick-up truck had been left far behind. Between the hideous billboards, they caught glimpses of the Sandias to their right. As she began to praise the dogs for their excellent behavior at Zippy's house, Delia was aware the traffic behind them was still heavy.

"What excellent animals you are," she told the hounds in her praise-voice. "Regular gents. You are both to be commended for your graciousness to your hostess — Zippy, I mean — and for not racing around the living room after her and knocking over that cello. To be frank, I was a little worried about that. That cello was not well positioned, but you good, good dogs, caused no harm." At the phrase, "good, good dogs," each animal cocked his head and wagged the tip of his tail. Delia knew they understood she was pleased with them.

Suddenly, because she was turned backwards, she became aware of a sedan speeding up from behind. Jean-Paul, she knew, saw it, too, for she heard him mutter under his breath, but there was no break in the right lane for him to get out of the way of the fast approaching car.

"Lie down!" she commanded the dogs, thinking if they were hit from behind, at least the dogs wouldn't sail over into the front seat. They obeyed and she resumed her forward position. The speeding car was only inches behind them when Jean-Paul was able to move into the right lane. He waved his hand as the offending car started to speed past.

His gesture apparently infuriated the passing driver who slowed down and glared at Jean-Paul and Delia. There were four rough-looking young men in the car—throwing fingers and making rude gestures, all while the driver raced beside them at eighty miles per hour.

Their assailants resembled a speeding cage of infuriated apes. Abruptly, a youth in the back seat opened the window and held up a metal wheel rim, gesturing that he would fling it out the window at them. What a weird weapon! A wheel rim! But it could do a lot of damage. Delia supposed if it broke the driver's window, it could catch Jean-Paul in the head, possibly killing him. The back-seat ape continued to gesture with the wheel rim. The offending car veered closer and closer until Delia was sure they'd be run off the road. She glanced at Jean-Paul's face, which wore an expression of grim concentration.

Jean-Paul began to brake. Little by little he reduced his speed. The offending car did the same, sticking like glue. The apes were shouting, screaming, shaking their fists and the wheel rim. Delia was certain they'd either get side-swiped or rear-ended. Drivers behind them in both lanes, trapped by these dangerous shenanigans, began to honk their horns. The traffic in front had sped ahead and there was a growing space of road as Jean-Paul and the attackers slowed.

The furious horns continued their cacophonic chorus of rage and frustration. This was becoming a mobile community of the crazed. An exit suddenly appeared and the offending car, its threats witnessed by many, abruptly sped up and cut across the lane in front of Jean-Paul. It disappeared around the off-ramp.

Delia took a deep breath. Rumpus and Hark, sensing a crisis had passed, resumed their sitting positions and stared out the windows.

Jean-Paul and the vehicles behind resumed speed as though nothing had happened. The sudden normalcy of the highway was surreal.

"What was the matter with those crazy monsters?" Jean-Paul asked.

"Drunk? High? Escaped from a mental hospital in a stolen car? We were all within inches of death. Good god! And out of nowhere! I must say, you handled it brilliantly."

"Instinct. Pure instinct. But such fury! Let us hope we do not encounter that gang again. Delia, did you bring your weapon? Perhaps we must protect ourselves from such violence. Perhaps the stories of the Wild West are true."

"Yes, I have it. But it's tucked in the well beside the spare tire. We could pull off the road and get it, but we'd have to unpack the entire back of the car."

"Umm, *non*. Do you have your mobile phone in your handbag?"

"Yes."

"Turn it on and if we see those villains again, call nine-eleven for assistance. Do you not think that the better idea?"

"I do—and certainly much easier. But I don't think they'll be back. They were so drunk—or whatever—they've probably already run off the road, killed themselves, or passed out—or all three."

"*Tu as raison*. They were without wits. Your weapon, it is too much trouble to retrieve. You may tell Detective Scott he should have advised us to travel with spare wheel-rims. You say wheel-rim?"

"Yes, my love, I think that's the right term. I'm not an expert on automotive parts, even though I did think I was becoming somewhat conversant with the more conventional types of weapons. They are not usually my favorite objects, as you know. But clearly we need to get more creative about protecting ourselves—out here in the Wild West."

In the last year, Delia had twice aided in police investigations. She'd worked with several police officers, one of whom, when he'd heard about their proposed trip west, insisted she take a pistol with her. She'd been reluctant. What if it were stolen from the car or she'd inadvertently left it in a motel? But Detective Scott was adamant. He'd gone ahead and seen to a license. America, he insisted, is a lawless place and New Mexico is a primary drug channel from south of the border. It's a state with a high crime rate.

So Delia asked a lawyer friend for advice. "Cops like everyone armed," he's remarked simply, and wasn't particularly opposed to her packing heat. Finally, Delia relented and had hidden her Beretta in the well of the spare tire, hoping the car wouldn't be stolen as they slept.

Although the car could be replaced, she'd hate to lose that Beretta. After her second adventure in aiding the police, she and Jean-Paul had spent a month at his French château. He'd happened to show her his treasured Beretta shot gun, which gave them the idea of taking a short trip to Italy, and stopping at the Beretta atelier in the Alps. Since the police indicated they'd appreciate Delia's help in the future, she and Jean-Paul decided to invest creatively in her self-protection. Together, they'd spent a fascinating day choosing a weapon of great artistry, with graceful engraving and a stock fashioned from the root wood of Turkish walnut. The pistol was not only lethal, but a work of art—a treasure she'd hate to lose.

The traffic thinned and the speed limit increased. Delia and Jean-Paul began to relax. The landscape opened up and the blue sky spread endlessly above them. From time to time, as the gusts of wind increased as they drove north, Jean-Paul had to make an effort to hold the car steady.

"Your cousin Alice, is she not a kindly person? I like her very much," Jean-Paul mused.

"Um, yes. One of those people who is comfortable in their own skin, comfortable in their world."

"The situation of your sister is most distressing, but is it not fortunate that the discovery was made from this genuine person—not a person of complication and facade?"

"I hadn't thought of that, Jean-Paul. Of course my dismay would be deeper if I'd learned about Dorothy from someone..." Delia hunted for the right term, "from someone hiding behind a persona—someone with an agenda. That would have made the situation even more fraught."

"I was thinking just that," Jean-Paul said in a contemplative tone.

They came to a long steep hill. An extra lane had been added to the right for traffic slowed by the grade. "This," Jean-Paul said, "will be the ultimate test of our new car. Certainly, my old Peugeot—packed with the luggage, two people and two hounds—I do not doubt, would slow. Let us now see what we can do."

Delia had long observed that this was the type of challenge many men love. In her experience, a woman would probably take the long hill in stride, and if her car began to slow down, would automatically move into the truck lane. But she now noticed the speedometer held steady at seventy-five, and the car flew up the hill effortlessly. "Bravo!" she had time to say before being rendered speechless by the dramatic landscape spreading before them.

A high snow-covered mountain range appeared to the East while to the West, at a further distance, was another long, high range. Between was open, snow-covered land as far as the eye could see.

"*Regards!*" Jean-Paul cried. "That must be Santa Fe—there, against the mountains. How charming is the setting!"

They were both excited by the sudden unexpected change in environment. And, at least at this point, not a billboard in sight. Just open land, low shrubs and sometimes, where the land dipped into a draw, large bare trees along the banks. Delia and Jean-Paul were unaccustomed to these types of vegetation and unable to recite their proper names. "Those large trees," Delia suggested, "must be cottonwoods. We saw some earlier, I think. We need to get a book. So many new species to identify... And Alice said the draw is called an arroyo in New Mexico."

"And the mountains. Can you find their names?"

Delia could access the names by checking her phone, but both she and Jean-Paul were addicted to the tactile satisfaction of paper. They liked hefty Sunday newspapers and the silky pages of magazines, and the weight of a good book in their hands. She therefore pulled their atlas from under the seat. She'd previously noticed the publishers had placed the map of New Mexico after the map of New York. All the other states were in proper alphabetical order. She'd also noticed the national weather person on television usually stood in front of New Mexico when giving the temperatures or forecast news and seldom mentioned it, although

Arizona and Colorado got plenty of coverage. Was there a mystery here? Did folks consider New Mexico a small and insignificant territory?

"Hmm. The near mountains..." she tilted the book, "I wish they'd print the names bigger... looks like the Sangre de Cristo range. Alice spoke of them. Blood of Christ, I guess."

"Yes," Jean-Paul agreed. "Alice mention that as a favorite Santa Fe name — for everything, except perhaps, the laundry. She said they have a Blood of Christ Water Company. What can that mean, wine comes from the water tap?"

Delia laughed. "Oh, no doubt. A special New Mexico wine, which when used in the washer won't dye the sheets pink."

"*Je t'aime*, Délie. You are adorable. What are the mountains there to the West?"

"Looks like the Jemez Range..."

Before leaving Maryland, Delia and Jean-Paul had made a point of studying New Mexico history, culture and architecture. They knew about the pueblo Indian settlements, the later arrival of nomadic Indians, the advent of the conquering Spanish and the consequent Spanish settlements to hold the land against other European powers, and then finally the arrival of the United States forces. It was, they'd learned, a blood-soaked land.

They had not, however, read a great deal about the landscape. Nor had they imagined the vastness, brilliance and dramatic configuration of what they now saw. No photograph or painting adequately portrays the sensation of clear dry air, nor the vast dramatic contrasts.

Eventually the highway circled around the south of Santa Fe. "Look, Jean-Paul, there is the Old Pecos Trail Exit. That's what we want. Clearly this is a smaller place than Albuquerque. Not so commercial. Yes, just follow along there."

As they entered town, they saw that snow had been shoveled to the sides of the road where it stood in melting walls. In shaded places the road was snow-packed, but where the sun hit, a river of melted snow ran through the street, splashing high against the cars.

Holding Alice's map, Delia said, "Let me see if I can find the number of the property agency. Yes, there! We can turn in there."

Delia and Jean-Paul parked beside a low adobe building with a narrow porch. A porch, they remembered, was referred to as a portal. The parking lot seemed unpaved, but the snow was packed. It didn't look as if they'd get stuck. The sun had moved westward, providing enough shade to leave the hounds in the car with the windows cracked open.

The Garcia Property Agency, attached to several other offices and a tile shop, was located in a narrow adobe building that looked as if it had existed for several hundred years. Its mud walls seemed to be melting back into the earth. Large, irregular patches of missing plaster revealed eroded adobe bricks beneath. Although the structure's future gave cause for alarm, Delia and Jean-Paul would soon learn that this was merely one aspect of "Santa Fe charm," and that its location on Old Pecos Trail made it a highly desirable property.

They were surprised that in this land of heavy snowfalls, the roofs of most buildings were flat. Snow was now melting rapidly from the midday sun and flowing copiously out wooden canales to the earth below. Each canale waterfall created a small rounded lake below with walls of snow surrounding it. The shaded canales had long, shimmering icicles hanging from them. Everywhere, the snow glistened like multicolored jewels and the air felt cold and fresh against their faces. The scene was so bright that, despite their wide-brimmed hats and dark glasses, they were tempted to shade their eyes with their hands.

As they opened the office door, a string of bells announced their arrival. The office was small and cluttered, with a tiny corner fireplace where a fire of vertical logs burned cheerily. On the whitewashed walls were two framed, slightly faded posters from past years of the Santa Fe Opera. They looked as if they might have been painted by Georgia O'Keeffe. A dark, middle-aged woman sat at a wide desk peering into a computer screen. She looked up as they entered. The nameplate on her desk read, "Rose Martinez".

"Good afternoon, Ms. Martinez, we are here to see Mrs. Garcia," Jean-Paul said courteously. "We are Mr. and Mrs. Duval. We have an appointment."

"Just a minute," the woman said brusquely. "Sit there." She indicated several wooden chairs resembling nineteen-thirties kitchen chairs, lined against the wall. "I'll check." She moved slowly toward a door, opened it, closed it behind her and was gone several minutes.

Returning, she said gruffly, "Go in now." Still no smile.

"We must have caused offense," whispered Jean-Paul to Delia in French.

They entered a second room with two small windows facing the backs of more ancient, jumbled buildings. This larger office was similar to the first except the walls were decorated with large photographs of New Mexican landscapes. In the foreground of one stood a movie star in jeans, a tee-shirt and handsome Indian jewelry, together with a signature which read: "Best wishes, Ali McGraw." Delia thought Ali looked terrific.

Kimber Garcia emerged from behind her desk. She was a large, middle-aged woman, dressed in a gray suit — a very professional outfit — except for the red cowboy boots. Maybe the boots were snow-determined. Delia, because of the last name, had expected a person of Spanish descent. But no, Ms. Garcia was decidedly Anglo, as Delia and Jean-Paul had learned to say. (Jean-Paul was a little ambivalent to learn from Alice that since he was neither one of the Indian People, Spanish New Mexicans, nor among the recently arrived group from south of the border, he was considered an Anglo.) Ms. Garcia had a round freckled face, heavily made-up gray eyes and extremely pretty, short hair that flared out from her head like spun gold.

She offered her hand and in a voice as high as a child's said, "Hi, I'm Kimber. Delia, glad to meet you. You too, Gene." Delia and Jean-Paul hadn't got used to the western predilection for addressing people by their first names upon a twenty-second acquaintance.

"*Jean*," corrected Jean-Paul cordially, pronouncing his name in the French manner. Except for the Deep South, where Delia and Jean-Paul had stopped off on their drive west, men in the United States didn't have double names. In a gas station in Mississippi, however, they'd met two brothers called Billy-Bob and Hugh-Jack, which Jean-Paul noted with interest. Although it was common in France, he knew by now not to expect the automatic use of his double Christian name. It was one of the numerous small conventions that kept him forever feeling foreign despite his many years in the U.S.

"Oh," replied Kimber, "sorry, I thought I'd heard someone say Gene. John, then. What can I get you? Coffee? And Rose brought in these wedding cookies this morning. Here, have some."

Still standing, Delia and Jean-Paul each took one of the sugary little pastries. They were light, sweet and delicious. Kimber went over to a filing cabinet and poured out three mugs of coffee from a machine. "Cream?"

Jean-Paul said, "Thank you," before realizing his mistake. The "cream" was a powder substance from a jar, which Kimber stirred into the mugs with a flat wooden stick. It was going to taste awful, but the black mugs were nice. Delia liked the silver sketch of a full moon rising above a mountain range. Underneath was written, "New Mexico... Land of Enchantment."

Kimber motioned to two steel and "leather" chairs, only slightly more enticing than the ones in the front room, before sitting behind her desk, leaning back and crossing her large legs. Watching her smooth her gray skirt, Delia thought the outfit would have looked better if either the boots or the skirt were longer.

"Now," said Kimber, smiling, "I'll tell you about the property." Her voice had lost some of its childish quality. "It's an old structure with a historic plaque, very well located and beautifully renovated. Delia, I'm sure you'll appreciate the kitchen." She then turned to Jean-Paul. "I have to hand it to you French. You know how to set up a kitchen. Bill was very particular about that. When he bought the property, he did a lot of restoration, but the kitchen was where he really focused. Would you believe there are homes in the Santa Fe area, especially among the high end, that lack full kitchens? Just a serving station with shelves, microwaves and electrical outlets for caterers to use as a staging area. But Bill wouldn't have put up with that for a moment." She sighed. "The kitchen is a dream."

Puzzled, Jean-Paul asked, "Who is Bill?"

"Bill Duthuit, the owner—the opera star."

"Oh, Bill," said Jean-Paul with a touch of irony, turning to Delia. "Guillaume Duthuit."

"Right," said Kimber. "We call him Bill. I think that's how his name translates."

Jean-Paul nodded. Delia ducked her head to hide her smile. She studied her mug. They were certainly right about this being the Land of Enchantment, despite their tendency to slaughter names.

"Excuse me one minute." Kimber got up from her desk and walked to the front office, the heels of her cowboy boots tapping with efficiency. Delia overheard her say, "I need the keys for the Duthuit place, Rose. Better give me two sets." Returning, Kimber handed one set to Delia and placed the other one for Jean-Paul on the edge of her desk in front of him. Then she sat down in her swivel chair again, rocked slightly and leaned forward earnestly. "I understand you won't be paying rent and Bill has agreed to pay utilities. And, since you're friends, he has also waived a damage deposit."

Delia detected a hint of disapproval, maybe skepticism in Kimber's voice regarding that last comment, but she moved on with her instructions: "These keys are for the doors to the main house. There is also a storage area and attached guesthouse, which I assume you won't be using. You'll see a three-car garage on the roadside. Bill keeps an old jeep in one spot. You can use the other two spaces for yourselves, for guests' cars or storage. The garage doors face the road, and a second set of doors lead into the patio, so it's best to keep them locked. In fact, it's a good idea to keep everything locked."

Leaning across the desk, she handed Jean-Paul a small map and explained how to navigate through town onto the Paseo, follow it round to the Pink Masonic Temple, turn right on Bishops Lodge Road, go up and down the big hill and just before the village of Tesuque turn right onto a road going off across a little bridge. "Drive up there and Bill's place is the third driveway. It's on the right. The other two residences are on the left. If you go too far, you'll come to Forest Service land. There's a locked gate, but enough space to turn around in. The mailbox at Bill's drive says one-zero-three. The road will be plowed for you, and Joseph, who is the handyman who takes care of the house and orchard—he comes from the local pueblo—and will take away trash on Tuesdays. Just put it out in the bin and leave it outside. We've cleaned up after the last tenants—who were here after Bill left at the end of opera season—so you'll find the house in good shape. Anything you need—just call me. You've got my number, and," she once again reached across her desk, picked up a business card from a stack, and handed it to Delia, "here's my mobile number. Any questions?"

"Perhaps we should say," Jean-Paul began, then hesitated before pronouncing, "Bill—err yes, Bill is not a friend of ours. We do not know him. He is the client of my son-in-law in France. We understand he is concerned about his house and wishes us to detect the source of problems." Jean-Paul still held his coffee mug, and because, as usual, he gestured with his hands as he spoke, the coffee was in some danger of escaping its container. Delia gently removed it from his hand and placed it on the desk. Kimber didn't show any emotion as she picked up the mug and walked it back across the room to the file cabinet. She resumed her seat and folded her arms across her chest.

"Perhaps," continued Jean-Paul, glancing at the map, folding it, and putting it carefully in his parka pocket, "you might offer us some idea of the nature of the problems. Perhaps we have misunderstood..."

Kimber picked up the plate on her desk and offered them more cookies. They were awfully good, weren't they? Delia and Jean-Paul each took another. For a moment there was silence. Ali McGraw continued to beam down from her mountain meadow. Then Kimber's little-girl voice returned: "Frankly, we've had trouble keeping tenants. Depending on the opera schedule, Bill's only here in the summer. When he's not, he likes to rent the property for a whole year. Otherwise, we rent it out for the winter season. People come for the fall aspen color, for skiing and during Christmas. Be sure to pick up brochures about Christmas activities from Rose's office when you leave. You're here at a good time. Everyone loves the Santa Fe Christmas." Kimber smiled benevolently. Her front teeth were slightly crooked.

Delia wondered if Kimber was avoiding the subject. "Ms. Garcia, is there something we should know about this property?"

"Oh, please, call me Kimber. We don't go in for formality here." She tittered nervously. "Well, to be truthful, I don't know what to tell you except we have trouble keeping tenants. They tend to leave after a few weeks. We're trying to ascertain the problem and, of course, you might help us. The tenants always seem vaguely embarrassed and say stuff like, 'Oh, well, it's too cold here. We've decided to go to Tucson.' So I ask them if the heating is inadequate. Bill put in a new furnace and we've checked the radiators, which are old, large and more than adequate. But they say it's okay. I've actually had the plumbers up there to check on things. Then the tenants come up with other excuses like they've got to meet friends unexpectedly in San Diego. To be truthful," she looked first at Jean-Paul, then Delia, with an expression of puzzled exasperation on her round face, then said with a sigh, "I don't know what to do. Bill's a nice guy with a good property. He's getting fed-up and may change management. Well, to be honest, that might be sort of a relief..." She stared off into space for a moment, then leaned back and re-adjusted her skirt.

Delia decided Kimber's skirt was definitely too small. She was sorry for Kimber, but couldn't ascertain whether she didn't know what was being said about the house or was holding back. Delia decided to take the bull by the horns. "We heard the house is haunted."

Silence. Delia looked at Jean-Paul to see if he disapproved of her bluntness. He winked at her. A little of the cookie sugar had fallen onto his parka. She restrained herself from getting up and brushing it off.

Kimber put her hands to her spun-gold hair, patted it gently and, seemingly reassured, returned them to her lap. "Rose said her brother-in-law told her that. He said there's an evil spirit loose up there that drives everybody out. His sister told him she'd actually seen the ghost. You'll meet Dolores. She's the cleaning lady. She comes on Tuesdays and Fridays to clean, but if you pay her extra, she'll do other stuff for you... ironing and helping with parties. Dolores says the ghost doesn't mean any harm, it's just upset and wants to have the place to itself."

"Sooo," began Jean-Paul, suddenly brushing away the sugar,

"Dolores is not bothered by the ghost. I do not suppose it is Dolores, herself, who would prefer to have the place to herself. Is she paid to clean whether there are tenants or not?"

"Well, yes, she is. I hadn't thought of that. But, you know...well," Kimber gazed out the little windows at the water falling from another ancient wooden canale, "somehow, I can't believe Dolores would make that up. She cleans several of our rentals. I've had her on my list for a long time. There haven't been problems with any other unit. And no one has ever complained about her."

Delia followed Kimber's gaze out the windows. Beyond the spurting water, it looked as if the smallest building was actually—at this very moment—melting into the earth; part of one wall had already crumbled into rounded steps. It reminded Delia of a Claes Oldenburg sculpture.

Returning her attention to Kimber, Delia asked, "What exactly are these problems the tenants complain about? Or do they just leave? Is that what you mean? Lame excuses and then they simply clear out?"

Kimber sighed again and hugged her arms closer around her gray jacket. She gave a tiny shiver. Then she looked from Jean-Paul to Delia, her mouth a straight line of tension. Delia was afraid she'd burst into tears. But Kimber only ran her fingers through her hair again. "We've never had a problem like this. I can't figure out what to do. If you have trouble, would you please tell me exactly what it is? I'd really appreciate that. You see, you're the first to take the property knowing there's something not quite right. Maybe that will make a difference—being forewarned is forearmed, so to speak..."

Jean-Paul stood up and Delia followed his example. He swept up the keys and said, "Let us not worry, Ms. ahh, Kimber." (He pronounced it Keember). We telephone you at the first sign of trouble and attempt to be specific."

They said their goodbyes, shaking hands all around. Using her little-girl voice, Kimber said, "Think you," which Jean-Paul later told Delia he had thought was an archaic form of the verb to think—a suggestion that they must think hard about the problems discussed.

As they left, they gave Rose Martinez a wave and a phrase of thanks for the delicious cookies. Rose stared after them stonily. The bells jingled as Jean-Paul shut the door behind them. And then they crossed the portal, the snow crunching beneath their boots as they walked to the car.

5

Jean-Paul opened the door of the driver's side for Delia; it was her turn to drive, though they were only a few blocks from the grocery store. The hounds wagged their tails in greeting. Jean-Paul unlocked the passenger side, got in and checked Kimber's map against the one Alice had drawn. "A match most perfect," he said.

Delia backed out carefully. It was difficult to see around the banked snow. They spotted the grocery store before they reached the traffic light and turned in. "Not much longer, guys," Delia reassured the hounds.

Though the store wasn't large, it was well stocked. Delia and Jean-Paul planned to buy enough for a few days, giving them time to check out the cupboards, unpack and get settled. They grabbed a cart and walked down the first aisle picking up items as they went. At the butcher counter, Jean-Paul emitted a sigh of contentment. "Real food," he said and told Delia he planned to prepare *coq au vin*.

"Splendid," Delia replied, "I see they have wine. While you're getting what you need here, I'll go pick up other stuff. I'll be back in a minute..." As Delia made her way to the front of the store, a stunning woman, talking with the check-out clerk as her groceries were being sacked, caught her attention. A black Stetson-style hat, sheep-skin jacket, form-fitting jeans, high brown leather boots and a large, clearly labeled Yves Saint Laurent bag, suggested a small fortune had been spent to keep this lady warm. Delia didn't want to stare; yet she was curious to ascertain why this woman emanated such entitlement. Her imperious carriage? The big, nervous gestures? The commanding voice? Her striking good looks? Though Delia didn't recognize her, she assumed the woman was another movie star; she hadn't realized Santa Fe was a Mecca for celebrities.

Arms full, Delia turned back to find Jean-Paul and deposit the food in his cart. She thought he could check out while she took the dogs for a stroll around the parking lot. She found him stocking up from the wine department, obviously delighted by the selection. However, his face wore a mixed expression of amusement and bewilderment.

"I ask the clerk if they have Macon Blanc. It is excellent for the cooking," he whispered to Delia. "The clerk said 'no', but I spy it here and say, 'Voilà, it is there!' The clerk, he look puzzled and said, 'You mean Makin Blank!' Apparently, that is what I meant. Délie, my treasure, I arrive in a rough and foreign land. Yet there are many wines of France! More than we find in Baltimore! We come to a Wonderland. C'est curieux, n'est-ce pas?"

"Indeed. We've got lots to learn. It's fun, don't you think? I'll go out to the dogs while you finish up and check out."

He flashed her his widest smile. He was having a good time.

Rumpus and Hark were glad to have a stretch and quickly jumped from the car. They liked the piled up snow and each took a bite of the cold, shining jewel-like substance. In the street, cars started and stopped as the traffic light changed, their tires making the special whooshing sound of vehicles traveling on packed snow. Delia's attention was caught by a large, round building cater-cornered across the street, surrounded by a veritable forest of snow-covered trees. From what she could see, a truly hideous sculpture awkwardly placed and of the wrong dimensions for the building behind it, commandeered the corner. Perhaps the composition of building, woods and sculpture looked more harmonious without snow. Delia certainly hoped so.

Delia and the hounds returned to the car to await Jean-Paul. She reached into her bag for the photograph Alice had given her. The discovery of a twin sister was fast becoming an obsession fueled by lack of information and a longing to know the rationale behind her enforced ignorance. She wished she understood her parents' attitude toward *her*—the one who had survived. Had their loving attention hidden complicated resentments? She felt as if she had entered a carnival fun house where happy memories became distorted.

Tilting the photograph toward the strong snow-light, she continued to examine it. She could make out the strands of her mother's pulled-back hair, her long, pretty, nose—not unlike Delia's—and her delicate eyelashes against her cheek as she tenderly looked down at the babies. How young she looked. The picture was infused with feminine delicacy: the antique broach at her mother's lacy neckline, the tiny dimpled baby hands above their frothy christening dresses and the trusting expressions on their identical faces.

She wasn't sure which child was Dorothy. Perhaps if she took the photo out of its frame, she'd find her mother or aunt had identified them on the back. But the worn velvet backing was tight in the frame; she'd need a sharp knife. Once again tears of confusion welled in Delia's eyes. Regardless of which baby was which, her family had betrayed her by withholding their secret. What could they have been thinking? Did her parents assume she'd never find out?

As Delia dabbed her eyes with a Kleenex, a pick-up truck with four large chrome lights mounted on top, its cab somehow held high above gigantic wheels, pulled in beside her. Amazingly, the truck slowly lowered earthward. Two youths sidled out and ambled off toward a nearby shop, kicking snow as they went. "Best not mention that," Delia said to the dogs. "It was an hallucination. This sister business has warped my mind." The hounds, their tails barely moving, peered after the boys as they disappeared into a coffee shop.

Glancing into the rear-view mirror, Delia noticed the handsome woman backing towards her in a snow-covered Land Rover while talking on her cell phone. She missed smashing into Delia's car by no more than an inch. Oh, great. It looked as if Delia's luck was improving.

She was relieved to see Jean-Paul coming towards them, pushing the grocery cart through the snowy parking lot. As Delia flipped up the car back, she wondered if the road was becoming icy. She pictured the

49

cocky youths ending up on their butts and hoped it wouldn't happen. After depositing several bags of groceries, Jean-Paul slammed the back shut and got in beside her. "Many good foods," he said with satisfaction. "Did you see the sight most peculiar?"

Delia decided to hedge her bets. "Peculiar?" she asked innocently.

"*Ah, oui.* That truck, it descended from a more high position. I see it from inside the shop. The check-up woman, she noted my surprise and explain that some young men of Spanish ancestry like vehicles of versatility. Some ride high and descend, while others sit low to the road. Those are called 'low-riders'. She thought it had something to do with ancient Spanish custom."

Delia laughed. "I'm glad to get this little bit of history. The hounds and I thought we were seeing things. Hallucinating from disorientation."

Jean-Paul leaned over and kissed her cheek. His breath was warm but his face was cold. "You are a woman of supreme psychic health! We experience unfamiliar sights. Soon we better understand our new context."

Delia smiled and said truthfully, "You are my context."

"Most certainly, my treasure. Never forget to need me. Remember how long it took me to gain you. Many, many years..."

Shifting his attention to the map he said, "The Santa Fe Post Office is en route. Shall we stop for mail? I should have had it forwarded to Tesuque, Alice said. It is a separate village. That I will correct."

They drove north through town, around on the Paseo to Washington Avenue. Turning west, they spied a modern post office incongruously set beside a stone Court House straight out of nineteenth-century Pennsylvania.

"*Attention! Attention!*" Jean-Paul shouted in French. An ancient pick-up truck headed straight for them. Delia swerved, throwing the hounds off balance, and slid into a parking spot.

"Good god!" she exclaimed, hitting the steering wheel with both hands. "I thought it was a one-way street."

"It is," murmured Jean-Paul peering after the truck as it weaved around a corner.

Delia too had turned to stare. "Isn't that the same truck we were behind on the highway? I vaguely remember noticing it lacked a license plate... The odd thing is — even with that guy driving the wrong way on a one-way street — no one honked or shouted. Maryland people would have fits! But here, people just got out of the way, as if there were no use objecting..."

"How strange this place is... Perhaps that is an ordinary occurrence." He wore an uncertain expression. "I shall retrieve our mail. You will be all right?"

"Yes, darling, I think I will."

Jean-Paul returned within a few minutes, holding down a stack of mail with his chin atop an enormous box. It looked as if he were about to lose his big hat. Delia jumped out to help. "You'll have to put it in the back seat with the dogs. There's no more room in the back. We don't have far to go, do we?" She saw there was a customs slip on the big box. "What on earth is that?"

"Our sheepskin coats from France. I had them sent from the château for I suspected here it would also be very cold."

"What a good idea. Squish over, doggies. We're almost at our destination."

6

Delia continued driving while Jean-Paul navigated. "*Oui*, yes, up and down the big hill says the map. Regard how the vegetation changes. As we descend to the valley, the trees enlarge. Ah, yes, there is the sign for Bishop's Lodge, now this wiggly road, *ah, voilá*, Délie, the little bridge and the skull of the steer nailed to the tree. Turn there at Calle C de Baca."

They crossed an icy brook and began to ascend a snow-packed road.

Delia remarked, "There's the sign for Alice's friends, 'The Ridgeleys'. There, on the left. Do you see it, darling?"

"I look forward to meeting them. They, too, will explain more of this land, *n'est-ce pas*? Careful, my treasure. The road, it is slick. Perhaps change the gear to avoid the skid."

Delia shifted just as she felt the wheels begin to slip. "And that is the second house on the left. We must be almost there."

"The orchard to our right—how pretty it looks in the snow. And *regards*—is it not extensive?"

"Quite a good-sized orchard. Our landlord must sell the apples."

Delia suddenly spied two figures, in the road ahead. "Gad, Jean-Paul, look at those Halloween spooks coming toward us."

But the orchard held his attention. By the time he'd turned around, the strange and menacing figures had disappeared.

"How peculiar," Delia muttered. "Maybe I imagined them..."

Jean-Paul continued his observations of the apple orchard. "The branches, they, I think, will break from the weight of snow so wet. But now it melts, I see. There must be irrigation. Oh! I spy shallow canals which run between each row of trees. (Delia loved the way he pronounced the word 'canals' like 'camels'.) We have that system in France. Do not look now. We will walk when there is time to explore the environs. And there, do you see the sign for Duthuit? Perhaps you park by the gate—not too close to avoid becoming stuck. Yes! Perfect!"

Delia smiled to herself. Not only was she excited to have at last, after two thousand miles, reached their destination, but she was amused by her husband's driving instructions. He was neither a bossy nor controlling man and she was an expert driver. But there was something about her being behind the wheel that inevitably brought out his need to tell her what she already knew. It tickled her because she'd never met a man who wouldn't prefer to be behind the wheel, making the decisions.

They jumped from the car and Jean-Paul opened the door for the hounds, which eagerly followed them through the high wooden gate.

"*Mon dieu!*" Jean-Paul exclaimed.

Delia squeezed his arm. "What a gorgeous house!"

"C'est fantastique ..."

They found themselves inside an enclosed patio where they stood taking in a magical scene. All was silent except for the drip of melting icicles from the trees and canales to the slick flagstones below. Time was eclipsed. The vast New Mexico landscape no longer existed. They had entered an unexpected world of protected domesticity. Standing completely still, they held hands and looked about in delight.

A covered portal ran along the north, west and south sides of the house. Its floor was brick — probably laid in sand — and the snow hadn't reached it. To the west and south stood a one-story, L-shaped adobe house of exquisite proportions, with double hung windows and faded pale blue shutters. This main house was connected on the south side to a smaller adobe building with a door — probably the storage area — beyond which a guesthouse was connected. Though built in the same style, it looked newer than the main house.

A thick, six-foot-high adobe wall, broken by a closed, road-sized, wooden gate, enclosed the east end of the patio, over which gnarly snow-covered wisteria vines hung. To the north, three connecting garages set close to the road, each with its own door to the patio, completed the enclosure. Delia suspected the garages had originally been a stable.

"Let us enter the house and explore our temporary home," Jean-Paul said in a voice full of anticipation. Delia dropped his hand as he pulled the key from his parka pocket. Like the windows, the main entrance in the west façade was surrounded by angled wood against a thick adobe wall. The double entrance door was plain but of graceful proportions. As Jean-Paul eased the key into the antique lock, Delia turned back to study the patio. The dogs were nosing around in a leisurely fashion, leaving yellow stains against one of the snowy apricot trees and sniffing at the base of the well. They too seemed to respond to the sense of peace, harmony and safety.

"I can't believe this place is haunted," Delia said in a low voice. "If it is, the ghost is benign." She realized she'd been unconsciously expecting a gothic structure with evil Victorian turrets and spooky woodwork.

Before opening the door, Jean-Paul looked down at her and put his hand against her cheek. "Beautiful, is it not? Our host, M'sieur Duthuit, is evidently a man of taste most profound. Let us leave the unpacking for a moment as we explore the interior."

Delia put her arm around her husband's waist, her spirits high to be sharing such a lovely place with such a lovely man.

They entered a long hall with a bare wooden floor lit only by the patio windows. Moving from right to left, they found four bedrooms and baths, a large one at the north end, two small ones in-between — perfect for their offices — and an even larger bedroom and bath adjacent to the living room. Delia and Jean-Paul noted that a landscape painting hung in each room, but they didn't recognize the artists: one by Blumenschein, another by Dasburg and two by someone named Victor Higgins. All very nice paintings of New Mexico.

The second Higgins — this one of autumn aspens — hung in what was obviously the master bedroom. "We shall take this room for ourselves." Jean-Paul walked to the three west windows with a springy step. Outside they saw a flagstone terrace beyond which a row of cottonwood trees stood guard against the western sun. "The big trees, when they leaf out, keep the house cool in summer," Jean-Paul murmured.

On this side of the house, they noted that the shutters were affixed to the inside of the windows. Each room was simply furnished in the Spanish Colonial style, with bright multi-colored wool bedspreads and chair cushions. Here in the main bedroom, the predominant color was a bright Mexican pink. Passionate pink, Delia thought as she eyed the queen-size bed with approval. It would do very well for their frequent, delicious lovemaking.

Jean-Paul's voice broke through her thoughts as he wheeled back from the wavy-glassed windows. "*Regards*, Délie, a fireplace in each room. How sweet to fall asleep to the glow of fire."

Rumpus and Hark trotted in behind as they entered the living room where two windows faced west; three more and a pale-blue door faced south. Above the fireplace, they recognized the painting of red hills as one by Georgia O'Keeffe. These red hills offered a contrast to the vast green, white and blue view outside the windows. Opening the door to the terrace, to further examine the view, Delia and Jean-Paul felt the remaining sun warm against their faces. They looked out over orchards to the west and south beyond which were acres of sloping hills of snowy piñon trees. Off to the east, the high white peaks of the Sangres de Cristos had already become tinged with pink as the sun began to drop in the western sky.

"What a place!" Delia gasped. "Did you ever expect anything like this?"

"Not even in my dreams." Jean-Paul stood behind her and hugged her. She backed up against him, feeling his spare body against hers, enwrapped by his puffy parka. They stood enchanted for some moments, watching the few long skinny clouds as they reddened. The hounds plopped down at their feet.

Delia laughed. "Dogs don't like views. Let's finish our house tour."

They reentered the house and moved to the dining room, which had three beautiful windows to the south; opposite were two more to the inside patio as well as a large fireplace. A refectory table stood in the center of the room surrounded by a dozen chairs. Two more country tables stood against the walls for use as serving tables.

"Does it not look like a farm house of France? Ah, Délie, indeed, I did not expect this. Here is where a family of many cousins collects!"

The dogs led the way like little real estate agents to the adjoining kitchen, a large square room with windows and a door to the patio on their left and an eating alcove jutting out and surrounded by windows in three directions, on their right. Large clay pots of blooming geraniums — red, salmon, pink and white — stood upon the wide sills. Delia went over and plucked off a yellowed leaf which she crinkled in her hand. It gave off its pungent smell. "Geraniums love sun, and especially in the morning — there must be plenty coming in here."

She entered a small adjoining room and saw it contained a furnace, hot water heater and laundry, with a lavatory beyond. She noticed a locked door, presumably to the storage area for which they had not been given a key.

Jean-Paul remained with the hounds in the kitchen, looking about. "Ah," he said meditatively, "we have breakfast there, warmed by the morning sun." Then he impulsively flung out his arms. "*Ou la, la!* What a kitchen! I can not wait to begin the preparation of dinner!" Delia knew many days of horrible road food whetted his appetite for his own cooking.

In the space of one room they had traveled from colonial Spain to modern France. Though, like the rest of the house, the floors were wood and the walls adobe with a ceiling of dark vigas, the cabinetry was new — white painted wood with glassed in shelving. The utilities were of the latest and most luxurious French models with a work island in the center beneath a hanging rack of bright copper pots.

Delia stared at the stove, her hands clasped beneath her chin. "Joy and rapture! Eight gas burners! And the counters aren't too high for me... thank heavens. I'd pictured our benevolent host as a big man — a barrel-chested, opera-singing man — and there has been no mention of a nice little wife."

"*C'est formidable!*" Jean-Paul agreed. "*Quelle bonne chance, chérie,* you will not have to climb upon the little stool to work here..."

The hounds had run to the doors beneath the sink, which stood under the patio window. They growled and Rumpus began to bark.

"What's the problem, little fellows?" Delia asked, opening the cabinet doors. "Oh, oh, a mouse. Shoo! Shoo! Go back where you came from!" She quickly grabbed the dogs' collars and shut the cabinet door with her foot. "Did you see that, Jean-Paul? This place looks clean, but we'll have to call the exterminator. Alice said rodents here carry plague. She gave me flea powder for the hounds. Oh, dear, oh dear, trouble in paradise."

7

After unpacking the car, parking the bags and boxes in the long hallway, Delia and Jean-Paul decided to leave the rest for the next day. Delia pulled the dogs' beds into the little room she intended to use as a study and then soaked in a long hot bath. Jean-Paul came into the bathroom with the excuse of asking when she wanted a drink and stayed to towel her off and wrap her in her terrycloth robe. Later, he produced a glorious *coq au vin* with tarragon, onions and carrots, which they ate at the long dining table in front of a blazing fire.

That night, although Delia woke once to the rasp of wind against the windows, there were no ghostly encounters. Even Rumpus and Hark slept late the next morning.

After cutting their grapefruit and exclaiming over the fine selection of knives, Delia and Jean-Paul enjoyed their usual breakfast of *café au lait* and croissants. Delia decided to organize the kitchen while Jean-Paul unpacked and exercised the dogs. She'd noticed the night before that the food cupboard was full of duplicates and left-over flour, sugar, canned goods, partially used cereal boxes and, alas, a large can of honey in which floated another mouse—this one quite dead. What a way to die, Delia thought. The sorry spectacle offered a lesson in the dangers of greed.

She threw most of the contents of the cupboard into a large garbage bag and tried to remember what Kimber had said about when Joseph from the Pueblo would pick up the trash. As if her thoughts conjured him up, a man appeared at the kitchen door, who, Delia suspected, must be Joseph, himself. As she opened the door, he said by way of introduction, "I'm Joe." He was a short, stocky, well-built, dark-skinned man of indeterminate age, with dark, canny eyes and straight blue-black hair bound into a ponytail. He was dressed in a heavy grey hooded sweatshirt, wide-legged jeans and black running shoes. Each hand held the hand of a tiny Indian girl, also in jeans, with pink parkas, black braids and inquisitive black eyes.

"Hi," Delia replied, "I'm Mrs. Duval. And who are these charming little people?"

Joe laughed good-naturedly. Delia could see they noticed the gaping garbage bag full of discarded food. She experienced a pang of guilt for throwing out so much and wondered what the new arrivals were thinking. But they made no comment and Joe answered her question.

"These are my goddaughters, Lizard-Breath and Rocks-and-Sand." As if suddenly propelled into action by the announcement of their names, the two solemn little girls turned on the elderly man and began beating him with tiny fists.

"No! No! No!" they sang, jumping around him in fury. "We are NOT Lizard-Breath and Rocks-and-Sand! No! No! No! Tata! No! We are not!"

Joe smiled at them and said, "Okay. Okay, okay. This is Elizabeth and this is Roxann."

Although there were a few Native Americans living in Maryland, Delia was unfamiliar with their ways. For a moment she had actually believed in the validity of the girls' unusual names. Why not? Didn't the Indian People live close to nature? Still, 'Lizard-Breath' and 'Rocks-and-Sand' were bordering on the absurd. She knew the traditions of the Native American People were far from absurd.

Delia held out her hand to each little girl, who, after a slight hesitation, smiled and shook her hand. Each child had chipped pink nail polish on her tiny nails.

"What's your name?" Elizabeth, whom Delia guessed was about six, asked.

"Mrs. Duval."

"No! No!" chorused the little girls again. "We mean your *real* name."

Delia understood they were asking for her first name and said, "Delia."

They looked puzzled for a moment and then giggled. "Deal ya another card," Roxann said in a singsong voice. Delia certainly didn't know what to expect from this set.

Joe said, "I got work in the orchard then I come for the trash. You put it in the patio, Deal-ya." He spoke as if each word puffed from his mouth on an exhale.

"Sure," Delia replied. "Thanks very much." She expected the girls to follow their godfather, but they slid out of their parkas, letting them fall to the floor, and scooted over to the breakfast room. "You got cocoa, Deal-ya?"

Delia hadn't factored in baby-sitting duties and decided she'd better make that clear. They were beguiling little imps, but there was other work to be done, especially the establishment of a writing schedule for her syndicated garden columns, which, because of the research involved, were time-consuming. And even though it was now only December, she had to stay several months ahead, which meant she was heading into spring, the busiest garden-preparation time. Readers expected clear and creative instructions and ideas. In fact, this was moving toward the time when she'd begin to get reader inquiries that she did her best to address in the text of her columns.

"We'll have cocoa some other day, but today I'm very busy, so perhaps it would be a good idea for you to go down to the orchard, too." She smiled at them in a kindly fashion, meanwhile guiding them into their parkas and toward the door.

Elizabeth looked up into her face with concern. "Deal-ya, you afraid to be here by yourself?"

She finally had them both out the door, so she figured it was probably safe to exchange a few words with them on the portal. "No, why would I be afraid? Besides my husband and dogs will be coming back soon. I'm not afraid."

The girls exchanged looks. "Ghosts," Roxann murmured almost inaudibly. "Bad ghosts can get you."

"Well," Delia said slowly. "Maybe that's just a story. You know sometimes stories get started and they're not really true. But people tell them anyway and other people begin to believe them. That's just something that happens."

"Oh, but lots of people seen the ghosts," said Elizabeth.

"Yeah," added Roxann flinging out her arms. "They seen a hundred ghosts!"

Oh, dear, Delia thought, this conversation could go on all morning.

"Well, girls, I guess I'll just have to make friends with them."

They looked at her with wide eyes before scampering out of the patio, banging the wooden door behind them. Delia sighed. I do hope they don't run into Jean-Paul and the hounds. They might very well attach themselves and be back in the kitchen expecting cocoa. Jean-Paul is so good-natured, he's likely to make it for them — and then where will we be? Babysitters at the beck and call of two hard-to-resist little girls.

She tied up the garbage bag and lugged it onto the portal. She noticed there was a sort of outside cabinet attached to the wall under the kitchen sink window and suspected that must have been where the mice got in. She'd telephone Kimber about an exterminator and then unpack her clothes, laptop and writing materials. But no sooner had she started to call Kimber than there was another knock, this time at the front door. So she scooted down the corridor hoping it wasn't the little girls again. She was thankful that despite her work clothes, she'd applied a little make-up. At least she didn't look totally scruffy for this unexpected stream of visitors.

She opened the door to find a handsome man smiling at her, hat in hand. Though about her own age, he exuded an old-world style. He wore a Norfolk tweed jacket over a fine wool shirt, a silk foulard, beautifully cut cord trousers and stout oxford shoes. He resembled a nineteenth-century country gentleman — not what she'd come to expect in Northern New Mexico. No jeans, no boots and no wide-brimmed cowboy hat. He examined her face calmly with pale blue eyes set in a well cared for beardless face with large, even teeth.

Delia was so startled by his dapper appearance that for a moment she didn't speak. He reminded her of an actor in an Edwardian play.

"Good morning, Countess. I am Steve Kovic, your neighbor from across the road." He pulled off his gray glove and extended his hand. "I fear I am disturbing you, but my wife asked that I drop by to invite you and the count to join us and a group of friends for drinks this afternoon at five."

Although his English was perfect, Delia detected a European accent. Her first thought was to wonder where he'd gotten their title information. Now she and Jean-Paul would be in for all sorts of questions and misperceptions, and damn it, she really didn't want to cope with all that.

Realizing she still hadn't said a word, she took his hand and smiled as graciously as she could. "Why, how very kind of you, Mr. Kovic. Do, please, come in."

"I will stay only a moment, but we intend to make you welcome. Guillaume has become a great friend and he told us you and the count would be here over Christmas — and perhaps for some weeks afterwards?"

Oh, so that's it. Guillaume Duthuit would of course have mentioned they were coming and this Steve Kovic, probably European himself, would naturally use her title in greeting. If she could stop him from spreading the word, it would make life easier for her and Jean-Paul. On second thought, perhaps it was better than being called by their first names on immediate acquaintance. They'd never be comfortable with this western custom, yet to object seemed unfriendly. She shivered in exasperation: this name business was silly.

Meanwhile Mr. Kovic was still standing on the threshold. "Please, come in," Delia said. As she shut the door behind him she detected a pleasing and no doubt expensive scent of after-shave lotion. Her visitor was rather a dandy.

Delia led the way down the hall to the living room, which she remembered from her readings was referred to as a 'sala'. As they entered, she noticed a mysterious little pile of dirt on the floor to the right of the sofa. She stepped around it, pretending she didn't notice it.

Even without a fire, the room was pleasantly warm, thanks to the old-fashioned radiators which held the heat when the furnace was off. "Please," Delia smiled as she took his elegant dove-gray hat and gloves and laid them on a Spanish Colonial side table beside the door. He was a continental character straight out of a Henry James novel. All he needed were spats and a gold-topped cane. She, on the other hand, should be wearing a long sweeping gown with a bustle. Don't laugh, she told herself: he'll think you're nuts. Aloud, she asked, "May I offer you coffee or a glass of sherry?"

"Thank you. I shall stay only a moment. I know you must unpack and get settled."

There was a sudden clatter and the hounds raced in followed by Jean-Paul looking wind-blown and exhilarated. Delia wished she too had gone walking and left the organizational chores for later. "My dear, this is our neighbor, Mr. Kovic, a friend of Guillaume Duthuit, come to invite us for drinks this evening."

"How do you do?" responded Jean-Paul, taking Kovic's hand. "It is a pleasure to meet you."

"Yes, Count, as I was mentioning to the countess, we have friends coming this evening and hope you might join us."

"That is most gracious of you," Jean-Paul said. "Please, will you not sit?"

Delia noticed the hounds were less than thrilled with their visitor. Normally they danced around with wagging tails when people arrived, but now they stood behind Delia, tails still and seeming ill-at-ease. Delia bent down and patted their heads. They stayed close to her as the three humans sat on the sofa and adjoining easy chairs.

Their visitor leaned back, grasping one knee with well-manicured hands. Delia noticed a gold signet ring studded with two discreet rubies. "Guillaume is very pleased you are here—he prefers this house to be occupied." Kovic smiled broadly, his large teeth shining. "Unfortunately, he is seldom here except during opera season. He requested that my wife and I look after you. I understand you are already acquainted with our neighbors, the Ridgeleys, through a cousin of the countess, I believe..."

"Oh, if you please," Jean-Paul interrupted, "we do not use the title in this country. It can seem peculiar and a little ridiculous. Please, I am Jean-Paul Duval and my wife is Delia Hager Duval."

"Certainly... Jean-Paul and Delia." Kovic made a barely perceptible bow of acknowledgement.

"And where are you from?" Delia enquired politely.

"I am a citizen of the world," replied their opulent visitor grandly, "although I grew up in France. In Marseilles. My mother was French; my father was Polish. He owned a shipping company based in Marseilles."

He unclasped his knee and sat up-right, one hand on each leg. "But, you, Jean-Paul, are purely French, I detect, and you, Cou... Delia, where are you from?"

"Maryland. Near Baltimore. That's where Jean-Paul and I met. My husband has been living there for many years."

"Oh, yes, the Baltimore Museum of Art and the great Cone Collection of Matisse and Picasso. I recall the museum also has a charming collection of watches from different periods, if I'm not mistaken. I am in the international jewelry business. Import-export, which in a round-about way grew from my father's shipping concern in Marseilles." He smiled benevolently again and rose suddenly. The hounds started but remained quiet. "I've enjoyed meeting you both, but I must not keep you. Please come anytime after five o'clock. We are the first drive on the opposite side of this road."

Their visitor hesitated. Smiling charmingly, he said, "I hope you are not disconcerted by the tales concerning this house." He paused.

"And what tales may that be?' Jean-Paul enquired.

"Oh, a ridiculous rumor that the house is haunted. The locals have circulated the idea for years and it seems to have stuck. Nothing – nothing to it, I assure you."

Jean-Paul looked searchingly at their guest and replied quietly, "Actually, we have indeed been advised of a resident ghost. Do you suppose it will become a nuisance?"

Delia couldn't tell if Jean-Paul was serious or just stringing the man along, which he did sometimes when he thought someone was absurd.

"No, no, certainly not," Mr. Kovic hastened to assure them.

Rumpus and Hark leaned heavily against Delia's legs. Perhaps they were becoming anxious about the ghost. Perhaps they were awed by Kovic's remarkable elegance. Delia was a little overwhelmed herself.

Everyone laughed uneasily. Delia noticed Rumpus and Hark had padded through the mysterious pile of dirt, sending it across the floor and down between the old floorboards. They all proceeded together down the narrow hall.

After they'd seen their guest out the door, Jean-Paul turned to

Delia, "*Eh bien, mon ange,* it is certain our neighbor most dapper is no Frenchman."

"No? Well, I couldn't be sure. But he's European of some sort, I suppose. We forgot to ask about his wife. We don't even know her name. And we never got around to telling him we don't actually know the Ridgeleys nor Guillaume Duthuit. Too bad about the invitation tonight. We haven't even unpacked. But I couldn't think of an excuse."

Feeling harassed, Delia sighed and brushed her hand across her forehead. Between the honeyed mouse corpse, Lizard-Breath, Rocks-and-Sand, and the opulent mystery-man, it had been a distracting morning.

8

Delia and Jean-Paul decided to walk the short distance to the Kovic house. They wore their long sheepskin coats and carried walking sticks and flashlights, which was safer, they thought, than driving the slippery road.

The wind from the southwest blew cold against their faces. A few lights twinkled faintly from the village below and there was a fragrance of wood smoke in the air. The now overcast sky obscured moon and stars. A thin outline of red sunset lingered far to the west behind the Jemez Mountains.

A pick-up truck with a snowplow attached chugged up the road shoving snow to either side. It stopped at the side of the Kovic driveway. An elderly couple slowly maneuvered themselves from the truck and, with a friendly wave in Delia and Jean-Paul's direction, headed rapidly through the cold toward the Kovics's decidedly grand front door. The driveway was slippery, but their fellow guests clung to the parked cars as they made their way toward the gigantic house.

"I never saw guests arrive at a party in a snowplow," Delia commented to Jean-Paul.

"We see it frequently in France," Jean-Paul lied merrily. "And everyone also has this type of lighting."

Delia knew Jean-Paul was being droll and had never in his life seen a snowplow party arrival nor this particular type of lighting. Candles in sand were set in paper bags outlining the drive and offering a wavering light for the arriving guests. Farolitos also mounted the formidable staircase to the heavy, baronial front door, which Delia suspected came from Morocco. She saw more farolitos in rows along the rooftop and recalled their host's large, shining teeth.

The light in the entrance hall was unexpectedly dim. The glamorous woman Delia had noticed in the grocery store greeted them inside the front door. "Hello! Hello! You must be Jean-Paul and Delia. So glad you could come—especially on such short notice. I'm Wilma. Steve ran down to the village market to get more gin. We discovered we were nearly out."

Wilma, who was of medium height, held herself majestically, enhancing her aura of entitlement. Her dark hair was cut extremely short and her face, with its smooth, even features, could only be described as beautiful. (Delia knew only the gorgeous got away with very short hairstyles.) Unlike her husband, Wilma spoke with a mid-western twang—strong r's and flattened vowels. It was rather charming and she did, indeed, seem happy to see them. But her movements were jerky and nervous. Delia wondered if her hostess was uncomfortable meeting strangers.

A small, faded woman stood ready to take their coats. She had dry, yellowish hair, sallow skin and darting suspicious eyes. Delia's immediate impression was of a person deeply uncomfortable in her world. Wilma's nervousness could simply be excitement; this woman's anxiety put Delia on edge. But Delia gave her a friendly nod and sat on the edge of a tall hall chair to remove her snow boots. She'd thought to bring her leather pumps in her coat pockets. In the dim light of the vestibule, she noticed several other women had also left boots in the hall.

Jean-Paul continued to stand with Wilma, but because the faded woman was determined to take his coat, he handed Wilma the bottle of French wine from the cache he'd bought the day before. In France, it was usually considered bad form to bring wine to the hostess, but here it seemed a fitting gesture. Jean-Paul shrugged off his sheepskin coat and the faded woman finally staggered off to unknown realms with their two heavy coats across her arms.

Liberated from her coat and boots, Delia moved back toward Jean-Paul and their hostess. Wilma resembled her husband in the flashing brilliance of her smile, which, at the moment, she beamed upon Jean-Paul. Delia saw that Jean-Paul, a connoisseur of feminine beauty, was drinking in Wilma's. Her oval face was even-featured and made-up with a model's perfection. Her glowing skin was as smooth as a child's. However, despite Wilma's projection of assurance, her expression suggested uneasy astonishment. She seemed too young to have undergone one of those face-lifts where eyes are transformed to perpetual wonder; perhaps it was simply the width between them that suggested surprise.

"What a magnificent house!" Delia exclaimed. (She told herself she wasn't saying she liked it, just that its grandeur was remarkable.)

Wilma looked around her as if seeing her house through Delia's eyes. "Yes," she said tentatively, "we're here to show people how to live."

Delia was intrigued by Wilma's mixture of arrogance and bewilderment. She was curious to know more about this beautiful woman who appeared quite different from the people Delia knew on the East coast and Europe.

Together they descended brick steps into a brilliantly lit, two-story room with balconies on opposite sides. Heavily curtained windows stood to their left; an enormous fire roared in a medieval-sized fireplace on the opposite wall. A fluffy white cat warmed herself on the hearth.

Amidst six huge potted plants, groups of people stood talking, drinking and eating in small clusters. A few were formally dressed in suits and ties, but most of the men and some of the women wore jeans with festive shirts or jackets. There was much Indian jewelry in evidence and several women sported handsome antique concho belts around their waists.

Delia shifted her attention from the perfection of Wilma's face and now noticed she was attired completely in black and wore a dazzling collection of jewelry that reflected the lights from the ferocious fire—not Indian jewelry but precious jewels in sophisticated settings. Steve had mentioned he was in the jewelry business, and Delia decided that Wilma was the perfect model for his wares. A large gold star set with brilliant diamonds hung from a chain around Wilma's neck. Her matching earrings cascaded gracefully down either side of her long, straight neck. On each arm Wilma wore diamond bracelets set in glittering gold and, though her right hand was bare, her left hand sported an enormous carved ruby ring surrounded by diamonds and sapphires. It was a breath-taking display that enhanced Wilma's natural glamour.

Delia had come to New Mexico with no jewelry except her emerald wedding rings, a modest watch, one set of small gold earrings and a narrow gold bracelet, all of which she wore at the moment. And although her pale fine-wool sweater and trousers were becoming, she felt woefully underdressed compared to her hostess. She and Wilma belonged to different species, of which Delia's was the inferior. But Delia reminded herself she was not in a competition: her husband found her sexy and charming and had waited many years for her, his abiding love known only to himself. Feeling inferior was a perverse indulgence. Besides, by almost any standard, Wilma's masquerade as a jewelry display counter was definitely over the top.

However, it was also clear that Jean-Paul was keenly aware of the remarkable feast of his hostesses' appearance, though for the moment, he had torn his glance away to take in the unexpected grandeur of the room. It was, Delia thought, what current real-estate parlance referred to as a Great Room. The ceiling was so high and the furnishings—the lamps, tables and chairs—so large that they reminded her of pictures she'd seen of robber baron-era hotels. If she sat in one of the chairs, her legs would stick out like a two-year-old's.

Wilma suddenly clutched Delia and Jean-Paul each by a hand (not unlike Joseph and his little goddaughters, Delia thought) and led them to a group for introductions. "Jean-Paul and Delia, you know the Ridgeleys—

cousins of yours, I believe. I'll just let them introduce you around..."

"Well, actually," Delia began, "we've never met..." But Wilma's attention had wandered. Several more people had arrived and Wilma moved off with a stately gait to greet them. It was remarkable the way she managed to transform her average height into such stature.

But here was the elderly couple who'd arrived on the snowplow. The couple Alice had described as her 'dear friends'.

Ethan and Molly Ridgeley beamed at Delia and Jean-Paul. It was immediately clear they qualified as what Delia's mother had called 'real people': their expressions were so genuinely good-natured and their looks so unaffected.

Ethan wore heavy khaki trousers and a pink shirt with a tartan tie under an ancient tweed jacket. His white hair was parted in the middle over a long, sensitive face with thick, bushy white eyebrows. He was of medium height with a slim, strong, small-boned body, not unlike Jean-Paul's. Ethan's stoop, however, betrayed his age, which must be somewhere in the late eighties, Delia reckoned. The firelight played against his features in such a way as to heighten the severity of his beak-like nose and the furrows of his brow. His white-lashed eyes were good humored, sage and penetrating. He looked intently at the newcomers and smiled a charming, welcoming smile.

Molly, by contrast, was short—smaller than Delia—and plump, without being fat. Delia remembered that Molly's métier was food and writing cookbooks—skinny cooks don't necessarily inspire confidence. Molly wore no make-up on her round face, which was surrounded by curly, gray, helter-skelter hair. Her good-natured, golden-brown eyes were small and jolly. She was dressed in wide-legged black pants, an attractive, short red corduroy jacket decorated with bright embroidered hollyhocks, and comfortable-looking tied black suede shoes.

The Ridgeleys introduced themselves with cordiality. From their voices it was evident they were from New England. New Mexico seemed to be as much of a conglomeration of accents as Europe; and Delia was becoming increasingly aware of the nuance of pronunciation.

"So you're Alice Spencer's cousin! I recognize that beautiful nose.

Welcome, Delia dear. Welcome, Jean-Paul!" Molly flashed them a light-hearted, infectious smile. They all shook hands.

"We didn't expect to meet up with you so soon," explained Ethan, "although Alice had told us you'd probably arrive last night. Are the Kovics old friends?"

They explained how they'd met Steve Kovic only that morning. Jean-Paul asked if they were not the couple they'd seen arriving on the snowplow.

The Ridgeleys both laughed. "It's not our usual habit," Ethan assured them. "But since we have it, we take the opportunity to keep the road plowed. The village snowplow gets to us last. When we leave, we'll swing by your place and smooth it out a little."

"So you hadn't met the Kovics before?" Molly enquired.

"No," Delia replied. "What are they like?"

"Well, the Kovics are friendly folk." Ethan seemed subtly amused. "They've lived here—on and off—only a few years and probably know five times as many people as we do. They are do-ers and serve on a great many boards and committees."

"This certainly is a grand house," Delia remarked again. "I didn't expect to see anything so elaborate in this part of the world."

"Nor did we," Ethan replied. "It's rather startling, wouldn't you say?"

"Grandiose." Molly supplied the word they were all thinking, but hesitating to use. Delia liked people who articulate the unspoken, especially if it's done with good humor.

Delia and Jean-Paul laughed. He suggested, "It must have been a building project of magnitude. How long did it take?"

Ethan and Molly replied in chorus, "A long time!"

Ethan explained, "That's how it seemed to us. We live at the bottom of the hill, you see. You can imagine what it was like to have the equipment rattling past starting early each morning—the dust, the dirt, the noise, the commotion. We thought it would never end!"

Molly sighed, "We were sad, too, because there was a rather attractive old adobe house here. This big house gobbled it up. Somewhere within the bowels of this place we'd find remnants of the old, I suppose... Actually we've never seen the entire new structure except from the outside. While it was being built, we'd come up on Sundays, walk around the construction site and try to guess what was coming next."

"They started by simply adding on — then it seems there was a fresh supply of funds and the new structure devoured the old." Ethan shook his head and took a sip from his glass of wine.

"An image most sinister," Jean-Paul remarked thoughtfully.

Molly nodded in agreement. "But in the long run, it all worked out. Construction finally ceased and we all became friends. The Kovics make an effort to be welcoming and hospitable."

"And you? Have you been in New Mexico long?" Jean-Paul enquired, snagging two glasses of wine from a guy with a tray. Handing one to Delia, he smiled and turned his attention back to the Ridgeleys whose glasses were still mostly full.

"Goodness." Molly laughed. "We've been here since the beginning of time."

Jean-Paul, whom Delia considered the most courtly of men, replied seriously, "Ah, but surely not..."

"I sense you are New Englanders," Delia ventured.

"Perceptive lady," Ethan replied, carefully setting his glass on a nearby table. "We're originally from Vermont. But after our marriage — almost sixty years ago — and my finishing medical school, we moved to the Navajo Reservation. Our son was born on the reservation. We remained until he was ready for first grade. Then we moved to Albuquerque, which is where we met Alice and her husband, Miles. After I retired, we decided to come here to be close to the Santa Fe Opera — one of our chief delights. We got tired of those late summer-night drives back to Albuquerque." When he smiled his lined old face became a road map of mirth. "Now I study music and bird watch, but my dear wife, as you may know, has never retired. She keeps right on finding another cookbook to write — having started with food of the Navajo Nation, going on to Northern New Mexico cooking and Santa Fe-style cooking and on and on and on." He patted his wife's shoulder affectionately.

70

"Indeed, yes!" Jean-Paul interjected. "We know the books very well, *n'est-ce pas, mon ange?*" He turned to Delia for collaboration.

Delia sipped the excellent chardonnay and then said, "I think I have five of your books, Molly, and we both depend on them. Jean-Paul is a brilliant chef, but we both occasionally run out of inspiration. We often turn to you!"

It was apparent that, although they'd just met, they were establishing a warm rapport. Delia's realization that they had two new sympathetic friends cast a happy glow on the prospect of their temporary life in New Mexico. They chatted on together; the Ridgeleys introducing them to several more guests before inviting them for Sunday lunch at their house.

Delia was sorry when Ethan and Molly left; she was having fun discovering their opinions and thoughts about New Mexico. Delia was particularly struck by their rendition of the devastating history of the Northern New Mexican Spanish: how they were abandoned by country and church, their terrible conflicts with the Comanches and their loss of land and livelihoods when the U.S. federal officials moved in. It was a cruel and terrible history.

After the Ridgeleys' departure, Jean-Paul fell into conversation with a stranger to whom they hadn't been introduced. Delia took the opportunity to slip away so she might walk around and examine the several large western-style paintings that hung between the windows. She was taken aback to see price tags attached to the picture frames. Prices ran from thirty-five thousand for a small painting of a crow, to a hundred-fifty thousand for a cowboy roping a steer. Perhaps it was the western custom to inform your guests what you paid for your possessions. She had noticed the word 'sharing' had become au courant; maybe this was its hospitality and/or decorating form.

She felt a seductive hand on the back of her neck as she studied the layered paint of the cowboy painting. Assuming it was Jean-Paul, she said without turning, "Well, I don't think much of that!"

But it was not Jean-Paul's voice that replied, "Neither do I. It's not one of his best."

Delia wheeled around. Her splendorous host stood beside her looking slyly amused.

Embarrassed, she drew back from his hand. "Oh, I am sorry! I thought you were my husband."

"It's quite all right. I do not care for the painting either. Too garish. The color is over-done. I am happy to say we do not own it. Wilma has a gallery on Canyon Road. You and the c... your husband must pay a visit. You will receive an invitation for a Friday night opening. That is when many Santa Fe galleries hold their openings. It is local custom—a sort of ritual. Everyone comes into town and visits the new exhibits. Sometimes Wilma brings some of the art home to hang here temporarily, hence the price tags."

Delia noticed again that though perfect, Steve's English was rather unnatural and stilted. Like his outfits, it seemed overly precise and studied. Tonight his speech struck her as even a little prissy.

But turning her attention back to the painting, she also decided it was a relief that the piece came from a gallery and was actually for sale. The idea of otherwise announcing the cost of one's possessions disconcerted her. She recovered her equilibrium and looked around for a painting or object she could honestly compliment to redeem her manners. Spotting an oil portrait of two handsome children in an ornate frame, she said with enthusiasm, "Now there's a painting I really like! And I hope you own it!"

Steve followed her glance and together they walked across the room to the portrait, stopping along the way for a few words and introductions to some of the other guests. As they stood side by side, examining the children's portrait, Steve said, "These are Wilma's children by her first marriage, Gillian and Jonathan. They are grown up now. Gillian is at Princeton and Jonathan goes to Yale. You'll meet them. They are off with friends at the moment, but they have already arrived for their Christmas holiday."

Delia nodded and continued to gaze at the enchanting subjects of the painting: a girl about eight, with her mother's wide set-eyes, and a boy only slightly younger. They were dressed informally in striped tee shirts and navy blue shorts. The little girl wore leather sandals, held a cloth doll in a gingham dress and sat tilted slightly toward her brother. The little boy was barefoot, sporting a band-aid on one knee and holding a small brown teddy bear by its foot. The bear dangled precariously and seemed to project out from the picture plane toward the viewer. Although there was a prevailing sense of peace about the composition, both children seemed about to spring into action, as if their ability to hold the pose was coming to an end. The canvas managed to convey such a sense of the moment that Delia wondered if the artist had painted the portrait from a photograph.

The background constituted a marked contrast to the subjects. Behind the rattan settee upon which the children were seated, tall, curved-topped French doors stood open to a formal garden of many-hued greens and blues. The curve of the children's seat echoed the curve of the doors and the curve of a lovingly painted dappled tree branch, all of which offered a sense of airy space and openness into which the children would run. The formality of the location contrasted with the informality of the children's positions and clothing, giving the painting an appealing tension and interest. Delia bent to read the signature of the artist in the lower right corner, but couldn't make it out.

Steve, meanwhile, had moved close to Delia, his sleeve touching her arm. He bent slightly toward the canvas, as if he, too, were examining the painting for the first time.

"Do you know the artist?" Delia asked, stepping back and turning towards him.

"Actually, I don't, Countess — Delia. It was someone, I think, who also lived in Lake Forest — outside Chicago — which is where Wilma and the children lived with her first husband. I think perhaps the artist was a classmate of Wilma's at the Art Institute, where she studied for some time."

"Oh, does Wilma paint, too?"

"Unfortunately, she gave it up because she grew allergic to oil and acrylic. She does sketch some — with graphite — and sometimes works in pastel. But her energy is absorbed primarily by running galleries. She is extremely successful — an excellent business woman, I am happy to say."

"May I ask what happened to the children's father?" Delia glanced again at the enchanting portrait.

"Well, that is rather a sad chapter. Soon after this painting was finished, Wilma's husband died of a rare blood disease. The doctors did not diagnosis it in time, but even if they had, there was not much they could have done. It was very traumatic. Everyone says he was a nice chap—and barely forty. One of those things..." He waved his hands and shrugged his shoulders in a European way.

Delia was fascinated by people's personal histories and found that they were usually delighted to talk about themselves.

"And you met Wilma in Chicago?"

"Actually, no. In Paris. She had come to a jewelry show at which I exhibited. She was thinking of opening a gallery and offering jewelry as well as sculpture and painting. Jewelry is art, too, you know," he said defensively.

"Well, yes, certainly," Delia hastened to reassure him. "But I gather she decided ultimately to stick to painting?"

"And sculpture. I convinced her she would do better as my model as opposed to a jewelry outlet—and then," he laughed triumphantly, "I married her."

"I see." Delia thought she may have asked too many personal questions. Turning back to the painting, she murmured, "They certainly are beautiful children. I look forward to meeting them."

A waiter came by with the drinks tray. Steve took Delia's empty wine glass from her hand and put it on the waiter's tray. "Will you have another?" he asked politely while staring into her eyes.

Because of her extraordinary emerald eyes, Delia was used to people staring at them, but Steve, she knew, was flirting. She wasn't terribly comfortable with that. "Thank you, I think not," she replied, shifting her gaze from his and turning once again to the painting. She was beginning to tire of this discussion.

Steve remained next to her, pondering the painting almost as if he'd never seen it before, and their discussion hadn't already taken place.

Rocking back on his right foot, his left hand under his chin, he looked like a Rodin sculpture in expensive clothes.

Delia sighed inwardly at the awkward situation. She couldn't quite figure out how to end their conversation without seeming rude so she asked, "Do the children like New Mexico?"

"They like the skiing. And I think they like getting away from the dreary east-coast winters. Especially Jonathan, who frequently remarks that New Haven is 'a dump'. Between you and me, Delia, I think he is right." Steve smiled at her as if she no doubt agreed with him.

"They certainly are gorgeous—and beautifully painted..." Delia was definitely feeling the combined effects of her strenuous morning, the glass of wine, the high altitude and the present tedium.

She was finally saved by a lively little woman dressed in a cowboy hat, fringed leather dress and ornate cowboy boots, who ran up to their host, grabbed his arm, and drawled in a pronounced Texas accent, "Steve, Steve darlin', you've got to come meet my houseguests! Excuse us, Honey," she said, turning to Delia, "but my friends just love foreigners! They've traveled to just about every country on this little ol' planet and I'm dying for them to have the chance to visit with Stevie here!"

Steve turned to Delia apologetically and allowed himself to be dragged off to meet several similarly dressed people who had just entered the room. (One of the men still wore his handsome cowboy hat.) Delia waved sympathetically to her host and looked around for Jean-Paul, whom she spied nearby having a conversation with a tall, red-headed, pink-faced man in a bolo tie. She was more than ready to leave the party and had begun to wonder where their coats were. As she sidled up to Jean-Paul, he put his arm around her and introduced her to the man who's named was Slim Fellows, a local architect.

Delia thought "Slim" was an odd name for this large, puffy-faced guy who surely weighed over two hundred pounds. He wore glasses with pale blue plastic rims possibly chosen by a small child. And behind his glasses, a pair of tiny, watery eyes almost disappeared in his fleshy face as he smiled and said hello to Delia. But his smile was genuinely friendly, and though his voice was twangy, it was unexpectedly melodious.

"Sure am glad to meet ya, Delia. Seems like your husband and I have a whole lot of common interests."

Delia liked him, but after shaking hands, she apologized for her sudden exhaustion and proposed that she find their coats. Jean-Paul nodded and said he'd just like to get Slim's contact numbers; so Delia moved off toward the door at the other end of the room. She hadn't seen where the pale woman had put their coats, but she had the feeling it might have been in this direction.

The adjoining room, three steps up, where another sweet-smelling fire burned merrily in a corner fireplace, was obviously a study. The room was furnished with more art, including a sculpture of a buffalo (no price tag), gigantic leather chairs, and an imposing desk with computers and phones. Delia suspected it was from this room that Steve ran his jewelry business. However, there was no sign of the coats, so she pushed on into a small hall where she saw what she took to be a closet door. Opening it, she found herself in a large storeroom, which automatically flooded with light as she entered. She saw various tall, free-standing closets and shelves with labeled boxes, as well as a well-stocked area of office supplies. Clearly she was in the wrong place, but what an enviable storage space! Perhaps their coats were in a hall closet near the entrance after all; she'd have to find her way back there. Turning to leave, she noticed four boxes labeled Wig I, Wig II, Wig III, and Wig IV. Mystified as to why the Kovics had wigs, it occurred to her that perhaps Wilma had had cancer, requiring chemo treatments. Her hair must have fallen out, which would explain the extremely short coif. How awful for her! So stunning a woman as she, obviously caring a great deal for her appearance, would naturally do all she could to maintain it. Delia intuited Wilma's suffering and experienced a pang of sorrow. Brave, brave Wilma...

This, however, was a secret to which she was not privy. Embarrassed for the second time, Delia shut the door firmly behind her and hurried back through the study. Here she encountered the fluffy white cat striding majestically across the desk, methodically sweeping a stack of papers— page by page—to the floor with her paw. Delia stooped to retrieve them and return them to the desk. When she placed them under a stone paperweight—too heavy for the naughty kitty to remove—she noticed the writing was in the Cyrillic alphabet.

She certainly was rapidly becoming Madame Snoop-Of-All-Time, inadvertently gathering information that was none of her business. Jean-Paul's comment that Steve Kovic "was no Frenchman" was probably accurate: Frenchmen seldom communicate in Cyrillic.

As she backtracked into the Great Room and the chattering sounds of the party, she saw Jean-Paul wending his way toward her, their coats over his arm. "We give our thanks now to our illustrious hosts," he said with a wink. It was going to be fun to talk about their various impressions when they got home.

"Where were the coats?" Delia asked puzzled. "I couldn't remember a coat closet in the front hall."

"Actually, unless you had watched the maid as I had when you remove the boots, you would be fooled. This closet was hidden behind a panel most clever, which maintain the symmetry of the façade. This place, it resembles a misbegotten castle, does it not?"

"Built to impress," Delia replied, smiling up at him. Though Jean-Paul's words were jovial, Delia sensed something was wrong. There was an unusual tension between them. He was uncomfortable in some way, but he was trying to hide it. Perhaps it was nothing and would pass before they returned home.

9

Outside, most of the farolitos still glowed, but a dusting of snow had fallen during the Duvals' sojourn inside the house. Much to their surprise, Rumpus and Hark greeted them ecstatically as they descended the steps of the Kovic mansion.

"*Eh bien*, doggies," began Jean-Paul, once their greetings had subsided. "How the devil did you get out? Neither of you were invited to this soirée, is that not so?"

The hounds loved conversations with their owners, whether in English or French, and began their low-slung and comical dance of gladness all over again. They were wet with snow, as though they had been outside for some time. But, as usual, they refrained from divulging the details of their adventures.

They all moved off together toward the road. The footing was slippery and the sky had closed in. The Ridgeleys had obviously plowed their part of the road upon their departure, but the falling snow was quickly covering the scraped surface. Delia and Jean-Paul were glad they had their flashlights and sticks as they trudged along; glad, too, to be moving upward instead of down. The snow was now falling so heavily their footprints were quickly obscured.

Through the whirling, wet night, they began to make out the lights of their house. In fact, the entire house was ablaze with light. When they reached the roadside gate, they saw that not only was every window shining with light, but the front door stood wide open.

Jean-Paul held Delia back. "*Mon ange*, where is the Beretta? I suspect you would not have thought to bring it," he said with a tense sarcastic laugh.

A frisson of fear ran through Delia as she tried to think. What had she done with it? She actually didn't remember ever bringing it in from the car.

"I think it's still in the tire well."

"*Bon.*" Taking the keys from his pocket, he pulled her gently back to the road and called the dogs. "We leave the house for now, retrieve the weapon and telephone the police from the car."

Delia had begun to shiver. The night was dark and damp except for the bright lights of the house. But now as they stood on the roadside of the patio wall, the lights were no longer visible. Only the shine of their flashlights illuminated their way. Delia held the beam for Jean-Paul as he used his key to open the garage door, which luckily slid upwards from the snow that had begun to pile against it.

"Let's leave the patio gate open so if the snow gets deep, we won't have a problem," she suggested.

"No worry, *chérie*. We may enter the patio through the inside garage door."

They got the dogs into the back seat and pulled off the wheel well cover in the far back. Delia's little weapon lay snugly where she'd packed it before leaving Maryland. With her gloved hand she reached in, grabbed it and slid it into her coat pocket. Jean-Paul replaced the cover and slammed the trunk closed.

Grasping the steel in her pocket, Delia walked back to the road but saw no one. Her feet were beginning to throb with cold despite her heavy boots. She suddenly realized she'd left her leather pumps in the Kovics' front hall. The evening was not ending well.

As Delia and Jean-Paul got settled into the front seat, he handed her the cell phone. It was better for her to make business calls to strangers who sometimes had trouble understanding Jean-Paul's accent. (He made the official calls in France, she in the U.S.) She called 911 and got through to the local dispatcher. She started to explain the situation, but the dispatcher interrupted her when she gave the address.

"Oh, yeah," he said. "We know—one-oh-three Calle C de Baca. Don't tell me. That house is haunted. We get calls about that place all the time. You the new tenant, lady?"

Taken aback, Delia could only reply, "My husband and I have been here only one night."

"We can send someone over, but we won't find anything. Want us to come take prints? Nothing is ever stolen, just messed up. You can get the locks changed. Gives work to the locksmith, but it won't do any good. My advice to you is: get over it or leave."

"Good heavens, really?" Delia was thoroughly confused. "Which do you advise?"

"Can't say, lady. It's up to you."

"But there are never any thefts, you say?"

"Never have been. Look, lady, I've got calls piling up. Snow's causing accidents. I'll send someone over, if you want, but it'll be a couple of hours..."

"Well, never mind, I guess. I'll call you back if my husband thinks otherwise..."

Click. The dispatcher went off the line.

"Well, I'll be damned." Delia shook her head and told Jean-Paul what was said.

He burst out laughing, and for the moment the tension broke. "*C'est ridicule*. It is a fool who plays the joke. I doubt we are at risk. Except your jewelry — which you must always wear — we have nothing valuable except the laptops. Can we not lock them in the car when we go out? The car, it is not haunted. Is there such a thing as a haunted car?" He laughed again and Delia joined in.

"I'm thankful we're not paying the heating bill. With the front door wide open for who knows how long, the furnace must be roaring. Still, it feels a little as if the house is merely a campsite with permeable parameters." Delia was now more perplexed than frightened.

"Come, gang," said Jean-Paul, emerging from the car. "Let us investigate."

Humans and canines trudged from the garage to the patio and into the brilliantly lit house, where they found nothing amiss except one overturned chair in the hall. Delia, however, kept her hand in her coat pocket as they trooped through the house and vowed to always keep her weapon nearby. She suddenly felt grateful to her friend, Detective Scott, who had insisted she take it and her permit with her. Although Jean-Paul was officially a U.S. resident, he was not a citizen, which is why it fell to Delia to carry the gun. Even with a license, there might be questions in some states — the sensible ones, Jean-Paul suggested — if he were found with a concealed weapon.

They went through the entire house securing doors and windows with Rumpus and Hark trailing behind, overseeing the project. Jean-Paul turned down the thermostat while Delia went around turning off lights. Nothing seemed to be missing. But Delia was still on edge and shivering.

She didn't tell Jean-Paul that in each room she peeked in the closet and under the bed. Her fears, she knew, were infantile; she was looking for ghosts as well as burglars. If there were someone hidden in the house, the hounds would immediately root him—or her—out, so her actions were absurd.

But it wasn't just the possibility of an intruder that upset Delia, rather a general unease about the entire evening. The Kovics, no doubt, were hospitable people, but Delia felt a twinge of annoyance that she and Jean-Paul had been pulled into the local social scene so soon. Perhaps that was why Jean-Paul seemed tense during their departure. The Ridgeleys, of course, were charming and, in their own way, the Kovics were, too. But maybe the Kovics were a little too pushy... too *something* she couldn't quite figure out. As she checked the hall coat closet for goblins, she wished Wilma wasn't quite so gorgeous. She wished, too, that she hadn't noticed Jean-Paul so obviously aware of Wilma's allure. She took a deep breath and reminded herself that any local entanglements would be temporary.

When she entered the kitchen, she saw through the window that Rumpus and Hark were outside again; Jean-Paul had already fed them dinner. Now they were happily nosing around the patio while the snow continued to fall. There'd soon be a yip at the door as they sought re-admittance.

"I shall reheat last night's dinner," Jean-Paul said.

"And I'll make the salad." As Delia turned to the fridge, she thought she saw her husband give her an odd look. Depositing the greens by the sink, looking around for a salad bowl and another in which to mix the dressing, she glanced at him again. He was adding wine to the casserole, but Delia had the distinct sense that he was avoiding her glance.

"I'll set the table when I finish this, Jean-Paul. Where do you want to dine? In the other room?"

"*Ah, oui.*" He handed her a glass of wine, still without looking at her.

She dried her hands on a paper towel, tossed it toward the trash basket and missed. Then she burst into tears.

Her usually sympathetic husband looked up from his preparations, clearly annoyed. He said nothing, but she heard him sigh. Yes, he was behaving abnormally and she was becoming unhinged. The party had been taxing, the wide-open house scary, and the idea of her unknown twin still disturbed her. She dried her eyes on her apron and reached for the glass of wine. She'd probably had enough wine at the party, but the present occasion called for more.

"What has happened?" she cried out. "Why, why is there this tension? Yes, I know it's not nice to come home to an invaded house, but is there something else? Jean-Paul?"

He turned to face her now and said with deadly calm, "I do not like that man flirting with you and you reciprocating. It is demeaning. I see the two of you apart from the party being cozy in the corner. I noticed."

Delia was stunned. Kovic was a good-looking man, but she wasn't attracted to him in any way. The last thing she wanted was a flirtation — no matter how innocent. Jean-Paul had never before evidenced jealousy. It wasn't his nature. But what was most ironic of all was her own discomfort over *his* manner — attraction? — toward Wilma. She knew she was staring at him, but she was momentarily speechless.

Then she started to laugh. The bewildered expression on her husband's face made her laugh all the harder until she was crying again, leaning against the counter with her hands over her face. "I have got to pull myself together," she said as much to herself as to him.

She walked over to him and leaned against him, seeking the comfort of his body. "You never, never have to worry about me and that man — or any man for that matter! He can never be anything to me. He's just a rich, puffed up... I-don't-know-what." She looked up into Jean-Paul's face. "The funny thing is — well, I guess it's funny — I was worrying about you and Wilma. She's so fabulous! I thought you were smitten."

His features finally relaxed and his eyes crinkled into his usual wonderful smile. Then he, too, laughed. "I hate her vowels," he said emphatically. "Vowels most horrible!"

This struck Delia as so unexpected but so typical of her husband that she began laughing again, and this time he joined her. "Her vowels! Her vowels! Oh, gad... You are wonderful! The only man on earth who

sees a beautiful woman and can't stand her vowels! Oh, I do love you!"
Tears of mirth ran down her face.

"It's funny," he struggled to say, "but it is true..."

Delia and Jean-Paul both knew the crisis had passed. But Delia inwardly acknowledged that life in New Mexico was presenting challenges. Particularly the discovery that she'd had a sister. This was not going to be an easy holiday.

10

Delia stood with a group of gigantic men, some of whom where animatedly discussing a football game, some of whom were vying for her attention. She, however, was angling to see around them — to find Jean-Paul in this crowded party of strangers — without offending the raucous men. She didn't know where she was. She didn't recognize any of the guests.

Claustrophobia closed around her. She couldn't breathe and was beginning to panic. Across the room she spied a small, pretty woman with short, light brown wavy hair. The woman looked familiar: she was dressed in a dark brown dress and wore small gold earrings and a slim gold bracelet. Delia knew this woman, but couldn't quite place her.

With what she hoped was an appreciative smile to the men, Delia excused herself. While trying to make her way to the woman in brown, it dawned on her that the woman was herself.

Now wait a minute. It couldn't be her, since she was standing alone in a crowd, not sitting on a sofa with several others across the room. She hugged herself to check her existence. She was where she thought she was.

She understood the other woman was Dorothy. Her sister, Dorothy, who wasn't dead after all. Delia experienced a jolt of shock, then a sweeping wave of gladness. She'd be reunited with her lost sister. Nothing terrible had ever happened. No death. No betrayal. It was all a mistake. Delia jumped with delight, enveloped in a mist of pure golden happiness.

But she couldn't get across the room. Hands reached out for her. Everyone insistently claimed her attention. And when she finally broke lose and ran toward the sofa, Dorothy had disappeared. The sofa was empty. There was no one to ask where the small woman in the soft brown dress had gone.

Delia awoke with a start. She lay still in the enveloping night. Jean-Paul slept beside her, his breathing rhythmic and even. Her nightmare had awakened only her. Her mind raced over the images of the dream. At least Jean-Paul was really there. She gently slid against him, not wanting to disturb his sleep, but wanting the reassurance of his warm, masculine body.

Dorothy's existence had now entered the depth of her psyche. Ten days before, she'd never suspected she had a sister. She'd had no doubts about the purity of her parents' love—nor her own self-image as an adored single child. Now, part of her core identity had been warped by the insecurity of ignorance. It was not a good feeling. Far off in the night she heard a woman moaning. But it was just the wind, echoing the disturbance of her mind. She lay for a time, agitated but still.

When she awoke, Jean-Paul was gone from the bed and the brilliant morning light filled the room. The snow-brightened sun lifted her spirits and banished dark thoughts. Their last few days in this beautiful house had been uneventful and peaceful. It was good to be off the highways, to have come to a halt in this magical place, with or without a ghost.

Delia and Jean-Paul had taken the week off from work to explore their surroundings. They found the orchard out front was indeed fed by little ditches, which Joseph confirmed were called 'acequias'. Allocated by ancient law and tradition, each property was allotted a certain volume of water that flowed during the warmer months. The flow and the conditions of the acequias were monitored by a *mayordomo*. This year, according to Joe, Ethan Ridgeley had been elected to that position.

Later, Delia and Jean-Paul discovered the wide arroyo that ran along the property opposite the road. They supposed it constituted Duthuit's southern property line. It was a terrific place to walk the dogs, what with its sandy bottom and ascending wooded sides. The Texans, they remembered, called it a 'draw', for it drew off the melting snow and the pounding summer rains. Sometimes there were dangerous flash floods. But for the most part, the arroyo resembled a long, protected beach, which in winter held a fascinating, ever-changing mixture of snow patterns on damp sand. This one ran for miles, from the foothills of the Sangres down into the Santa Fe River and eventually into the Rio Grande.

It became their habit to have a ramble each day. They saw rabbits and chipmunks. The dogs gave chase, baying their joyous hound cry. Once they caught sight of a bobcat rushing into the underbrush. Deer leaped across their path. A coyote trotted blatantly along the bank. When encountering large or ferocious animals, Rumpus and Hark pretended not to notice, which suggested considerable wisdom on their part.

A flock of crows often joined them, swooping through the tree branches and carrying on animated conversations. Delia sometimes joined in, imitating their cries. She and Jean-Paul were pretty sure the birds answered. They seemed such clever creatures; it crossed Delia's mind that perhaps they were involved in the invasion of the house. She knew crows sometimes rang doorbells to get food, broke windows and even stole objects from patios and gardens. This flock seemed to want to play a game with the hounds. They flew down and circled the dogs, chattering all the while. The hounds wagged their tails and raced after them on their short legs. One crow descended quickly and playfully tugged Hark's tail. Rumpus ran at him, managing to catch a few feathers in his front teeth. From then on, Rumpus and Hark growled and barked if the crows flew close, and the birds kept their distance.

Hardly a day passed that Delia and Jean-Paul didn't walk in the arroyo. Sometimes the sand was packed and walking was easy, sometimes it was damp and the snow deep. On those days, they turned back sooner.

But it was a perfect place for exhilarating exercise. (Delia was secretly charmed with Jean-Paul's pronunciation of the word 'arroyo', which didn't lend itself very well to the use of his French R.)

They drove into town to explore Santa Fe. Christmas was approaching and transforming the town for the holiday. They watched workmen stringing lights on the trees in the Plaza; and strolled beneath a long portal at the Palace of the Governors, viewing Indians selling their wares. Further along Palace Avenue, they found restaurants and shops in the adjoining patios. Sena Plaza was their favorite with its enclosed garden of ancient trees overlooked by the handsome Sena residence, now converted to shops and offices.

Come Friday evening they planned to attend an opening at Wilma's gallery on Canyon Road, where many of the galleries were located. No doubt they would meet more attractive, sophisticated people. Jean-Paul remarked on the international awareness of New Mexicans — so far from Europe, Asia and Africa, but so attuned to art and culture in every form. He was particularly impressed by the Santa Feans' concern for the plight of Tibet, remarking on the many bumper stickers proclaiming: FREE TIBET. He wondered if there were preparations for war with China. He'd read nothing about it in the paper, but, after all, New Mexico was traditionally a violent territory. In any case, Delia and Jean-Paul congratulated themselves on their choice of Santa Fe for a winter vacation.

Bang, bang, crash, jingle. It was Jean-Paul and the hounds returning from their morning walk. Delia had lain awake so long in the dead of night that she'd overslept and missed their walk. She glanced at the clock: it was twenty past ten. She thought she heard several voices besides Jean-Paul's.

He and the dogs burst into the room. "Délie, my treasure! So at last you awake!" He raced to the bed and hugged her. His face, hands and parka were freezing against her exposed body in a scanty, silk nightgown. Rumpus and Hark jumped against the bed, big paws on the duvet. They were all three beside themselves with exhilaration from the dry, cold New Mexico air.

"Oh, well... hi, guys!" Delia brushed her hands over her eyes in an attempt to wake up. "I see you're all feeling superior for not only being awake, but having completed your exercise."

"We ARE superior!" joked Jean-Paul, teasing her by running his freezing hands along her bare arms.

"Oh, you brute! You feel horrible! Get away from me!" Delia attempted to escape under the covers.

Jean-Paul laughed a lecherous laugh but said in a lowered voice, "How hot and delicious you are. I would get in that bed with you, right now, except there have arrived two people. It is the cleaning woman, Dolores, and her granddaughter, Carla. What do I tell them? They say it is their day to clean the house. What do you want done?"

"Oh, good heavens," Delia said, sobering up from her hopes of an incipient playtime. "I can't think. I'll get up. Let's see... Jean-Paul, would you please tell them I'll be there in a few minutes, but that they can carry on with their regular routine? I'd forgotten all about them. Silly day to sleep late."

The hounds had sunk down in front of the warm radiator and were already snoozing. Jean-Paul kissed Delia's neck—he was still cold—and said he'd relay her message. "I thought there would be one cleaner only. The local tradition must be to bring the granddaughters..."

When Delia had dressed in her jeans and wooly sweater, she went in search of Dolores and Carla. They were together in the utility room, preparing to run a load of laundry. There wasn't a great deal to wash, but Dolores had gathered up the towels and cloths from the kitchen.

"Hello," Delia said, hesitating only a moment before saying, "I'm Delia." Dolores smiled and held out her hand. She looked to be a sensible woman, the prototype of Northern New Mexican Spanish, with dark graying hair pulled back in a bun, honey-colored skin, dark eyes and a short, sturdy body. Though not pretty, there was character in her face. She wore green knit pants, running shoes and a short-sleeved green print tee shirt. Delia wondered if this obviously intelligent and capable woman would be cleaning houses if Hispanic history had been different. Even in the twenty-first century, Delia supposed the opportunities for education and advancement were inadequate.

Dolores's granddaughter, Carla, a pudgy teenager, had her grandmother's coloring, but wore tight jeans and a denim jacket decorated with a pattern of hearts. Her dark eyes were heavily made up, and her lips were accented in pale lipstick. Delia judged that Carla was about fourteen and assumed she was on Christmas vacation from school. As Delia came forward to greet them, Carla stepped back into the light and Delia saw that beneath her heavy makeup were some nasty bruises along the side of her face and neck.

Perceiving Delia's glance, Dolores said, "I'm Dolores. My granddaughter is Carla. She's been in a car accident so I'm bringing her to work with me 'til she feels better." Her words were clearly enunciated and her voice had the same slight singsong quality Delia had noticed in Rose Martinez's. She suspected that was the influence of the Spanish language. Delia realized there was much about this culture she'd like to know.

Delia turned to Carla to greet her as well. Carla merely grunted and moved back toward the hot water heater. Delia supposed she was shy and so turned back to Dolores to discuss how best to proceed with the chores of the day.

Clearly Dolores had a routine: after starting the laundry—and she expected to wash the sheets and bathroom towels as well—Dolores would clean all the rooms of the house, starting with the north end. Carla meanwhile would sweep the portals, shovel back any drifting snow and throw sand from an old wooden box on patches of ice.

And so the morning began peacefully with Delia drinking her coffee in the sunny alcove, Jean-Paul working in his little office on an East Coast design project and the hounds sleeping by the radiator in the big bedroom. Knowing the kitchen was well supplied with basics, Delia decided on a whim to bake a pie with the apples they'd gotten at the store.

As Delia was taking the pie from the oven, she heard piercing screams from the patio. She could see through the kitchen window that Carla was backed up against the wall, the broom held before her like a shield and her eyes wide with terror. What frightened her?

Delia ran to the window but could still see nothing. Dolores shot out through the front door. Jean-Paul and the hounds appeared beside Delia.

"*Mon dieu* ! What is happening? Délie, why does that person scream so?" His eyes were also wide with alarm, yet his concern was primarily for his wife. He gently took the pie from her hand, set it upon the counter, and put a protective arm around her shoulders. The hounds leaned against her legs. Delia felt at once defended and at the same time a feminine island of safety for her man and beasts. She reached into her apron's big pocket, where, without thinking, she had earlier deposited her weapon. Although she was no longer rattled by recent events, she had decided it was prudent to keep the gun near.

Carla continued to scream hysterically. Her cries came in terrible waves of alarm. She seemed frozen in place by dread, her mittened hands still clutching the broom handle, her eyes riveted on some appalling ghastliness above. It occurred to Delia that she looked like a martyred saint in a fifteenth-century Spanish painting.

Dolores attempted to calm her and eventually enticed her back into the house. Carla turned back just before the front door shut to look reluctantly but with apparent fascination at the unseen apparition above. Delia, Jean-Paul and the hounds met them in the hall.

"What is it?" Delia asked. Jean-Paul's arm remained reassuringly on her shoulder.

Dolores turned towards them and said in a shaky voice, "I'm sorry for the outburst. She's okay now. The car accident has destroyed her nerves."

Delia instinctively stepped toward the distressed girl and gently laid her hand on Carla's arm. To her surprise, Carla grabbed her hand and held it to her, then broke out in fresh sobs.

"Come," said Delia. "I've got a piece of fresh baked pie for you and will make you some herb tea. Would you like that, Carla? Come into the kitchen and you can tell me what happened."

Jean-Paul, seeing the crisis had passed, retreated to his study. Dolores hesitated and then, with Rumpus and Hark, followed Delia and Carla into the kitchen.

Delia indicated that Carla should sit in the breakfast nook. Carla sank into the chair with a shuddering sigh, rubbing at her eye, makeup now streaking down her cheeks. Delia handed her a plate with a slice of the warm pie. Carla held it flat, warming her hands.

"Now, how 'bout some chamomile tea?" Delia asked. "Do you think you'd like that? It's very calming."

Carla wiped her face on her jacket sleeve and nodded. Delia rummaged in the cupboard for the herb tea, found it and a small pot and lit the gas under the kettle. Dolores, Rumpus and Hark stood silently watching Delia's movements with hypnotic interest.

"How about you, Dolores? Would you like some pie?"

Dolores started, as if waking from a dream. "No, no. Thanks. I've got to get on with cleaning..."

"Lie down, doggies. Tea is not for you," Delia commanded gently. They sank to the floor still watching her intently.

But Dolores hadn't moved except to shift her gaze toward Carla. Her face looked worn and held an expression of exasperation and pity.

"What happened?" Delia asked quietly.

Dolores hesitated and turned her gaze back to Delia, giving her a long look as if assessing how sympathetic or receptive she might be. Dolores then folded her arms in front of her and sighed. "Well, you see, Carla saw the owl sleeping in the apricot tree."

Delia waited, mystified. It wasn't much of an explanation.

"This house is haunted," Dolores said firmly. "It is haunted by La Llorona—a woman who takes the form of an owl when she wants to travel. Carla is afraid of her. The trees around this house should be cut down."

"Oh, I see..." Delia responded. Actually she didn't see, and couldn't imagine cutting down the lovely old apricot trees in the patio nor the big cottonwoods out front. But Dolores's explanation seemed to calm her granddaughter, who now sat quietly staring at her piece of pie. Delia watched her fork off a piece and raise it to her mouth.

After her first taste, Carla burst out, "*Eeeeee –ho- lay! Que bonito, essay!*" or at least that's what Delia thought she said. She didn't really know what Carla was saying, but clearly she approved of the pie and the crisis was over. At least for now.

11

D elia felt sure that when they returned from the Canyon Road galleries, the house would again be wide open. The intruder would realize they weren't home and strike again. Some people live to create chaos. Delia wasn't amused, but there was so much of interest in the area, she was determined not to let the tricksters spoil her and Jean-Paul's western adventure. She did, however, put on her few pieces of jewelry, and she and Jean-Paul secured their laptops in the car, along with Rumpus and Hark and some warm blankets. The dogs had gotten so flexible from their travels that even a cold evening in the car didn't bother them.

The sun was setting behind the Jemez and the sky was streaked with scarlet and gold clouds. The flock of crows sailed slowly toward the arroyo, large and black against the glowing sky. Delia wondered if they too carried the souls of witches or goblins. She and Jean-Paul hadn't seen the offending owl again; in fact, most birds seemed to have flown south.

As previously arranged with Wilma, Delia and Jean-Paul stopped off at the Kovics' to pick up Delia's shoes. Steve had gone to Las Vegas, Nevada, where he had a jewelry gallery, and Wilma, they knew, would already be at her gallery on Canyon Road. The same pale woman again opened the door and handed Delia her shoes in a sprightly polka-dotted gift bag. Delia tried to have a few friendly words with her, but she apparently didn't speak English. She certainly didn't look Spanish or Indian; Delia wondered where she fit into the Kovics' picture.

The light was beginning to fade. Stars and a new moon were already visible as they drove south on Bishops Lodge Road. The roads were clear now although snow was piled along the shoulders. At Wilma's suggestion, they parked in a lot behind what had been the Loretto School and locked the dogs in the car. Rumpus and Hark settled down for naps.

Before turning back to Canyon Road, Delia and Jean-Paul stood to admire the territorial-style architecture of the school which now functioned as offices and a tourist bureau. It reminded Delia of a scaled-down version of the Greek Revival buildings in Maryland. Jean-Paul thought this territorial style actually derived from Greek Revival. In fact, it was quite similar in feel to Duthuit's house. They noted it, too, had blue doors and window frames. Jean-Paul had read that New Mexicans believe blue frames represent "the sacred blue eyes of Christ" which repel evil spirits. "*Naturellement*," Jean-Paul murmured, "Jesus would not have had the blue eyes."

"Ah," Delia countered, "that no doubt is true, but in the sacred art of the western world, blue is the color of purity. Hence, the Virgin's robe is usually depicted in blue." Then she laughed and added, "Like the blue packaging of over-the-counter drugs... Pure as the driven snow."

"Speaking of which," Jean-Paul answered, thumping his hands together in their sheepskin gloves, "I become more interested in the warmth than the purity. Let us save our architectural conjectures for a more warm day and race to Canyon Road before the frost attacks the bones."

"Yes, yes, darling." Delia tucked her hand under his arm. "But isn't it interesting that there is so much concern here for evil spirits? I suppose that also happens in France, but I don't remember hearing much about it in Maryland. I'd like to learn about benevolent spirits, too. I'm going to start asking around for good ghosts." She stopped suddenly as they stepped onto Canyon Road. "Oh, how pretty the Christmas lights are! Look, the trees are totally covered. That's charming!"

They began their trek up Canyon Road where the Christmas decorations became even more lavish and imaginative. Some of the lights were in the shapes of animals, some covered outside sculptures, and some ran along the tops and facades of the low adobe buildings. There were farolitos burning everywhere — along the low walls and lining the snow-packed walks and steps to the galleries. Groups of bundled-up people slipping in and out of galleries trudged about the road in thick snow boots. The clear, freezing air was perfumed with a delicious fragrance of burning wood — piñon wood, Alice had told them.

"The buildings are unassuming. They are plain, yet the decorations are extravagant. Is it not an unexpected combination?"

Delia agreed with Jean-Paul. "Oh look! There's the Snyder-Kovic Gallery! Just as my toes were beginning to suffer. That's the name on the card Wilma gave us. I guess her name is actually Snyder. We never did ask."

They jostled against a good-natured crowd of art lovers as they maneuvered through the low front door. Inside, the gallery was bright and warm. It must have once been a house, for the rooms were small, each with a corner fireplace burning that sweet-smelling wood. There was lots of hanging space, which made it ideal for a gallery. However, the crowd of people in heavy coats made it difficult to see the art. "We must return on a day more calm to see the art properly," Jean-Paul suggested, bending toward Delia and planting a kiss on her forehead.

As they glanced around the gallery, they were surprised the art was by the same artist: some canvases were large and abstract, others small and minutely drawn, some overlaid with thick paint and wild brush strokes, others, subdued and pale. Obviously, the artist was superbly versatile.

They pulled off their gloves and opened their coats, slowly wending their way through the crowd. Towards the back of the building they encountered Wilma dressed in a spectacular orange and brown jumpsuit encircled by a heavy concho belt and tucked into beautiful toast-colored cowboy boots. Around her neck was an intricate, Indian squash-blossom necklace. She certainly stood out in the crowd. They exchanged greetings and Wilma asked if Delia had gotten her shoes.

"Indeed and thank you. Wilma, your gallery is lovely and your Indian jewelry absolutely fabulous!"

Wilma's hand flew up to her necklace. Delia noticed a spectacular turquoise and silver ring on her index finger. "Oh, thanks. It's pawn jewelry. Navajo. I seldom wear it because Steve likes me to model new pieces he's got for sale, but since he's away, I thought I'd take a break from the European stuff." She smiled a greeting and waved to someone across the room.

"So... isn't this an interesting artist? He's actually from Peru but has lived in New Mexico for twenty years. He's amazingly versatile, as you can see. In the back room you'll find some of his sculpture — which I think is quite phenomenal."

Wilma was distracted, looking around the gallery as she spoke, her eyes darting from person to person. Delia wondered if she were expecting Steve's return. Wilma's agitation made Delia feel transparent — as though Wilma were looking right through her. But Delia was also not wholly attentive to their conversation. She strained to hear Wilma's vowels to understand for herself what Jean-Paul meant. Jumpy Wilma was gorgeous; her accent, however, was not. In fact, Wilma's voice grated. Odd she hadn't noticed it before. Delia supposed she'd been previously distracted by Wilma's physical perfection. She felt a smile twitching around the corners of her mouth as Wilma talked. Yes, her vowels were indeed 'horrible'. She glanced at Jean-Paul, who caught the gist of her amusement and winked.

"By the way," Wilma continued, unaware of what passed between the spouses, "Gillian and Jonathan — my children — are here this month. In case I forget — they asked if they might visit you. Jonathan is studying photography at Yale and wants to take pictures of some local structures for a project. And Gillian is writing a paper on eighteenth- and nineteenth-century American architecture and would like to make some notes on the interior of Guillaume's house. Do you think you could put up with them for an hour some time before the New Year?"

Delia glanced inquiringly at Jean-Paul. "*Mais, oui*," he responded. "It is our pleasure to receive your children."

"Hello, Duvals," said a friendly voice. Ethan and Molly Ridgeley had come up beside them. "Hi, Wilma," Ethan said. "You're looking perky this evening."

Wilma looked both taken aback and displeased. She stepped aside and—for a fleeting moment—glared at Ethan. Obviously, 'perky' was not a description she appreciated. However, she soon recovered, forced a smile and replied, "You're looking pretty cute yourselves." Then with a nod to Delia and Jean-Paul, Wilma asked, "You see anything you like?"

"Actually, yes," Molly said. "We're thinking of that charming little sketch of the Chimayo Church... Delia, Jean-Paul, have you been to Chimayo? There are two churches there worth seeing. It's only a few miles north of here."

"Not yet, but we're glad to know about it," Delia replied. "Maybe you'd give us directions. Or perhaps you'd like to come with us."

"Good idea," Ethan replied.

"Let us see the sketch Molly favors," Jean-Paul suggested.

They found the picture hung with a group of small drawings with several people standing before them examining them at close range.

"These will go fast," Wilma warned. "Molly—Ethan ... is that the one you like? Excuse me," she said, smiling at the viewers, "may I just scoot in here for a minute?" The group parted and Molly pointed to one sketch that was particularly well executed. Wilma leaned back toward Molly and whispered, "I'll let you have it for nine hundred."

Delia noticed each work was priced at eighteen hundred dollars. Although they were nicely matted and framed, she thought even nine hundred was a steep price for a sketch of no more than three-by-three inches. On the other hand, art should be supported.

Molly turned to Ethan with a questioning look. He nodded. "Yes," she said to Wilma. "Most definitely!"

Wilma seemed to expect that answer and instantly took a small red sticker from her jumpsuit pocket and placed it in the corner of the frame. "I'll just go write up a contract, Molly. You can pay anytime." Wilma moved off toward her office with one of her nervous smiles.

"That is most charming," Jean-Paul complimented Molly and Ethan. "You will enjoy that little church. It is drawn with much delicacy and love."

Ethan smiled contentedly and Molly said, "We expect the two of you for brunch Sunday. You may bring the hounds, if you like. There's lots to talk about, Chimayo included. What about Alice? Would she like to come? We'd still be an intimate group."

Delia was grateful, but replied, "She's off on a lecture tour. We're not quite sure when she gets back. But when she does, we'll make a point of including her with the two of you another time. I know how fond she is of you both."

Since Molly had mentioned Rumpus and Hark, Delia was reminded that the dogs were still locked in the cold car and they'd better get home. Also, in the corner of Delia's mind was the desire to foil the inevitable intruders. Maybe there was some way they might sneak up and catch them in the house. Delia patted the pocket of her sheepskin coat to make sure her Beretta was in place. She'd gradually been making up her mind that she and Jean-Paul were not going to be bullied by the clowns amusing themselves at the opera singer's expense. There were times when you simply had to take a stand and say, "No! We're not having this situation any longer! *We* are taking charge of this property, not you — whoever you are!"

There was something quite invigorating about this place... this town. She realized she was feeling increasingly liberated from the usual cautions and constraints.

They trudged back to the car and drove home under a sky lit with more stars than they'd ever seen. The brilliant canopy of stars seemed so close they could reach out and touch them.

Delia's pulse raced as they drove up the snowy road. To her surprise their house was dark, with only the gate, portal and living room lights visible. Would the front door be wide open? No, all seemed exactly as they'd left it.

12

elia told Jean-Paul she was looking forward to meeting Wilma's two beautiful children. Although their portrait had been painted over a decade ago, she didn't doubt that as college students, Gillian and Jonathan would be lovely.

Jean-Paul had an appointment to meet the architect, Slim Fellows, whom he'd met at the Kovics' party, for coffee at La Fonda, the inn on the plaza. He was interested in hearing about an environmentally sensitive development west of town that Slim's firm was planning. Delia had a column to write. She thought she could probably get some work done while Gillian and Jonathan took notes and photographs for their assignments.

Not long after Jean-Paul left, the doorbell rang. Rumpus and Hark scampered to the front door with their chorus of welcoming barks. Delia opened it to find two dreadful looking young people. Perhaps they were the spooks she'd glimpsed briefly as she and Jean-Paul first drove up their road.

"Hi," the young man said. "We're Jack and Jill—naturally awaiting our next disaster."

Both were dressed entirely in black leather. Gillian—or Jill—had orange-tufted hair that stood out from her head in horns. There were rings through her lip and nose, and the head of a tattooed snake appeared above her collar on the side of her smooth young neck. Jonathan—or Jack—had a Mohawk haircut. His head was completely shaved except for a scarlet fringe of hair that stuck up along the top of his head like a brush. He looked like a demented bird. He, too, came equipped with rings in his ears, one eyebrow and nose. They were both excruciating to look at, which Delia suspected was their intention.

Well, well, Delia thought, so much for the Ivy League style of the twenty-first century. Though the siblings were hideous, they seemed friendly enough.

"Do come in," Delia invited as she stepped back and smiled. "This is Rumpus and this is Hark. You'll find them friendly and no doubt deeply interested in your projects."

Jack picked up a bag of camera equipment he'd set on the portal bench before ringing the doorbell. He handed his sister his tri-pod as he moved everything into the hall. Jack and Jill smiled as they looked around. They smiled at Delia and smiled at the dogs. Jill fell to her knees beside the hounds and received kisses on her chalk white face. Delia hoped that whatever makeup Jill was wearing wouldn't upset the hounds' digestion.

"Oh, you're lovely creatures!" Jill crooned to the dogs. Then, looking up at Delia, she said, "I love Bassets! Aren't they great, Jack? Take some photos of them for me, will you?"

"Sure. Let me get shots of the house first and then, with Mrs. Duval's permission, I'll shoot the dogs."

Mrs. Duval. Mrs. Duval! Delia noticed the East Coast manners and smiled. These two young people may look awful, but they were gracious. She was getting used to all this first-name business, but she hadn't yet learned to like it. It made the young people's relative formality all the more noticeable. And they did seem vaguely familiar. Maybe they'd been the apparition on the road or perhaps she'd somehow run into them on the East Coast.

"Of course you may photograph the dogs. In fact, I'd like a good picture of them myself. Is there anything I can get you two before you start work? Would you like some coffee?"

"We're fine, thanks," Jill replied. "But I would like to ask you some questions about your experience of living in this house. I've got this idea that architectural styles affect people's attitudes and moods. I mean if this were a modern glass house as opposed to an old adobe, you might experience your visit differently... if you see what I mean. I'm not only writing a paper on architecture, but I'm doing a project for psych class about the effect of the work environment on people's production. Mom says you're a writer."

"Yes, I am. You mean you'd like to interview me concerning my reactions to this house?"

Jill nodded. "And, if you don't mind, talk about how conducive it is to your—and your husband's—work."

Jack held up his hand. There was a tattoo of a black hexagon on the palm. Delia wondered what that meant.

"I'll start in the kitchen, if that's all right with you, Mrs. Duval," Jack interrupted.

"Certainly. Jill and I will be in this bedroom. The fire's still going." The hounds and Jill followed Delia. Before Jack turned the corner, the sun from the living room windows lit up his head and Delia saw the black roots of his hair beneath the red dye.

Delia and Jill settled themselves in the two easy chairs before the fire and Jill took a small notebook from the pocket of her leather jacket. "I do love your dogs, Mrs. Duval. We used to have Irish setters, but they died. They were pretty old. It didn't make sense to get more dogs when Jack and I are off at school and besides, we all travel so much. Seems as if we're never in the same place for more than a month."

"You mean this isn't your permanent home?" Delia was surprised. Their property across the road seemed substantial and settled. And there was the matter of Wilma's gallery.

"God, no." Jill stuck her legs straight out in front of her and slid down on her spine. Hark got up from his place in front of the radiator and sniffed at the bottoms of Jill's boots, where little clumps of mud clung, despite the snow she must have trudged through to get here. "We're here essentially for the skiing and Mom likes to be here at Christmas because there're so many tourists who buy from the gallery." Jill laughed. "Mom says a lot of 'em don't know what they're buying. She always tries to have a really good show at Christmas, because of course there *are* people who appreciate good art, but she thinks if she hung a bunch of garbage she'd make just as much money." Jill laughed derisively.

Hark sat down beside Delia's chair; she reached down and rubbed his ears. He stared across at Jill with woeful Basset eyes, his tail wagging ever so slightly. Rumpus, still lying in front of the radiator, began to snore. Delia got up and poked the fire. Jill suddenly stood, took the poker from her and asked, "Shall I throw on another log from that basket? When Jack and I leave we'll bring in more wood for you from that pile on the portal..."

Delia nodded. "Oh, thanks..." Jill and Jack may look like hell, but they seemed angelic. Delia also noted that neither spoke with the nasal quality of their mother's speech. She wondered where they'd grown up.

The fire jumped into a glorious purple-orange blaze. It made the hissing sound Delia loved. The chimney drew beautifully, and the smoke rose straight up into it, leaving the wonderful wood fragrance to fill the room.

"Doesn't your mother need to keep an eye on the gallery? Can she leave it for long periods? It seems a serious business."

"Oh, it is. But she's got a manager. Also, by traveling, Mom discovers new artists, and she likes mixing things up. There are some galleries in Santa Fe that stick to one kind of art. You know — Western or nineteenth-century or Asian — but Mom likes being eclectic. She says it gives her an excuse to travel and, of course, she can take a tax deduction for her trips."

Delia wondered how many people's lives were ruled by the tax code. She supposed that since she and Jean-Paul lived both in France and the U.S. they might be wise to look into the tax implications, but so far there had been so many personal events informing their time, they'd neglected to do so.

"How long will you stay in New Mexico?" Delia realized she was the one doing the interviewing. She also wanted to find a tactful way to inquire about Wilma's health. She assumed her cancer must be in remission.

"Well, I'm not sure how long Mom and Steve will be here this trip. But by spring vacation they'll be in Tobago. Spring in New Mexico is horrible! We call it Beige Time." Jill gave the fire one last poke and turned back to sit down again. Hark moved over to sit next to her. Jill's note pad still lay on the floor beside her, seemingly forgotten. Hark's tail, when he sat, covered it.

"Goodness, I didn't know spring was horrible. I imagined New Mexico would be rather lovely with lots of trees and plants leafing out. I pictured the apricot trees in the patio looking splendid."

For a moment Jill didn't answer but stared distractedly into the fire.

The colors of the fire mirrored the orange of the sticky-out horns on her head. Now that Delia was getting over the shock of Jill's appearance, she saw that beneath the repellent persona the girl was every bit as beautiful as her mother. And a lot more relaxed.

As if awakening from a dream, Jill sighed. She talked of the seasons while patting Hark gently and rhythmically on his head. "Those old apricot trees are protected by that walled patio. And it's true, lots of people have walled gardens. But with this high altitude, you can get snow right up through May. It also usually freezes at night, so whatever blooms — trees or flowers — gets killed anyway. The snow begins to melt during the day... everything dries out. The wind blows and there's dust everywhere. You do not want to be here in the spring! It can be really nasty! Not to mention allergies! Of course, it's gorgeous everywhere else in the world, so everyone who can, leaves. If you look around, Mrs. Duval, you'll notice a lot of empty houses in and near Santa Fe. Quite a few people come for just a few months in the summer, for the Opera and Indian and Spanish Markets — when the rest of the world is too hot — and then, in a month or two, they're gone. Some of them have four or five other houses. That way they don't belong anywhere and avoid paying taxes."

"I see. Nomadic like the Comanches used to be." Delia couldn't restrain herself from adding, "It's not very good for the community, is it, or for the less rich people who need the services those taxes would provide?"

Jill appeared to think about that but said nothing. She ran her finger along the spirals of her notebook, which she'd finally picked up from beneath Hark's tail. Her nails, Delia noticed, were painted black. Unlike the little Indian girls', they weren't jagged nor was the polish chipped. Evidently, Jill's personal style choices were carefully selected and maintained.

Delia was intrigued by the lifestyle Jill was describing. She supposed she and Jean-Paul knew others who lived like high-style nomads, but she couldn't think of any specifically. If Jean-Paul hadn't recently inherited his uncle's estate in France, they, themselves, would certainly not own two properties in two different countries.

She leaned forward and asked, "So you go to Tobago? Why Tobago?"

"Oh, Steve is a developer, you know. He's building a luxury development on what used to be a banana plantation. It gets too hot to go down there in the summer, but early spring is terrific."

"No, I didn't know your step-father was a developer! We only just met your parents and don't know much about them. What do you and Jack do when you go to Tobago?" She still wanted to enquire about Wilma's health, but the question seemed out of place at the moment.

Hark had moved back to Delia's side and Rumpus continued to snore across the room. The fire threw out a lot of heat and the piñon fragrance continued to perfume the room. Delia had promised herself she'd work on her column this morning, but she wasn't begrudging this time with Gillian. She enjoyed what was becoming a cozy and informative chat.

"We usually take a gang of friends down from school. There's a reef there that has an enormous variety of sea life. Really, really wonderful for snorkeling and diving! Everyone loves it. And we've got a glass-bottomed boat!" Jill was as gleeful as a child.

"The only bad thing is the Moray eels. They're horrible. They live in the reef and have huge sharp teeth. If they bite onto your arm, someone has to cut your arm off. When I first learned about them, I had nightmares. I fantasized about how scary they would look. Then I actually saw one in an aquarium. It was worse than I'd even imagined!" She took a deep breath and shuddered. "But other than the eels, the place is paradise. And they grow cocoa there, too—as well as bananas. You can't imagine how delicious their hot chocolate is! I have to be careful not to make myself sick. Jack and I really love it there—but not to live fulltime. Islands get to you, you know..."

This was all news to Delia. "But I thought your step-father was in the jewelry business."

"Oh, yeah. Yeah, he is. He's got outlets in Las Vegas, Antwerp and Cape Town."

"Cape Town, South Africa?" Delia asked.

"Un-huh. He says he's considering buying a diamond mine in Kimberly, near Johannesburg. The seasons are reversed in South Africa, you know. Although the winters in Cape Town don't get terribly cold. Not like here." Jill continued running her finger back and forth over her notebook's spiral binding.

Delia was surprised and curious at what Jill was telling her. "And what about your mother? Does she travel with him? Does she have galleries in all these places?"

"Not South Africa. She says it's too dangerous. But she does have a gallery in Antwerp, and Steve has a fabulous jewelry outlet there. But he just told us at breakfast that he's thinking of developing a luxury resort in Cape Town, too. Almost all his lots in Tobago have been bought and he could do pretty much in South Africa what he's doing in Tobago. Club house, spa, pools, nice grounds... you know."

"But surely the topography and culture are totally different..."

"Not completely. Sort of African, basically, you know. Besides, he says if you standardize your layout and repeat it in other places, you save a lot of money. It's financially more efficient. To tell you the truth, Mrs. Duval, Steve isn't much into culture. He and Mom both like turning profits. That's the point of it all."

"Gad," Delia said. "Your parents certainly are energetic!" Clearly, if Wilma were unwell, she wouldn't be traveling.

"Jill, don't you need to ask me questions about this house? I seem to have been interviewing you instead of the other way around. Is there something I can help you with?"

Jill pulled a pen out of a pocket along the leg of her black leather trousers. For a pensive moment she held it against her cheek. "Actually, you're the first person I've talked to about this idea. I haven't exactly formulated my questions yet. Hmmm."

Delia thought perhaps she could help. "Are you trying to get at whether architecture influences mood — or production — or something like that?"

"Work, really. It's been suggested that the more elaborate a place is, the more people produce."

"I see," mused Delia. "Would you call this house elaborate?" Delia and Jean-Paul considered it beautiful — but in truth, it was very simple.

"Well," Jill gazed around the bedroom, her wide-spaced eyes ringed with cosmetics. "It's a lovely house, isn't it?"

"My husband and I think so. I've just had a thought. Both he and I have projects we plan to continue here. But we haven't been here long enough to know how well that'll work out. I usually get a certain amount written in, say — a month — and he, well, he's a landscape architect, and he usually has a certain amount of billable hours. How about if we show you logs of our working hours and contrast them to what happens when we're working at home? Would that help you? Then you could compare that to what other people report in other environments. It wouldn't be very scientific, but I gather it's the architecture you're really focusing on, and it might add some interesting conjecture for your report."

"Great!" Jill stood up with a look of genuine relief on her face. "Would you and Mr. Duval really do that for me?"

"Well, I think he'd probably agree to it. It's an interesting concept. Oh, here's Jack."

Jill turned toward Jack as he entered the room energetically and, it would seem, with considerable good humor. "I got all the photos I need. Thanks, Mrs. Duval. Jill, are you ready to leave?"

"No, I just need a few more minutes in — well — maybe the dining room and living room. Oh! And Jack, would you take some pictures of Rumpus and Hark now? And we could give some to Mrs. Duval as well..."

Jill went off to take notes and Jack set about photographing the hounds. They always enjoyed any sort of attention, although they hadn't previously done much photographic modeling. Within a few minutes the visitors had finished their projects and proceeded to bring in several loads of wood. They left with many thanks and affectionate compliments to the dogs. Despite their suggestive nicknames, no disaster had occurred, or at least none that Delia was aware of then.

She managed to get some work done before Jean-Paul returned for lunch. The snow, she noticed from her study windows, had begun to fall again. The wind was up and the flakes were whirling down slantwise. She heard that faint moaning sound she often noticed at night. It must be the wind in the chimneys.

She thought vaguely that the exchange with the young people had been pleasant, although their appearances were certainly surprising. It wasn't until several weeks later, however, that she and Jean-Paul would realize the dire consequences of meeting Jack and Jill.

13

On Saturday night, Delia and Jean-Paul had fallen asleep in one another's arms after a particularly delicious lovemaking. As she drifted off, Delia listened for the moaning wind, but all was quiet. The night outside was bitter cold and still; their sleep was deep and comforting.

Towards dawn, however, terrible screams penetrated Delia's consciousness. She jerked awake suddenly and strained to listen. At first there was no sound except the pounding of her own heart. Still fearful, she decided she must have been dreaming, so she snuggled close to Jean-Paul, ever the sound sleeper who continued to breathe evenly.

Just as she slipped back into sleep she again heard the piercing screams. Someone, somewhere, was in trouble. Maybe the ghost existed after all — what was she called? La Llorona? A cold sweat broke over Delia's body.

Jean-Paul stirred, so she suspected he, too, had heard the shrieking this time. The dreadful sounds were not just a figment of an overwrought imagination. Surely, they should try to help — or call for help. They mustn't let the screams go unheeded.

"Jean-Paul! Jean-Paul!" she whispered urgently. "Darling, I hate to wake you, but something is happening."

He rolled over and turned on the bedside light. "My treasure," he said in French, "what is it?"

Before Delia could answer, another wail reached their ears.

"Did you hear that?" Delia whispered urgently.

"That is indeed a horrible sound," Jean-Paul, now fully awake, said in English. "But do not be alarmed, my angel. You hear the conversation of the coyotes who communicate across the night. They only call to one another to telegraph their positions."

He smiled indulgently, turned off the light and pulled her close beside him.

So much for Delia's new found courage and calm.

Sunday morning was brilliant and crisp. Delia felt foolish about her nocturnal fears and interrupting her lover's sleep. Though she didn't believe in the supernatural, she and Jean-Paul had entered an environment where others did. But the bright morning was reassuring. Daytime offered rational living; it was nighttime which brought a world of dreams and the unexplained. Like the Tobago reef of Jill's description, here was beauty mixed with lurking dangers.

Jean-Paul returned later than Delia had expected, but he had finally managed to find a copy of the Sunday *New York Times*. "The village market, it sold out. I arrive too late so I go to Santa Fe to find the paper. You must guess who parked next to the dogs and me at the DeVargas Mall."

As he handed her the newspaper and threw his parka on the hall chair, Delia saw merriment in his dark eyes. He seemed to have forgotten about the disturbance of the night. Something or someone had amused him.

"Hmm. Someone we know?"

"*Non...*"

She laughed, patting his arm and looking up into his face. "Then how can I be expected to guess who it was?"

"A-ha! Because it is someone you know *of*." He stepped back, put his hands in his pockets and looked at her expectantly.

"Someone famous?"

"*Oui.*"

"Well, let's see..." Delia was amused by the guessing game because Jean-Paul obviously enjoyed it. He was in a high good humor.

"I know!" she exclaimed, clapping her hands together, "John McCain!"

"Not even close, Délie. *Eh bien,* on the second thought, she is perhaps to be considered also the political person."

"Oh, it's a woman... I know: Hilary Clinton! You saw Hilary Clinton in the parking lot surrounded by a troop of Secret Service people! No doubt, she was looking for a *Washington Post.* Right?"

"My treasure, you are a terrible guesser."

"Okay, I give up."

"Jane Fonda!"

"Really? How'd she look?"

"*Belle. Très, très belle.*"

"Are you sure it was Jane Fonda? Did you talk to her?"

"*Naturellement.* She hear that I speak French with the dogs. Then in French she speak to me. Very nicely. We exchange the words."

"Oh, ho! I see! Let me tell you something, Jean-Paul Duval: if I were Jane Fonda, I, too, would speak very nicely to you. Because you are so attractive, sexy and courtly. Like Jane, I, too, wouldn't miss that opportunity! But I hope you told her that you understood she had already had a French husband and that you are the only one your wife has and that she isn't giving you up, even for the most glamorous movie star on earth! Did you tell her that, M'sieur le Comte?"

"Of course, I tell her that. And Rumpus and Hark, they tell her, too, in their most correct French. So she smile most sadly and drive away."

"Poor lady," Delia murmured looking down at the headlines. "What a dreadful disappointment for her."

Jean-Paul had read only three pages of the front section, and Delia only two editorials, when Jean-Paul rose from his chair, shaking the newspaper and looking at his watch—the beautiful gold one Delia had given him when they'd first fallen in love. "*Mon dieu, mon ange*, at what hour are we to be *chez* Ridgeley?"

"Whoops," said Delia, looking at her own watch, "in five minutes. I completely lost track of time. We'd better be off. Let's walk and take the hounds. They said we could."

Delia thought people and their houses, if they'd lived in them a while, had a tendency to look alike, like people and pets. Although the Duvals always passed the Ridgeley property on the way up and down the road to Duthuit's house, because it was hidden behind a stand of trees and a high wall, they hadn't had a good look at it. Like Duthuit's, the house faced south, but the drive was also on that side and visitors entered through a south patio and a narrow portal.

The driveway had been plowed and a path shoveled to the portal entrance. Delia and Jean-Paul knew that the little river ran close by on the west side and must be pleasantly audible in the summer. Beyond that was the road, and as they entered the patio, the whir of a few passing cars was audible. What surprised them was that the house was built of stones, which must have come from the river. It looked quite different from the other houses in the area, though mellow in color and texture.

Jean-Paul dropped the iron knocker against the door. Rumpus stood to one side, Hark to the other, their tails moving slowly in anticipation. Almost immediately Ethan flung open the door with a hearty greeting. Warmth and the aroma of something wonderful cooking inside assailed the visitors.

The front door opened directly into the living room, which was small, comfortably and informally furnished with sofa, easy chairs, many pillows and a baby grand piano piled high with books and photographs. Delia noticed a number of clay pots on a shelf that ringed the room. She presumed from her reading that they were pueblo pottery and immediately sensed the harmonious feeling they emitted, as though the potter herself were present. There was no doubt that to achieve such nourishing results the potter had to be perfectly centered within herself when she formed them from the earth. It was as though the pots themselves were sacred objects. It occurred to Delia at that moment that creativity counters violence. The pueblo people, she understood, were not warriors. She made a mental note to question the Ridgeleys and learn more about these powerful objects.

Ethan hung their coats on a rack beside the door and led the guests to the room beyond, which turned out to be an enormous kitchen with deep-set windows at each end. A large oval table stood in the center and a clutter of pans and every cooking implement imaginable, as well as fragrant bunches of dried herbs, hung from racks throughout the kitchen. Fresh herbs grew in pots on the windowsills.

Molly moved from the stove, wiped her hands on her apron and hugged Delia and Jean-Paul in turn. She was a vision in pink: a round pink face, pink dimpled hands, pink sweater and skirt, and a pink gingham apron. "Hello, people! Hello, dogs! Have a seat at the table! Make yourselves comfortable. Sherry? I'm experimenting with a new concoction."

Molly returned to the stove to stir a rich stew with the sent of bay and mint. The dogs tried scooting under the table, but Delia pointed to the living room door and commanded them to move out of the kitchen. She'd learned the hard way that animals under foot mixed poorly with cooking activities. Ethan, Delia and Jean-Paul pulled chairs from the table and arranged themselves at three of the set places so they might face Molly at the stove. The atmosphere was one of warmth, comfort and creativity.

Delia spied the little drawing of the Chimayo Church, which was propped at eye level against a row of cookbooks. Following her glance, Ethan said, "Wilma let us have it yesterday. We haven't yet decided where to hang it."

"Maybe the bedroom," Molly said tentatively, "which faces north and is the only room in the house without direct sunlight. That can be a problem for paintings, drawings and photographs here. With too much light, they fade. I guess the graphite would be okay, but that subtle lavender matting is just right—and certainly that color would fade in direct light. After lunch, maybe you'd walk around the house with us and help us decide where to hang it..."

That was the sort of little project Delia and Jean-Paul both enjoyed. But for now, they were suddenly made ravenous by the stew's aroma. As they sipped their sherry, Molly took cornbread from the oven, transferred it to a basket wrapped in a napkin printed with musical notes, and put it on the table before them. "Start on some of that while it's hot. Nice to nibble with your sherry..."

Delia wanted to know more about the Chimayo churches they planned to visit together next week.

"There's an inn there where we can have lunch. The house of an old Spanish ranch," Ethan suggested. "Actually, we could start early and drive all the way to Taos on the back road, if it's not too snowy. You'd enjoy the scenery and villages, which look a lot like those of Spain."

"There are so many layers of culture here," Jean-Paul observed. "From what Delia and I observe, the Indian, Spanish and..." he hesitated to say 'Anglo', Delia knew, because he remained incredulous that he, a Frenchman, should be included in that category, "Anglos are separate and distinct, are they not?"

Molly was preparing a citrus, walnut and endive salad. Her hands flew with great skill over the preparations. "Indeed they are, Jean-Paul. And you'll also find that the Pueblo Indians, who have been here the longest, are not only different from each other, with different customs and languages in some cases, but different from the Plains Indians who arrived later—about the same time as the Spanish. When Ethan and I lived on the Navajo Reservation, we were surprised to learn how specific each culture is."

"But do they not war with one another?" Jean-Paul asked.

"No longer," Ethan responded, "but neither do they mix very much. That's something Anglos new to the area often try to change. They hope to have Indian, Spanish and Anglo friends mixed together like—say—New York City. It doesn't usually work. There are exceptions, of course, but the groups tend to remain separate."

Delia took a sip of the excellent Spanish sherry. "Maybe New Mexico is the prototype for the twenty-first century. People will hang on to their own cultural identities while managing to live together in the same area."

"I must admit, I never thought of New Mexico as a world prototype, but perhaps you're right," Molly said as she put the large wooden salad bowl on the table, along with a stack of colorful ceramic plates. "By the way, how are you getting along with Dolores? She's an excellent cleaner, isn't she? Did you know she works for us, too?"

Ethan began to spoon the lamb stew into warm bowls that matched the salad plates. Rumpus and Hark, who had decided to lounge in the living room when banished from their preferred central kitchen location, trotted to the door looking hopefully at Delia, who shook her head at them. They sank down in the doorway, put their big hound heads on their paws and stared dolefully at their owners, no doubt convinced they were effective guilt-slingers. Delia and Jean-Paul, however, were immune. Almost always, the dogs' behavior proved that with proper training they could be more mannerly than many humans. And like gracious people everywhere, they were welcomed guests.

"No, we didn't know Dolores works for you," Delia replied. "And her granddaughter, Carla? Does she come along to your house as well?"

"Ah," Ethan said, pulling out his wife's chair for her and bringing a bottle of red wine to the table, "thereby hangs a woeful tale."

As everyone tasted the experimental stew with great satisfaction and expressions of delight, Ethan continued: "Carla has been refusing to go to school until her bruises heal."

"It must have been a bad car accident..." Delia offered.

"Oh, no," Molly interjected, "her boyfriend beat her up."

"*Mon dieu*," Jean-Paul said softly. "Terrible, terrible thing to happen. No wonder she is of the temperament most nervous." He told them about the episode with the owl.

Molly sighed. "I worry about that girl. She's either withdrawn or on the verge of hysterics. I have the feeling," Molly spoke tentatively while gazing off toward the potted herbs, "that Carla has already suffered so much tragedy that she may never understand there's joy in life. We all must learn to recognize joy when it's offered — to balance the inevitable pain of life. I fear she's not getting the chance..."

Molly halted and looked at her guests as if determined to return to the practical. "And she should be in school. Her poor grandmother—Dolores has got her hands full."

"But where are her parents? By the way, your concoction, Molly, is most superb!" Jean-Paul always enjoyed creative cooking. "You make the cookery into the art form."

Molly smiled her acknowledgment.

Ethan topped up everyone's wine glass and returned to the subject of Carla's misfortune. "Carla's mother is in prison on a drug charge and her father was killed in a shootout in Chimayo," he said.

Delia gasped. "How awful. And has Carla no siblings?" The minute the words were out of her mouth, the ache of misery concerning her own newly discovered sibling returned to her consciousness. In the last few days she'd begun to have some respite from her unhappiness concerning Dorothy, but the word 'sibling' brought it back in a flash.

Jean-Paul must have seen the sudden look of pain on Delia's face—he was very sensitive to her moods—and he leaned over and caressed her arm. Ethan and Molly, however, didn't seem to notice.

Molly said, "Actually, yes, Delia. Carla has a brother—quite a bit older. And he's a winner! After all the sadness and turmoil he's lived through, it's hard to see how he managed. Juan is the star of the family. He's incredibly bright, won a scholarship to the University of New Mexico and is now in his first year of law school. Unfortunately, it's as if all the confusion and hurt of the family settled on Carla. "

"We don't see much of Juan," Ethan added. "During college he had a part-time job in a grocery store and now he's also got some part-time work in an Albuquerque law firm. I suspect his time is pretty used up."

Molly had gotten up to offer seconds on the stew and corn bread. "And Dolores thinks Juan isn't keen on returning to the scene of so much family misery. I do think, however, that she wishes she had a little more help with his sister..."

Delia was only half attending to the conversation. The word 'sister' brought a flash of clarity to her distracting thoughts. Her misery was no longer the result of shock on learning of a sister, nor was it anger and hurt that she'd been kept in the dark about Dorothy's death, but rather the fear that her own existence had been a constant reminder of the lost child. Instead of bringing joy, she'd prolonged her parents' sense of loss. Oh, if only she could know how they'd really felt!

Ethan was passing the bread. She distractedly focused on his thin, lined face. Except that his white hair was parted in the middle, he resembled Woodrow Wilson. She felt herself smiling at the thought and made a point of offering a friendly glance. "Yes, I'd love more cornbread." She was back in the land of the living.

For dessert, there were poached pears in a delicate wine sauce and then coffee in demitasse cups that Molly said had come from Martha's Vineyard. Pretty little cups with a nautical motif. "Most unsuitable for New Mexico," Molly said laughingly.

"Speaking of New Mexico, I have a question," Delia said. "We hear Duthuit's house is haunted. Obviously Carla and Dolores believe La Llorona is an actual presence. Who is she? Why this particular woman?"

"Shall we go into the living room? Ethan, dear, maybe you'd light the fire in there... and we'll tell you what we know of La Llorona."

Rumpus and Hark were evidently glad to be joined by the humans. Ethan lit the fire and, as they settled around it, Molly refilled their cups from a matching nautical pot. Jean-Paul watched carefully as the rich brown liquid streamed into his cup. He usually didn't like American coffee, but he obviously enjoyed the fragrance of this one. He started to speak — Delia expected him to ask for the brand name, but instead he said, "We have burned much wood which we must replace. Where do you suggest we buy more?"

Molly, still holding the coffee pot, thought for a moment and replied, "You can always go to Rios Wood Yard on the corner of Canyon Road and Camino del Monte Sol — but you know — on Bishops Lodge Road, on the east side of the road, there are several places with NO PARKING signs. There's often a pick-up there filled with wood for sale. In our experience, the wood has usually been dried and burns well. They'll deliver. You could get some there and it might be cheaper."

"In the NO PARKING spaces..." Jean-Paul said meditatively. "In

New Mexico, tell me, there is a hierarchy of laws, *n'est-ce pas*? Some to be obeyed — others not?"

Ethan slid the fireplace screen back in place, turned to his wife and smiled. Then to Jean-Paul he said, "My dear chap, you are most observant! New Mexicans do indeed choose which laws to obey. I'm afraid it's rather lawless around here."

Molly placed the coffee pot on the hearth. "Hard to keep things hot at this altitude," she murmured.

Ethan regarded the flames with satisfaction and took a seat on the sofa beside his wife. "So... back to the subject of La Llorona. As far as we can make out, La Llorona is the Spanish colonial version of the Greek myth of Medea. You'll remember that Medea murdered her and Jason's two sons to revenge his leaving her for another woman. Then Medea wandered forever, wailing and mourning the loss of her children."

Molly interrupted, "I've always thought it a nonsensical myth. If Medea was distraught from the loss of Jason, wouldn't she want all the more to hold onto her sons? At least she'd have them to love. But her actions and crazed regret must speak to the human psyche because the myth continues to live. Here in New Mexico, she is called La Llorona and believed to be a Mayan loved by Cortes. In this version, she is thought to have killed her sons because Cortes planned to take them away to Spain." Molly sighed with exasperation. "It still doesn't make a lot of sense."

"However," Ethan interrupted, "La Llorona's moans are associated with the sound of water, with the whoosh of water running through the acequias which irrigate the land. It's not a bad tale to tell children if you fear they'll fall into the irrigation ditch and drown. Many New Mexicans can't swim. No ocean. No big rivers to learn in."

"But... why does La Llorona haunt the house of Duthuit?" Jean-Paul asked.

"I suspect," Ethan said, "because there are an unusual amount of acequias running across the property..."

"And," Molly added, "at this point it's owned by a foreigner and often unoccupied. Vacuums are an abhorrence, so a ghost rushes in and takes up residence."

114

"Hmm," Jean-Paul murmured, staring dreamily into the fire, "an uninvited housemate for Delia and me." After a quiet moment, he asked, "The Spanish folk stories, are they all lugubrious?"

"By no means," replied Ethan. "If you get lost on your trip to Chimayo or are in danger—from the cold perhaps—you'll be rescued by the Christ Child. Or so it's believed. Across from the Santuario is a second Church to which people bring little pairs of shoes so the rescuing Child doesn't expose his feet to the snow or rough earth. You'll see all the shoes lining the altar."

Molly leaned down and patted Hark's head. "This belief probably comes from Spain. It's believed that the Spanish who were imprisoned by Moors were saved from starvation by the Baby Jesus racing from cell to cell bringing them food."

"A very charming image," Delia declared.

"And up-beat, wouldn't you say?" Ethan confirmed.

Their conversation continued into the afternoon, relaxed and informative, as they got to know one another. When Delia and Jean-Paul got up to leave, they were pleased by what seemed to be a nourishing day with new and sympathetic friends.

There was, however, a seed of suspicion growing in Delia's mind. The Ridgeleys possessed vast knowledge of New Mexico traditions. They knew a great deal about local society. Was it possible they knew more about the break-ins than they'd revealed? Were they hiding something? Protecting someone? Delia felt both unsure and a little embarrassed by her suspicions. She wouldn't say anything to Jean-Paul at present, but in the past, her intuition had usually proved accurate and she dare not ignore it.

By the time they trudged back up the road, the sun had melted most of the ice and rivulets of water trickled down the sides in the small gullies. Rumpus and Hark ran to and fro, their big paws gathering mud as they went. The sun slipped toward the west and their shadows lengthened, the darkness in sharp contrast with the still brightly lit snow. Delia tucked her hand beneath Jean-Paul's arm, which he pulled close against him. All was ostensibly fresh and harmonious.

Until they opened the patio gate and saw that once again all the doors and windows of the house were flung open.

"*Merde! Pas encore!*" Jean-Paul dropped Delia's hand and stamped his foot. The hounds with their muddy paws rushed into the house and began racing around, sticking their noses under doors and growling importantly. Jean-Paul marched in behind them. Delia stood on the portal amidst all the activity, feeling alone in an alien land. She slipped her hand into her coat pocket to feel her Beretta nestled there amongst the warm sheepskin lining. The gesture was becoming automatic.

14

The locksmith, who said his name was Eloy, arrived promptly at 8 o'clock Monday morning. Delia and Jean-Paul were still eating breakfast when the rusty bell sounded outside the patio. Rumpus and Hark were delighted to have a visitor and rushed out as soon as Jean-Paul opened the kitchen door.

Eloy, a tall, elderly guy in a brown parka and well-worn jeans and boots, instantly inspired confidence. He politely asked Jean-Paul what country he was from and, upon hearing that he was French, confided that his great-grandfather had also been French. Congregating in the kitchen, Eloy explained that his ancestor was a trapper who'd come down the Mississippi from Canada and trekked west over the mountains to New Mexico. "He wasn't the only one. Other trappers arrived the same way and married into Spanish families. It's said that's where the northern New Mexican pitched roofs come from. I heard they have pitched roofs back in France."

Jean-Paul confirmed that they did.

Delia added, "It certainly makes sense with all this snow."

"Yep. Yep. Sure does," agreed Eloy. "Let's hope we keep on getting it."

He then started his inspection of the house with Jean-Paul, Delia and the hounds trailing behind. "I've been here before. Guess you've still got a break-in problem..." He looked carefully at every window lock, worked and rattled them and pronounced them in good shape. "But I'll change the locks on the doors. What you got? One out here from the sala — hmm — to the south, one from that big bedroom to the west, two portal doors — hall and kitchen. Okay. We'll change them. It'll take a while. You know, you folks need a working burglar alarm. Looks like that one got disconnected."

"That is true," Jean-Paul replied. "But we understand it rang frequently, so the landlord, he decide to disconnect it to avoid the fines. Now a person breaks in, but nothing is taken."

Delia wondered if Jean-Paul would mention the ghost, but he said nothing, nor did Eloy bring it up. Delia suspected Eloy knew the story, however. A purpose of ghost stories is for everyone to know them. They never stay secret, despite the efforts of the property owner. Ghost stories leak like an underground oil pipe, spoiling the property and the owner's equity.

Eloy went to his truck to forge new locks while Rumpus and Hark supervised from the patio gate and the Duvals finished breakfast. Delia and Jean-Paul decided to keep the lock change a secret. Anyone with a workable key could create havoc. So until they departed for the East Coast, no one would know they'd changed the locks — not even Kimber. But was Eloy trustworthy? Might he be complicit in aggravating the problem? He'd profit by the series of lock changes. Delia would make sure she or Jean-Paul paid him themselves so he wouldn't send his bill to the management company.

Delia decided she'd also start questioning people about Duthuit's reputation. If he were resented, she wanted to know why. Certainly Cousin Alice and the Ridgeleys admired him, but she'd heard little about him from anyone else. She thought of grumpy Rose in Kimber's outer office.

Rose hadn't mentioned the opera star during their visit, but her demeanor had been less than friendly. She wondered if that had something to do with Duthuit. Had he insulted her inadvertently or intentionally? Rose certainly didn't behave in a sympathetic manner; she was barely polite. Delia planned to also ask Joseph and Delores for their opinions of Duthuit, although she doubted she'd get anything much from Joseph. Still, it was worth a try. There was something going on. Someone, somewhere, had to know what it was.

Delia had been invited to Wilma's for coffee that morning. Jean-Paul planned to meet again with the architect, Slim Fellows, who now had an influential client hoping to sell the state on the idea of a wildlife bridge across Interstate 25 at Glorieta Pass. For years the busy highway constituted a murderous strip through wooded areas rich in wild life. It was hazardous for motorists as well: they'd stop suddenly or swerve dangerously when wildlife crossed their path, causing deadly crashes. Jean-Paul had never designed such a bridge, which must be light and strong enough to withstand the weight of earth and vegetation. But he'd seen several wildlife bridges in Europe, where they'd been used for years. Jean-Paul was eager to share knowledge and learn more of New Mexico's problems.

He planned to take the hounds and the laptops to be on the safe side. He and Delia would have Eloy's new keys and their cell phones in case they needed to be in touch. And he'd not be away long. Nevertheless, Delia tucked her little weapon into her handbag. They hoped, however, the lock change would finally solve the intruder problem.

As Delia began her short walk down the road to Wilma's house, she realized it was the first time in a long while that she'd been alone. Since they'd begun their trip West, she and Jean-Paul had been constantly together — and for the most part, with the hounds as well. She didn't mind being on her own; there had been times she'd felt bereft during the interval after her first husband's death and falling in love with Jean-Paul, but even then, she'd usually been peaceful and fulfilled in her solitary life. Now, she admitted to herself, the thought of being alone had a different feel. Part of that was her consternation and pain over discovering the existence of Dorothy. But also, she'd become more self-aware—maybe a little more self-conscious and unsure of herself. Certainly she felt miniscule in this expansive New Mexico landscape.

The wind had gotten up, blowing strong from the southwest, and the remaining snow on the trees was cascading with frost diamonds glistering from the sun. The sky was a deep and brilliant blue, but Delia noticed dark, threatening clouds moving up from the south. Another storm was on its way. Her boots crunched against the snow and seemed to echo the vastness of the landscape. Here and there were treacherous patches of ice; Delia was glad she'd brought one of the ski poles she'd found in the hall closet.

A silver Audi with colorful New Mexico plates was parked in the Kovics' driveway along with Wilma's Land Rover. The Audi struck Delia as an odd car for New Mexico; she wondered how well it performed in the snow. As she passed, however, she saw it was actually four-wheel drive. That certainly made sense.

The majestic steps to the front door had been swept clean, but Delia judged they'd be safer with a railing. She liked houses where the front door was either at ground level or just slightly raised. Descending steps to enter, on the other hand, struck her as a little sinister and unwelcoming.

Delia rang the doorbell and leaned her ski pole against an exterior wall, thinking if she forgot it she could come back and pick it up without disturbing anyone. Expecting the silent, pale woman to open the door, she was surprised when Wilma, dressed in a black cashmere sweater, black jeans, a belt with an enormous silver buckle and elaborately decorated black cowboy boots, opened the door. She looked harassed, holding her phone to her ear, but waved Delia inside, grimacing and making a hand signal of exasperation as she closed the door behind her. When Delia shrugged off her coat, Wilma caught it with one hand and hung it on a hook inside the open door of the previously concealed closet.

While Wilma continued her harsh-voweled conversation in a loud and commanding voice—Delia assumed the call must be an international one with a less-than-perfect connection—Delia looked around. Sun beamed through the high hall windows where dust motes floated lazily. Wilma signaled for Delia to follow her. They descended the three steps into the "great room" where Delia noted four or five paintings stacked against a wall and the giant fireplace cold and dead. The fluffy white cat was nowhere to be seen, nor was anyone else. They climbed the two steps to the study with its grandiose desk and continued on through a hallway, Delia following Wilma who was still shouting into her phone. They arrived at the master bedroom.

For a moment, Delia stood stunned, astonished by the elaborate décor suggestive of a Moorish palace. In the middle of the room stood a massive, carved four-poster bed hung with majestic orange, pink and deep blue tapestries, and across from it, stood the largest flat screen television Delia had ever seen. The walls of the room were the pink of the tapestries and covered with a myriad of paintings in heavy gold frames, hung one above the other. (Delia was reminded of a photograph of the Cone sisters' apartment at the Baltimore Museum of Art, where every inch of wall space was covered with art.) Brilliant stripes and colorful floral patterns predominated throughout the huge bedroom. The effect was outrageously opulent. Somehow, Delia hadn't expected such extravagance in New Mexico. She supposed, however, that since many New Mexicans had Spanish ancestry, Moorish décor was fair enough—or at least that must be the underlying assumption. And, of course, there was that jarring Scottish Rite Temple at the end of Bishops Lodge Road—also bright pink and Moorish in style.

Beside a wide but small-paned window facing north were two large velvet armchairs upholstered in leopard-skin patterns with a massive claw-footed coffee table between them. A gleaming thermos, heavy ceramic turquoise-colored mugs with matching creamer and sugar bowl, as well as a platter of sweet rolls, were clustered on the table.

Wilma sank into a chair and motioned Delia to take the other. The chair was so large Delia feared it might devour her. There was nothing for Delia to do but curl her legs under her or sit on the edge of the chair with her legs dangling. Wilma's longer frame, however, settled comfortably as she waved to Delia to help herself to coffee. The thermos, Delia thought, was a good idea; she'd already learned that at this altitude nothing stayed hot for long. As for her hostess's continued phone conversation, Delia was becoming impatient. She could have brewed herself a fine cup of coffee back at the Duthuit house and been a damned sight more comfortable. She decided to forgo the coffee and buns until Wilma got off the phone. In the meantime, she'd gaze out the window at the snowy piñon forest. It was a healthy, wild forest for as far as the eye could see, affording privacy from neighbors and road. Delia liked that. It was a good choice to put the bedroom-sanctuary at this quiet end of the house. Perhaps she'd see that pack of coyotes that had awakened her a few nights past. So she sat, looked and waited.

Wilma finally concluded her conversation, clicked off the phone and stuck it against the cushion of her chair. "Sorry about that, Delia," she said airily. "Honestly, some people are fools. You can tell them the same thing over and over and they just don't get it. They probably don't want to get it! I've got a show coming up in Antwerp—a really important show of eighteenth-century European paintings—and it has to be perfect. I left an explicit diagram of exactly how everything's to be hung and my assistants—god! they're so arrogant!—have taken it upon themselves to alter my plan. I do sometimes wonder who they think pays their salaries! I could fire everyone in the flick of an eye, except that would cause me even more trouble breaking in a new staff." Wilma heaved herself about in her vast chair and groaned.

Delia felt Wilma was transferring her fury toward her staff to her. She wished she hadn't come.

"Oh, well," continued Wilma, picking up the thermos, "maybe I'll give up the whole damned enterprise. But," she looked up at Delia, "cream? It's lucrative. But I'm really not in the mood to jump on a plane and travel a million hours to Belgium. That's the problem with New Mexico. It's Siberia! It takes days to get here or get started to anywhere else!" Wilma sighed unhappily. She appeared to calm down as she poured herself and Delia mugs of coffee.

The room was cold, however, and Delia sank back into her chair-environment and cupped her hands around her mug for warmth. She consciously tried to put a pleasant expression on her face. After all, Wilma probably knew quite a bit about matters that were of interest to her.

From the recesses of her chair, Wilma's phone growled again. "Hello? No." Wilma answered. "I'm in a meeting. Call back later! This afternoon—as we had previously arranged." Wilma clicked off the phone and again shoved it down into the recesses of the chair. She seemed particularly jumpy this morning.

"Where is everyone?" Delia asked. "I don't even see your pretty white cat."

"Gone."

Delia noticed Wilma's large, linen napkins were decorated with medieval warriors in various suits of armor. Wilma passed Delia a sticky bun atop one of the napkins. It had a knight mounted on horseback with a long lance. Delia thought warriors a queer motif for morning coffee, but then it occurred to her that if she spread the napkin out over her legs, it might provide a layer of warmth. And it would catch the crumbs from the sticky bun as she ate.

"Let's see," Wilma continued in a startled voice as if she were just waking up to the fact that she was alone. "You're right. Everyone IS gone. The kids went to Taos to ski and Steve and Monika went to Las Vegas. Nevada, not New Mexico." Wilma gave a little laugh at the thought of anyone going to Las Vegas, New Mexico. Since Delia hadn't been to Las Vegas, New Mexico, she suspected she was missing Wilma's meaning.

However, Wilma did seem to be calming down. "As for the cat— hmm—I don't know what's become of her. Probably got eaten by a coyote..."

Wilma was surprisingly unconcerned at the fate of the white cat, so Delia decided to enquire who Monika was.

"Oh," Wilma said, taking a large bite of her sticky bun and wiping her fingers nervously across her napkin, "Monika is Steve's assistant. You met her at our party. She's not very memorable, I grant you—you may not have even noticed her."

"Was she the pale woman who took our coats?" Delia was dismayed to think that Wilma had somehow read her mind and then she felt herself blushing at the remembrance of her snooping in the wrong closet that evening.

Wilma appeared not to notice. "Yeah, she's pale and says very little. She doesn't speak English well, although I suspect she knows more than she lets on. She's actually Steve's sister-in-law and she's an absolute wiz with jewels. She knows everything there is to know, apparently. She can spot the good ones from the poor ones with the naked eye. Steve says it's quite incredible.

"Here, have some more coffee."

"Thanks, just a little," Delia replied. It was good coffee and helped to warm her.

Wilma refilled her cup and handed it over with her slim, black-clad arm.

"So they went to Las Vegas to buy jewelry?"

"No, they went to sell a shipment they just got from Europe. Steve's got an outlet—a shop there. It's a good venue. Actually, I'm thinking of opening a gallery there, too. Those tourists really buy. It's not that they understand quality as much as they simply like stuff. I think I could make a go of it there, for sure." She sighed again and smiled for the first time. "That is, if I could find a decent staff..."

"And, err, Monika's husband, your brother-in-law, did he go, too? You know, I don't think I met him at your party."

For a moment Wilma gazed out the window toward the piñon forest. Delia noticed the trees were much smaller than at the Duthuit place, which was higher. She found it puzzling that the big cottonwoods grew on the Duthuit property; she thought they'd have been more apt to thrive lower down by the Tesuque River. Someone must have set up irrigation especially for them; they were so large and handsome.

Wilma's cup tipped while she was looking out the window and a little coffee spilled. She dabbed at her lap with the warrior napkin. Turning her attention back to Delia, she said, "My brother-in-law was killed some years ago. It was pretty awful, I gather. Steve gets upset whenever it's mentioned. So I've learned not to bring it up. I'm sure you've found that in marriage, there are certain places it's wise not to go..."

Actually, though she'd been married twice, Delia had never found herself articulating that little piece of wisdom, but perhaps Wilma was right. She certainly sensed that Wilma herself didn't relish talking about her brother-in-law's death, so she changed the subject. "Tell me about Guillaume Duthuit. How do you like him? You know, it's interesting living in someone's house whom you've never met. You can't help but get an idea of what they're like. So, I'd like to hear your impressions."

"Oh, he's nice, I guess. Another European, if you know what I mean."

Delia didn't. Both Jean-Paul and Steve were European, but she wasn't clear what Wilma was suggesting. She decided to let it go. She had the feeling she and Wilma were talking past each other. It bothered her that they weren't establishing a better rapport. Delia liked to connect with people.

Later that afternoon when she thought over the visit, she wished she'd pursued Wilma's meaning about "being European". The label sounded pejorative. Her sense of Guillaume Duthuit was becoming as baffling as the break-ins and the La Llorona story. It must all fit together somehow, but Delia couldn't find the key to the puzzle.

Wilma brushed her well-manicured hand over her cropped hair and continued in another vein: "Have you heard Guillaume perform? He's quite phenomenal. Big bass voice. Very 'musical' is what people say about him. And he's terrific looking with lots of taste. I'd sure like to get my hands on some of those New Mexico paintings he's got in that house. They're very valuable. You'd think someone would steal them — with the house being empty so often and tenants from God knows where running in and out all the time." Wilma sighed and looked at the ceiling, which was painted day-glo green. "It's a wonder he hasn't married. Or, come to think of it, maybe he has and we just haven't met his wife. Lots of people hate travelling. Oh, I don't know..."

Wilma was losing interest in Guillaume Duthuit. She certainly seemed distracted. Delia wondered if she were depressed. Or ill again.

124

Maybe the cancer had come back and was beginning to sap Wilma's energy, though she looked well enough. Clearly, if she had had chemo treatments, it hadn't been recently.

Wilma's phone rang once again. Delia had really hoped for more information about her landlord. Her suspicions of him were growing. But Wilma checked to see where the call was from and then decided to answer it. Delia became seriously irritated.

"Yes? What is it?" Wilma inquired. Then turning to Delia she said, "Sorry, I've got to take this." Wilma rose from the chair, turned her back on her guest and walked toward what Delia assumed was an adjoining dressing room and closed the door behind her.

This, Delia decided, was no time for a neighborly visit. She wriggled out of the big chair, gathered up her bag and headed toward the study where she hoped to find pen and paper to leave Wilma a departing note. She stood for a moment to see if Wilma would return, but her barely audible voice continued behind the closed door.

Entering the study, Delia saw that although there were five or six trays of papers and documents on the big desk, there was neither pad nor pen. Without much thought, she opened a drawer in which she was startled to find another pile of papers, and a pile of passports held together by a rubber band, beside an exotic, or at least foreign-looking, pistol. The papers beneath the weapon were written in a language she didn't recognize.

An alarm clicked in her brain. She glanced behind her to see if Wilma had returned to her seat in the bedroom, then pulled her cell phone from her bag. It was a new phone with a camera and she wasn't sure she remembered how to use. But the pistol looked so ominous, intuition told her to photograph it and the document beneath it. She did so and then shoved the drawer back with her knee. Then for good measure, and without touching anything, she photographed the visible documents in the boxes on top of the desk. Some were written in Cyrillic, the others were also in languages she didn't recognize, certainly not French, as she might have expected. She hoped she had the camera the right way around. A photo of her own sweater would not be of much use in her investigation.

Hearing footsteps, she turned to see Wilma behind her. Her heart gave a thump. She shoved her phone into her bag, frightened that Wilma had seen what she'd done. "I was looking for a bit of scrap paper to leave you a note. And stupidly, I seem to have forgotten to bring a pen in my purse." Delia smiled in what she hoped was a casual, friendly way.

Thankfully, Wilma appeared not to have noticed and seemed genuinely distressed that Delia was leaving. "Oh, don't go! We haven't had much of a chat, yet, and I was hoping to get your and your husband's impressions of my Santa Fe show.

"You must think me awfully rude—taking those phone calls while you're here. Steve says I get carried away by my little businesses. He thinks I take them too seriously. I suppose I do. You must stay for another cup of coffee."

Delia glanced at her watch. She didn't want more coffee, but she figured it behooved her to stay a little longer if she didn't want to be seen as departing precipitously. It was almost noon. "Well, okay. Thanks. I could stay a bit longer..." She hoped she sounded natural. She was uncomfortable about her behavior, especially if she'd been seen. She wondered if Wilma even knew about the gun or if she were versed in the languages in the documents. There was clearly nothing stupid about Wilma. She was a canny woman, despite her inhospitable manners.

Delia stumbled on the steps to the bedroom, but caught herself before she fell. Watch it, she told herself, and willed herself to calm down. She needed to bring the conversation to a friendly level. So she complimented Wilma on her show and then moved on to her and Jean-Paul's interest in the adobe buildings on Canyon Road and their contrastingly flamboyant Christmas decorations.

Wilma told Delia about the local custom of a Christmas Eve stroll through the Canyon Road and Acequia Madre neighborhood and the reenactment of Las Posadas, the journey of Joseph and Mary from Nazareth to Bethlehem. She graciously invited Delia and Jean-Paul to drop by her gallery again soon.

Delia was determined to forgive Wilma her previous inconsideration and vowed that after Steve and Monika returned, she'd invite them for a meal—Sunday lunch, perhaps. She and Jean-Paul were hospitable people and they'd been accepting invitations from near strangers since their arrival in New Mexico. Now it was their turn.

Delia remembered to reclaim the ski pole as she left Wilma's house and began her trek up the road. The sun felt warm against her back and the ice on the road had become mushy. The dark clouds to the south had dispersed. Her throat felt a little dry as she wondered if there had been another break-in at the house. She hoped that Eloy had taken care of the problem. Still, there remained a prick of anxiety.

But Rumpus and Hark rushed out to welcome her home. Jean-Paul had already been back for twenty minutes. They heaved a collective sigh of relief that no one had gotten through the locks.

Giving her husband a hug, Delia said, "With any luck, our intruder problem is solved."

Jean-Paul pulled back, looked at his wife and planted a kiss on her forehead. "*Eh, bien,* my darling, you know what you always say, 'Assumption is not fact.' We must continue our vigilance. Though nothing has yet been taken, let us continue to remove with us our important possessions."

"Oh, yes! Isn't it lucky we have so little to protect?"

"*Bien sûr. La bonne chance!* The possessions, they tyrannize, *n'est-ce pas?*"

Leaving her bag on a nearby chair, Delia hung up her coat and replaced the ski pole in the hall closet. They walked hand-in-hand toward the kitchen with the idea of a little lunch. The hounds followed expectantly.

"And, my treasure, did you enjoy the morning with Madame Kovic?"

"Not particularly. She was on the phone most of the time. And that house is monstrous! So large and ill-proportioned. You wouldn't believe the bedroom! It's the Moorish salon from hell. And I really hate all those little steps between rooms. A real flight of stairs is one thing, but one or two steps between each room is dangerous."

"It is because a flat place was not bull-dozed before the house was built." Delia could tell Jean-Paul was seeing the construction process in his mind's eye. He had that far-away, scrutinizing look. "Ethan, he tell us the new part devour the old. I remember he say 'devour.' Additions are often difficult to build."

"Hmm, I know..." Delia responded, half-thinking of what to have for lunch. "So often the integrity of the original structure is breached. Couldn't they have built up the land—to make it flat before they began that monstrosity?"

"*Très difficile.* To bring in the earth make the problems. It will settle. The walls, they crack."

"Well, at least that was not how this house was built—one hundred years ago." Delia stopped speaking, cocked her head and listened. "Do you hear that moaning sound? What is it?"

Jean-Paul smiled. Then making his voice into a spooky moan, he replied, "La Llorona." He laughed. "Do you not sometimes hear that sound? I cannot find the source. It must be the wind in the cottonwood trees."

Delia suddenly asked with urgency, "Jean-Paul, what do you suppose is the purpose of the break-ins and the ghost story—which a good many people seem to believe?"

"To force our departure."

"But why? Whom or what does our presence disturb? And who is doing it? The help?"

"I think," Jean-Paul opened the refrigerator and brought out the container of homemade onion soup and some salad fixings. Delia took the fresh baguette from its paper sleeve and the cheeses from under their glass dome. "I think," Jean-Paul repeated, "it is not the servants. Does not Joseph emanate—you say emanate?—goodness and *les jeunes filles*, are they not too young for the behavior criminal?"

"Yes, and as for Dolores—she seems responsible and sensible. Carla. Well, Carla's a hysterical teenager who's had a hard time. But somehow I can't see her orchestrating this problem, even if her mother is behind bars. Of course, it could be some teenage prank, but her terror of La Llorona was genuine."

Delia got down a pan and carefully poured the soup into it. She loved their landlord's French enameled cast iron pans; their wooden handles were so comfortable to cook with. She carefully carried the saucepan to the stove, turned on the gas under it and stood, stirring from time to time with a wooden spoon. "Well, what about the women at the rental agency?"

Jean-Paul was setting cutlery, glasses and napkins on a tray to take into the dining room. "But the question remains, why? Would it not be against their interest if Duthuit got fed out with them and change to a different agency?"

Delia got down two ceramic soup bowls from the cupboard. "Fed up."

"*Ah oui*, fed up... Those ladies, if they lose the client, they lose the income." He prepared the salad: cooked green beans from dinner last night, tomatoes, young greens with basil and Delia's spicy dressing.

The French onion soup gave off a delicious fragrance. "We must sit down now, darling, before the altitude cools the soup."

When they'd arranged themselves at the near end of the big dining table, had spread out their napkins and begun their satisfying meal, Delia declared, "It must be a grudge against Duthuit that causes all this trouble."

"*D'accord*. Someone holds the grudge. And it is someone we have not yet met."

Jean-Paul's comment gave Delia a new idea. "What about Carla's dreadful boyfriend? He sounds like a thoroughly bad sort. Men — or boys — who beat up their girlfriends are perverted! She should get away from him! Dolores should get him out of Carla's life! He'll never straighten out if people accept that sort of destructive behavior!" Delia was getting upset.

Jean-Paul leaned across and patted her hand. "*Tu as raison*. But the teenage girls are they not determined to have their way? Dolores, I assume, cannot send Carla to a convent. Or can she? The Catholic Church has influence here, does it not? Ah, but then, would she not run away?" He suddenly smiled one of his glorious smiles. "The convent, it, too, is apt to have a ghost, *n'est-ce pas*? We know *la jeune fille* has the allergy to ghosts..."

"Oh, Jean-Paul, it's all so perplexing." Delia gazed out the window at the far away hills and a sky now full of mares' tails. "Can we find a motive for the boyfriend chasing away tenants?"

They sat silently, pondering. "Darling, your onion soup is particularly good. Do you want more cheese?"

"*Merci*." He leaned back in his chair. "*C'est curieux*. For me, there is the suspicion of the grudge for Guillaume Duthuit. He is here to perform, which means he is *probablement* distracted from local matters. He perhaps does not see, nor care to see the implications of what he say or ask of the local people. Someone has decided they do not like his manner."

"You think he's arrogant?"

"Perhaps. Not meaning it. Unaware. Perhaps he is unaware. And because he is the stranger, the resentment builds up. What do you think, my treasure?"

Delia served them each more salad. She knew the beans were cooked just the way he liked them: not too al dente, but still not limp and flavorless. "Why not telephone André in France? After all, Duthuit is his client. He must know him. You could get his opinion. But of course, this discussion could be moot. We could have solved the break-in problem simply by having changed the locks. Still, it would be nice to know why..."

15

Delia and Jean-Paul had at last begun to relax and enjoy New Mexico. Their beautiful house still moaned, but changing the locks seemed to have taken care of the break-ins. The sun warmed their days, though the nights were frosty; and Jean-Paul was excited about the prospects of the wildlife crossing. He gathered information from European colleagues for Slim Fellows, told Delia all about what he was learning, and became fascinated to know more about the New Mexican multi-leveled ecosystem.

They discovered walking trails and arroyos low enough to be mostly clear of ice and snow; and they visited churches and museums in Santa Fe. The Folk Art Museum enchanted them. They bought Christmas presents in the museum stores and the Christmas Shop on Palace Avenue for their friends back home. They were especially drawn to the Spanish retablos and the pueblo pottery crèches.

During their second week in residence they learned about the importance of Our Lady of Guadalupe and watched the procession to the Cathedral of St. Francis of Assisi. Then the Ridgeleys took them on a day trip to Taos where, on the way up, they stopped at the Santuario de Chimayo and also saw the little chapel where tiny shoes for the Baby Jesus lined the altar. Delia and Jean-Paul particularly liked the eighteenth-century mission church in Las Trampas. Jean-Paul remarked that the area around Peñasco reminded him of a school trip he'd taken to Spain as a boy. The country was ancient, beautiful and sparse.

The old town of Taos, with its ancient pueblo beside the rushing stream, seemed particularly poignant because of the high, snowy mountains surrounding it. They ate lunch at Doc Martin's Restaurant, where Jean-Paul admired the latias in the ceiling.

Returning home by way of the Rio Grande Gorge, they stopped to admire the dramatic view of the gorge cutting through the wide, flat plain. They left the car in a picnic area and hiked for several miles. Delia thought Jean-Paul looked Latin and seductively attractive in his wide-brimmed hat. They were both glad to have the wide brims as protection from the brilliant sun. Delia thought the Ridgeleys' old, felt cowboy hats were also particularly fitting for the environment.

They trudged over bare earth punctuated by clumps of snow which mimiced the shape of the small fluffy clouds floating above. Rumpus and Hark chased a rabbit in and around the gray-green sage. Jean-Paul plucked a sprig of sage and sniffed it. *"Ah, que c'est bon, ce bouquet!"*

Everyone had fun. Delia tried to reason with her suspicion of the

Ridgeleys. They were delightful! But still... there was something about them Delia didn't trust.

When Joseph, Elizabeth and Roxann arrived several afternoons later to invite them to the Christmas dances at their pueblo, Jean-Paul lit a fire in the dining room. They all sat around the table enjoying tea, hot chocolate, fresh baked croissants and brown bread and butter with sprinkles of cinnamon. Jean-Paul remarked the gathering resembled a "nice bourgeois French family."

Elizabeth and Roxann were too small for their chairs, so Delia got pillows from the sala. The little girls seemed comfortable enough kneeling on their pillows until Roxann fell onto the floor. Rumpus and Hark rushed over to console her, licking her face and making her giggle. Obviously she wasn't hurt. After a moment on the floor with the hounds, she raised her arms and commanded, "Sit me, Deal-ya!" Delia wasn't sure what she meant, but Joseph explained that she wanted to sit on Delia's lap. Apparently, what little Indian children want, they get. Joseph picked up Roxann and deposited her on Delia's lap, where she proceeded to wipe her buttery fingers over Delia's sleeve. Then Elizabeth clambered up onto Jean-Paul's lap. He winked across the table at Delia, obviously amused. Delia suspected he missed his little granddaughters with whom they had, until now, always spent Christmas.

Elizabeth then announced that their grandmother had a "whirl-chair". Again, Delia and Jean-Paul weren't sure what she meant until Joseph explained that the grandmother had fallen off the roof and broken her leg and was temporarily confined to a wheel chair. Although Delia and Jean-Paul were bewildered as to why the old lady was on the roof, they murmured their condolences.

"She rides in the seen-your-ceetzen bus to the Endin Hospital on Mondays," confided Roxann in serious tones.

"We go, too!" Elizabeth was so excited at the thought that she slid down from Jean-Paul's lap and began to dance and sing, "To the Endin Hospital!" Then Roxann wriggled from Delia's lap and joined her sister's dance. Soon the dogs were also jumping about, wagging their tails and howling their loud, hound song.

Delia expected Joseph to admonish the children—to tell them to quiet down, but he appeared not to notice and took another croissant. Jean-Paul passed him more jam.

Despite the bedlam, Delia thought the girls were awfully cute. She remembered that her new phone took photographs so she excused herself and went to get it.

"May I take your picture?" she asked when she returned. Elizabeth and Roxann immediately ran to Joseph and posed at attention beside him. "Délie," suggested Jean-Paul, "perhaps if you take your photograph with your back to the window light, it might be more successful."

Delia immediately scooted to the other side of the table, and the girls, like flowers following the sun, jumped to the other side of Joseph's chair. Her subjects were so photogenic, and the architecture of the background so charming, that Delia took several more with Jean-Paul included.

"I take one of you now, Délie, with our new friends."

Then, of course, the little girls wanted to take some pictures themselves, so Delia showed them how to aim the phone at their subjects. She figured the girls' photos might be poorly composed and she could delete them later.

She, Jean-Paul and Joseph posed together. As she reclaimed the phone, she remembered the pictures she'd snapped at the Kovics' desk. She'd completely forgotten them. She silently reminded herself to send them to Detective Scott in Maryland. At the moment, however, she could see no earthly reason for doing so. Still, she had them and she might as well do something with them. What her friend on the District of Columbia Police Force would make of them, she couldn't imagine. She simply had the feeling that she didn't want her snooping to go to waste.

Joseph told the little girls it was time to leave. The southwestern sky was turning rose and cantaloupe; and the sun gleamed gold from under a gigantic dark cloud. The snow on the eastern mountains, reflecting the celestial extravaganza, was turning pink.

As they walked toward the front door the little girls grabbed Jean-Paul's hands. They had fallen in love with him and skipped along the hall in front of Delia and Joseph, smiling and chattering, giving Delia the chance to ask Joseph in a subdued voice, "Is there someone at the pueblo who can get rid of bothersome ghosts?"

Joseph regarded her gravely and said, "Yes."

"Can they do that for Anglos, too?"

Joseph shook his head solemnly. "No, they can't do that."

"Goodbye! Goodbye, Deal-ya! Goodbye, Gene!" the little girls shouted as they drove away in Joseph's old pick-up. "Don't forget to come to the dance!"

"Goodbye. Goodbye," Delia and Jean-Paul called. "Thank you! We'll be there!" Delia, Jean-Paul and the hounds then raced under the cottonwoods at the front of the house to watch the biggest, brightest sunset they'd ever seen.

16

Christmas morning dawned raw and cold. A sharp wind blew from the north and snowflakes whirled ferociously through the air. Jean-Paul lit the bedroom fire and brought breakfast to their bed. Their minimal breakfast was the only meal they had to fix that day since Joseph had invited them to lunch at the pueblo and the Ridgeleys had invited them for Christmas supper. Delia had hoped cousin Alice might join them, but she'd only just got back from her lecture tour and had promised to join old friends in Albuquerque many months ago—colleagues with whom she and her late husband had taken turns going to each other's houses at Christmas.

It interested Delia to see how people who'd chosen to move from the east to the west, where they had no families, turned friends into "family" and proceeded with traditions as usual or established new ones, often mixing the old with the new. When she'd shared her observation with Jean-Paul, he'd suggested that holiday rituals were programmed into our DNA. Thoughts about genetic inheritance led Delia to thoughts of her long-dead twin. Christmases certainly would have been different had Dorothy lived. Probably even better. She sensed that the shock of discovery was beginning to turn into mourning for the sister she couldn't remember. Mourning, she knew, could be postponed, but should never be avoided.

But bewilderment over her parents' neglect in telling her about Dorothy's birth and death bedeviled her. Her bewilderment produced fury. The discovery of their betrayal called into question her trust and belief in their love for her. She'd even begun to question her own self-worth. Had they really loved her as much as she'd assumed? Wouldn't her very existence have reminded them of their terrible loss? Perhaps they even resented her.

Her innate sense of well-being and self-respect was shaken. But she reminded herself that a marvelous man like Jean-Paul could never have loved her if he hadn't found her worthy. Happily, she was certain of his love. And she well understood that dwelling on these unanswerable questions produced a slippery slope. She must seek a better way to cope. At the moment, however, that way escaped her.

"Merry Christmas, my darling," Delia said sleepily. She and Jean-Paul had agreed to give each other only one gift since it meant packing them in the car before leaving the East Coast. This was not an easy decision because they each enjoyed seeking out special things for the other, and in this particular venture they tended towards extravagance. But for once, practicality won.

When Delia opened Jean-Paul's gift, a gorgeous French silk shawl with cashmere lining, she immediately wrapped it around her shoulders with a sigh of contentment. She adored the woven silk design of peacock feathers in greens, blues and turquoise over the pale sea-green wool. The combination enhanced her own delicate coloring and she realized the turquoise would fit in very well with their southwest locale. And then a thought occurred to her and she reversed the lovely shawl, putting the green that matched her eyes on the outside and the peacock feathers underneath. Jean-Paul was indeed a genius of design, color and texture. And he'd managed to give her two gifts in one.

"I shall wear my new gloves to the pueblo today." Jean-Paul was clearly pleased with his gift. Delia had taken the train from Baltimore to New York to do her pre-trip Christmas shopping, not sure what she'd find when she got to Santa Fe. She'd been delighted when she'd discovered the fur-lined gloves of the softest caramel-colored leather in a luxurious little shop on Madison Avenue. Christmas morning in Tesuque made Madison Avenue seem very far away.

When breakfast was finished, Delia removed the breakfast tray and then quickly returned to remove Jean-Paul's robe and pajamas and pull him back under the duvet. He was as eager as she for what ensued. They even added several of their most erotic games, just for spice.

"A Christmas most perfect," he murmured. "*Mais, mon dieu, quelle heure* has it become? My treasure, we will be late for the pueblo dance."

"Hmm..." Delia snuggled against him. "I guess you're right. We must somehow manage to get there or Elizabeth and Roxann will be disappointed..." She turned toward him for his kiss and then struggled out of bed toward the bath. "I don't know what time the dance begins. You don't think they'll call it off in this weather, do you?"

Jean-Paul slipped from bed and stood warming his nude body before the fire. Delia thought he looked very desirable with his long, lean, strong physique. She was ready to seduce him back into bed. Perhaps he had the same idea for he shook his head slightly as if willing his way out of languor and desire before replying, "Do you not remember Ethan say he thought the dance would take place in a break in the weather and that it would not start until everyone is ready. Let us bathe, put on the warm clothes and then we proceed to the pueblo. Is it not charming of Ethan and Molly to invite the hounds to stay with them?"

They had decided to take a box of Swiss chocolate for Joseph and his family because they clearly liked chocolate. They rounded up the hounds, locked the house carefully and drove down the road to the Ridgeleys' house.

Rumpus and Hark, who had had their morning run on their own, were ready for a nap in front of the Ridgeleys' living room fire. "Are you certain you don't want to come with us?" Delia asked Molly. "I'm sure the dogs will be okay here by themselves."

Molly and Ethan, who were still in their robes, nodded toward the pile of gifts under their Christmas tree. "If we don't open these soon, we won't know what to thank everyone for when the calls start coming in. But thanks. You'll have a nice time."

"I see the snow's letting up a bit," Ethan said, peering out the window. "And I see you're warmly dressed. That's important."

"Just go and have a good time," Molly said. "We'll walk the dogs before you get back, then you can tell us your impressions while we have an early supper. You know, I'm always of two minds about trying to get the family here at Christmas. The plane schedules get crazy. It's almost a relief to keep things this simple." She kissed Delia goodbye and sent them on their way.

17

Once on pueblo land, Delia and Jean-Paul drove for a long stretch beyond the highway. The snow had stopped, though the clouds hung low, obscuring the mountains to both the east and west. "*Regards,*" Jean-Paul said, "the mountains, they have been removed!" They were, indeed, completely invisible.

A cold wind continued to blow from the north, buffeting the car as they continued over the rough road. The visitors passed ancient, falling down corrals in which fuzzy-coated ponies huddled together beneath open sheds. Finally Delia and Jean-Paul came upon the parking area, where a herd of cars, trucks and campers was already parked. A fat tribal policeman with a gun and a stone-faced expression directed them to the spot where they were to park. Delia remembered that the pueblo was a sovereign nation with its own rules and laws. She felt they had traveled to a far away place in a far away time.

The knife-like wind whipped against them as they walked toward the plaza where the dance would be held. They drew their sheepskin coats tight around them, wrapped their wool scarves around their necks and pulled up their hoods. They'd been wise to wear boots and two pairs of socks.

Following a crowd of people through tiny dirt streets between adobe houses in different states of repair, Delia thought she could distinguish the Anglos from the Hispanics. Some of the Indians, many of whom were wrapped in blankets, seemed also to be visitors. They continued to walk quietly as befits the approach to a religious service. Delia thought she was beginning to get the sense of who the New Mexican people were and where her own place might be.

There was a hush as they arrived at the dirt plaza, and soon the Rainbow dance began. Drums beat and men in white shirts, black skirts with a red and green line, a long sash and high white soft leather boots, which she thought were called kaibabs, appeared in a line, each carrying an evergreen branch in his left hand and a rattle in his right. On their heads were bands of blue, orange and yellow feathers. Delia saw only two women among the dancers, both wearing large turquoise necklaces and thick leg wraps. The chorus of men sang hypnotically and sprinkled cornmeal upon the ground.

The performance was deeply moving. Delia was suffused by a spirit of harmony, reverence and awe for the earth, for the universe and the other humans residing in it. The dance and song, she understood, were a prayer for fertility and health. There was an enveloping feeling of spirituality and thanksgiving; and Delia experienced a profound sense of union between humanity and other living things. Enveloped by a sense of completeness, she slipped her arm beneath Jean-Paul's. He seemed equally transported by the sights and sounds, patterns and colors before him.

As the dance ended, Delia felt a tug on her sleeve and looked down to see Elizabeth. "Desert Ray say you come. You bring Gene to our house and we eat now." Delia shook herself from her trance, got Jean-Paul's attention and they did their best to follow Elizabeth as she darted through the crowd away from the plaza. It turned out their destination was a house on an adjacent dirt road.

The wind still blew, and now that she was removed from the relative warmth of the surrounding crowd, Delia shivered. They were still not far from the center of the pueblo. Like an Italian hill town, there were few trees and only occasional shrubs along the road. The blowing wind in her face caused Delia to turn for a moment and look back. She'd been too absorbed in the dance to notice her surroundings. She realized there was a small church at the edge of the plaza which she hadn't noticed.

There was something protected and womb-like about these central plazas — both here at the pueblo and those she'd seen in Europe. But unlike the ancient Italian piazzas, where the lofty church spire dominated the area, the roofline of the pueblo church was built of soft adobe with a rounded, gentle outline against the sky. These Pueblo Indians, Delia understood, unlike most European cultures, dwelt with a feminine spirit. These luminous moments at the pueblo dance were worth all the effort of crossing the country and whatever problems she and Jean-Paul faced with Duthuit's property. This Christmas dance was an unexpected and nourishing reward.

The house where Elizabeth led them had a rounded oven, a horno, Delia thought it was called, off to the left of its entrance. But she was surprised to see that the house was no different from an ordinary tract house anywhere in the United States. Jean-Paul sensed her surprise and whispered in her ear, "Ethan says the house is provided by a federal government loan and is built to specification." Delia nodded. The United States government certainly lacked imagination. Government regulations were probably aimed at saving the taxpayers' money. Utilitarian but sterile housing was the unhappy result. The effect, after the biomorphic adobe homes, was jarring.

Elizabeth took hold of her guests' hands, and pulled them through the front door into a well-heated room where they saw a mixed-race group around a table, quietly eating a meal. Roxann clumsily propelled a small woman in a wheel chair toward them. The woman, seemingly unaware she might tip over at any moment, smiled up at Delia and Jean-Paul in welcome. "I'm Desert Ray. You sit there." She pointed toward a brown couch before a large television set on top of which sat several photographs of babies.

Elizabeth pointed toward a photograph and informed them, "That's me. I was a baby."

No sooner had Delia and Jean-Paul sat beside each other on the couch than Elizabeth climbed into Delia's lap and slipped her hand into Jean-Paul's coat pocket. Within minutes, more people piled into the small room, all standing quietly and talking amongst themselves. Elizabeth slid off Delia's lap and ran toward the visitors, jumping up and down excitedly. Though the situation was new and unexpected, Delia felt comfortable and accepted. Nothing seemed to be expected of her or Jean-Paul except their presence. After a few moments, she and Jean-Paul followed the example of the other guests and shrugged off their heavy coats. The old woman in the wheelchair spoke in Tewa to a tall teenager, who then gathered up the coats and took them to a back room.

Delia whispered to Jean-Paul, "Is her name really Desert Ray?"

"I think not," he whispered back. "*Probablement Désirée.* You know these girls enjoy to make name games."

Delia nodded.

Those at the table rose, murmured thanks and began to depart. Then it was the turn of the people on the couch to come to the table. Jean-Paul quietly greeted Joseph, who had been one of the dancers and had just entered the room. He pulled their gift from his pocket and presented it to their host.

"Thank you," Joseph said, dipping his head slightly and smiling.

After they were seated with strangers on benches at the table, they introduced themselves in subdued voices. All were people who lived nearby and knew Joseph's family. They greeted another teenage girl who brought a fresh round of lunch from the open kitchen behind them. She poured grape Kool-aid from a plastic pitcher for each guest and then served bread pudding, red chili with meat, posole and also cherry Jello as a sort of salad. For dessert there was prune pie with a thick crust. Very filling. Very hearty.

Meanwhile more chilled people piled through the door and awaited their turn for lunch. It had started to snow again. The new group stamped their feet and shook their wet coats before giving them up to Jackie, the tall teenage girl. Both girls turned out to be older sisters of Elizabeth and Roxann. Everyone seemed to be related and everyone, young and old, participated in one way or another in the festivities. There was a lot of food and surely a great deal of effort went into preparing it. But the atmosphere was so harmonious that Delia doubted the effort had caused hardship. The prevailing sense of gratitude and community was noticeable at all levels.

Later, at supper with the Ridgeleys, Delia and Jean-Paul shared their impressions and delight in what they had experienced that afternoon. They noted that despite the difference in cultures, the Ridgeley's home held the same simplicity and warmth as the house at the pueblo. Indeed, with the many Indian pots and baskets decorating Ethan and Molly's house, there seemed an overlap with the pueblo culture.

"We forgot to hang the little painting of Chimayo Church when you were last here," Molly said at the end of supper. "Come to the bedroom and see what you think..."

The painting was set to the right of a rounded corner fireplace, opposite the bed. "We thought we'd like to see it when we awake," Ethan said. "This room gets the northern light, which will illuminate the picture without causing damage."

"It reminds us of that happy day when we all went to Taos together," Molly interjected.

"Very charming," Jean-Paul affirmed. "Your home is a unique mixture of cultures. Is it not so, Délie, that in France, as in Maryland, houses reflect the layers of history of their specific place. In France, we see the history of France. In Maryland it is the history of Maryland that surrounds us. But here in New Mexico, it is a jungle."

The Ridgeleys looked confused. "Perhaps, darling, you mean 'jumble'?" Delia suggested.

"*Ah, oui, tu as raison.* A jumble. The three cultures, they invade one another."

"I see what you mean, Jean-Paul," Ethan said, leading them back into the living room. The fire had burned down, but still threw out considerable warmth. The hounds snoozed before it—having a minimal interest in art.

"You're very astute," Ethan continued. "The three cultures do invade one another, but they don't meld. They remain distinct. But I believe you're right: each aesthetic does seep into the life of the other. Actually... I'd never thought about that before. It's natural to acquire something beautiful. Perhaps we're not overtly aware that one object is actually Indian—pueblo or plains—another is Hispanic and still another is Anglo... We tend to buy because the object speaks to us. We expect it will enhance our life."

Molly glanced at Jean-Paul, standing beside Delia with his hand on her shoulder. "I think you're right, too, about that vertical heritage on the east coast. Certainly New Englanders are deeply aware of the style of their ancestors. It informs their visual choices. Now this," Molly continued in a dreamy voice, as if talking to herself, "might be an interesting subject for another book."

Delia asked Molly: "Wouldn't it be interesting to somehow juxtapose New England recipes with those from New Mexico? For instance, a Christmas dinner from the different traditions or a summer gathering—with corn, perhaps, cooked and served in different ways..."

"Oh, my..." Molly said, suddenly excited, "you've given me an idea for my next project!"

"Well, before you begin, perhaps the two of you would join Délie and me for a French Sunday lunch—family style." He looked towards his wife for her reaction.

"I was thinking the very same thing!" Delia echoed. "Shall we ask the Kovics as well and perhaps your friend Slim the architect... and cousin Alice? Wouldn't that be fun? This coming Sunday—if we can get hold of everyone..."

The snow was still falling heavily as they left for home, but with four-wheel drive the road up to their house was still passable. Fortunately, they'd left some lights on, so when they entered the patio it was pleasantly illuminated. At the east end, Delia spied the owl perched in the snowy branches of one of the apricot trees. "Oh, look, darling!"

"A Great Horned Owl," Jean-Paul ventured.

"A bulky creature, but awfully pretty, don't you think?" They moved quietly onto the portal out of the snow and continued to observe it. "Perhaps it's the same owl that frightened Carla," Delia suggested.

"*Ah, oui*, perhaps. Look, *mon trésor*, is that not the nest deep in the tree?"

Delia was getting cold and the swirling snowflakes made bird watching difficult. "I can't really tell...let's take a peek tomorrow when we've got more light. You know, sometimes I think that moaning sound comes from this patio. Maybe it's the owl's call we hear..."

Rumpus and Hark exhibited no interest in the bird. They waited in the kitchen expectantly for the humans to fix their dinner. As the hounds gobbled up their food, the humans rejoiced not only because of their interesting and celebratory day, but because the doors to the house were still locked—just as they'd left them.

Still, something told them they couldn't trust the present calm.

18

Jean-Paul checked his e-mails and reported disturbing news from France. "Alas, Délie, I must return to France. Do you remember that young man, Jacques, the son of Lili and Lucien?"

"You mean the handsome boy whose parents work at your château?"

Jean-Paul nodded, his dark eyes troubled. "Our château," he corrected her distractedly.

"I remember him very well. Such a nice young person! What's happened? Is he ill? Has there been an accident?"

Delia and Jean-Paul were cozy and warm now in their robes, treating themselves to a rare nightcap before the bedroom fire.

"There is the trouble most grave. He and a group of neighborhood boys are accused of arson—of setting a neighbor's hay barn on fire. They are being held in jail pending a trial. Lucien and Lili are deeply troubled."

"But surely Jacques couldn't possibly have participated in a crime! He has always been such an upstanding young person—the sort of guy who clearly inspires confidence."

"Well, *naturellment*, that is the mystery. And where is the motive for such an act of stupidity? But, my treasure, you know teenage boys— especially when they are formed in a gang. They make mischief on a dare."

"No," Delia said, shaking her head and reaching down to pat Hark, who was about to settle himself at her feet. "I don't believe it for a moment! Jacques is too level-headed."

"Ah, but apparently there are the witnesses. But I feel as you do, Délie. I have been asked to return to give the testimony of character. His lawyer tells his parents my reference will carry great weight."

"But there must be others who would testify to his excellent character—his teachers, the priest..."

"Just so. Nevertheless I must go." He sighed and shrugged his shoulders. Delia thought he looked tired and discouraged.

"It's because you're now the count. And the largest landowner. Yes...I suppose you have a duty to be there and your testimony is indeed necessary." Delia was weary, too. "Oh dear, I suppose you'll be away for New Year's Eve. Perhaps you'd like me to come with you? I could probably leave Rumpus and Hark with Alice. We could fly from Albuquerque and then back to finish our holiday here. I must admit, especially after today, I'm not particularly eager to leave New Mexico — and, of course, we'd have to come back to retrieve the car and dogs." The dogs looked up at her with some concern. They knew the word 'dogs' and they understood their owners were worried.

Jean-Paul considered her suggestion but shook his head. "I don't like to leave you, especially with the problems we experience... But the lawyer said I have only to make one appearance in the court... and then I return to you. Claire and her little family are still away visiting the in-laws. They will not return to Paris until the middle of January. No." Jean-Paul drained his cognac and put his hands together as if in prayer. "No," he said decisively. "If you do not mind, I shall go for three days only and return immediately to you here. Let us first have New Year's Eve together and then I shall depart the following day."

They both stared into the fire, which had begun to spit. Jean-Paul quickly stepped on a spark that had leaped onto the rug and then moved the mesh screen in front of the fire. Both hounds sat up and stared dolorously at him.

"Okay, that's settled then. Shall we go ahead and plan that lunch party for Sunday? I hope Alice can come, too. I'll call her tomorrow. Molly and Ethan already know. I suppose we really should have Wilma and Steve — and their children? And what about Steve's silent sister-in-law?"

"Most certainly. Twelve will fit the table. Perhaps also Slim, the architect." Jean-Paul was beginning to regain his usual *joie de vivre*. "Hadn't we thought to have him? He has no wife and another man is nice..."

Delia extended the invitations the next morning. Unfortunately, Alice had a previous engagement but vowed to come for a long weekend soon. Delia was trying to discipline herself not to dwell on thoughts of her twin, but she did experience a twinge of discomfort while talking with Alice. Neither woman mentioned Dorothy, but Delia suspected Dorothy was on Alice's mind, too. Of course, Alice was too tactful to refer to her, and Delia was grateful for that. Unbidden tears of sadness and anger welled in Delia's eyes whenever she thought of her sister. She feared choking up, which was both embarrassing and annoying. She knew she must somehow find resolution in the matter of her sister's death.

Wilma's children planned to go to Taos to ski with friends and wouldn't return until Sunday evening. The Ridgeleys, Wilma, Steve, the silent sister-in-law, Monika, and Slim all accepted the lunch invitation. Delia and Jean-Paul planned the menu and wines and on Friday Delia started to bake bread and a cake. With Molly's help she'd learned to adjust recipes for the high altitude.

As Dolores and Carla cleaned the house, they were soon assailed by the fragrance of baking. What was the occasion? Upon learning about the luncheon, Dolores suggested they return on Sunday to wait on table and clean up afterwards. Delia and Jean-Paul gratefully accepted. Dolores and Carla were eager for extra cash and their help would make the occasion more relaxed for the hosts.

The Kovics arrived at two o'clock with cheery hugs and festively wrapped gifts. Steve looked Edwardian in a gray corduroy smoking-jacket and matching trousers. Wilma wore a short, black, jersey dress with ruffles and fabulous, ruby earrings. Even Monika had dressed up in a blue velvet pants-suit, with a necklace of pale stones set in gold filigree. Delia didn't know whether the stones were citrines or actually diamonds. "That's a stunning necklace," she told Monika truthfully.

Monika looked pleased at the compliment and replied, shyly, in her thick foreign accent, "I made it, myself."

The Ridgeleys arrived a moment later, rosy-faced and wind-blown from their trek up the hill, dressed in bulky Santa-decorated sweaters. Slim appeared in jeans, elaborately tooled boots, a red flannel shirt and a bolo tie featuring a hefty chunk of turquoise. Delia concluded New Mexico party attire was totally unpredictable. She, herself, had decided to wear her new Christmas shawl to dress-up her beige blouse and trousers. Everyone complimented her enthusiastically. Slim patted her shoulder appreciatively and said, "Mighty pretty, ma'am, mighty pretty..."

After drinks in the sala, there was a long leisurely lunch of clear homemade chicken soup, tiny rolls of halibut with a lemony white sauce, sliced beef fillet with young root vegetables, sorbet, chocolate sponge cake and, later, coffee in the sala. The meal proceeded with good wines and good humor; even timid Monika managed a few words of praise for the meal. For once, both Wilma and Monika seemed comparatively calm. Dolores and Carla performed a splendid serving job, with Dolores whispering instructions to Carla on how to set out and remove each course.

The only negative note was Slim's news that he'd gotten word that the state legislature would vote down funds for the nature bridge across Route 25 at Rowe Mesa. Perhaps there might be a bond issue in the future. The bridge then had to be explained to the Kovics and Ridgeleys. Everyone saw how the bridge could reduce human and wildlife deaths. Steve began to describe a nature bridge he had seen in France. As it turned out, Slim had studied that same particular bridge in detail, so the two men were able to present a vivid description to the guests.

Jean-Paul excused himself and returned with computer printouts he'd procured from Kinko's the previous day. Everyone was fascinated, including the serving women, who took a moment to study the sketches when they were passed around.

"New Mexico is a poor state," Ethan said with a sigh. "It is such a brilliant idea and would certainly save lives and money in the long run."

"Yes," Molly agreed, "but I fear that until more lives are lost, there's little chance of shaking the funds loose. There really should be a bond issue..."

"Well," Slim said, laconically, his tiny eyes narrowing further, "I sure was lookin' forward to workin' on that thang. It would have been a big improvement. Yes, sir. And a big challenge. I'm here to tell ya, I'm real disappointed."

Jean-Paul refilled everyone's' wine glasses, and Slim looked a little happier.

It was almost dark when the guests departed. As they walked through the sala Delia saw that Molly was looking at yet another pile of dirt beside the sofa.

"Isn't that weird, Molly? From time to time we find a mysterious bit of dirt in that one place..."

Molly looked up at the vigas running across the ceiling. "I can tell you, Delia, that's a little problem old adobe houses tend to have. You see, there is a layer of dirt under the roof to act as insulation. That's the old way. And now and then, unless the ceiling is absolutely tight, which it never is, the dirt escapes. Just sweep it up and be glad it's not filtering down onto your bed..."

"Oh, I see." Delia was relieved. "I thought the hounds might have gotten into some annoying new habit, or some other little animal was bringing it in from time to time." She laughed and gave Molly a hug. "You're such a comforting source of information."

Dolores and Carla still had a way to go with the clean up but were glad of the extra hours of pay. Dolores would have to leave soon to pick up her aunt from her church group, but Carla arranged to stay on to finish, saying her boyfriend would come get her in an hour.

Delia, Jean-Paul and the hounds took off down the arroyo to walk off lunch while there was still light. The sunset was turning blood red across the western sky and even the snow beneath their feet reflected a pinkish tinge. "Isn't it sad dogs can't see color?" Delia murmured as they tramped through the snow.

"And some people, they also are color blind," Jean-Paul added. "Do you suppose they see the sunset as green or the trees and sky as the same color?"

Upon their return the hounds suddenly chased off after some interesting little creature, so Jean-Paul left the patio gate open for them. Since there was no truck parked on the road, Delia and Jean-Paul assumed the boyfriend had either not arrived or had already picked up Carla.

With sinking hearts, they noticed the kitchen door to the patio stood open. They wandered in and were met by a horrifying scene. Carla lay on the kitchen floor in a pool of blood. One of Duthuit's sharp kitchen knives lay at some distance from her. There were multiple stab wounds on her face, arms and body.

Delia gasped and Jean-Paul tore off his big coat and fell to his knees beside Carla's body. He groped for her pulse and, finding none, turned to Delia, who was stricken still as a statue. "I fear the girl is dead." He leaned close to her face to feel any breath from her nostrils, the blood from her terrible wounds now covering the front of him.

In the distance a siren shrieked, and just as Delia rushed to the phone to call for help, two uniformed police officers stomped through the open kitchen door. Delia almost fainted when one of the officers roughly grabbed Jean-Paul by the shoulder, pulled him back from the corpse and announced, "Sir, you are under arrest for murder." Before either she or Jean-Paul could speak, the other officer, in a slow and terrifying voice, read Jean-Paul his rights, cuffed his hands behind his back and marched him out the front door.

Delia pulled her coat tightly around herself and attempted to accompany them, but the officer commanded her to remain at the scene of the crime until his colleagues and an ambulance arrived. She could hear more sirens wailing in the distance and she stood for a moment shocked into confusion.

"Call my embassy!" Jean-Paul shouted in French as they shoved him into the squad car and drove off. Other official vehicles skidded up through the snow and screeched to a halt, their revolving lights casting weird shadows in the night.

Delia felt ill. She leaned against the wall as the ambulance attendants rushed past with a stretcher and men with cameras flashing brushed against her.

Jean-Paul was gone. She didn't know where. It occurred to her that the dogs had not returned, which she supposed was a good thing; they might have attacked the police.

Moving against the wall, making herself as small as possible and thankful no one took an interest in her, she slipped into the bedroom, rummaged through Jean-Paul's bureau drawer where he kept his cell phone and scrolled down for the embassy number in Washington.

"Please, please, someone answer..." she prayed in the darkness. "Oh, it's too late. I know it is. No one will be there. It's Sunday night. What shall I do? The ambassador. Is his number here? Yes, I'll call him." She was whispering to herself, leaning against the edge of the bureau, threatened with waves of nausea and feeling as though she were about to faint.

She punched in the ambassador's number. Miracle upon miracles, he answered. French. Speak French, Delia told herself.

"Mr. Ambassador — Victor! This is Delia Hager Duval calling from New Mexico."

"Countess! How nice to hear your voice! What an unexpected surprise! Anick and I were just speaking of you and the count the other evening!"

Delia tried hard to be coherent. She managed to blurt out the terrifying problem. "And I don't even know where they've taken him..." Sobs rose in her throat.

"This is indeed grave. But have no fear, Countess. I shall make inquires immediately and we shall unravel this mistake. You will stay at this number, please, and I shall return with news and instructions. Be tranquil, Countess. We will soon resolve this unfortunate problem."

"Thank you, Victor. Oh! Thank you! Yes, I'll remain with this phone line open."

She had somehow managed to move toward the bed and sink down upon it. Her head was reeling, but she was beginning to regain her composure.

Footsteps shuffled past the door and there were further sounds of activity in the kitchen. Then a door banged and all was suddenly, eerily silent.

Delia remained sitting on the bed, still in her coat and boots with the cell phone in her lap. What should she do now? Perhaps all she could do was wait. And wait.

She didn't know how much time passed, but finally she got up and shakily walked into the hall to take off her coat and hang it in the closet. She moved slowly, as in a dream, through the sala, the dining room —

where the shutters were still open to the now black night—toward the empty kitchen. Carla's body had been removed. Two chairs lay overturned and there was no sign of the knife. Jean-Paul's sheepskin coat lay at the threshold where he'd thrown it off upon first seeing Carla.

For a long moment, she stood staring, undecided as to what to do next. Then she stooped down and picked up Jean-Paul's coat. Holding it against her face, she carried it into the dining room and laid it tenderly upon the long table. Then in a decisive gesture she turned, went into the laundry room, grabbed a bucket and Clorox, filled the bucket with water and began furiously mopping the floor. No one had told her not to touch the crime scene. In fact, no one had told her anything.

Like every woman at some moment in her life, she wondered if she'd become invisible. A scene came crazily into her mind of herself trying to buy a drink at a bar at Kennedy Center between acts of the ballet. The barmen filled the orders of the men around her, but seemed literally unable to see her amongst the crowd. She never did get her drink.

Yes, perhaps she'd become invisible. Or at least, not considered worth noticing. She furiously sloshed Clorox all around the floor with the wet mop. If anyone had seen her, they'd think she was having a temper tantrum. But it wasn't fury that drove her activity. It was fear. Where was Jean-Paul? What was happening to him? Why had Carla been savagely murdered? And by whom? What a nightmare!

Then she halted. It suddenly occurred to her that the police had arrived before she'd called them. What accounted for their showing up at the instant she and Jean-Paul found Carla's body? There was something wrong with the sequence. There was something very wrong with everything.

Puzzling and lost in thought, she stopped mopping. Slowly she moved to the sink. The situation was surreal. Lost in thought, she lifted the bucket and emptied it down the sink, shoved the mop back into the laundry room and left the kitchen, gently but resolutely shutting the kitchen door behind her. Calmly, her mind recalled the bizarre events. Nothing made sense.

Jean-Paul's coat, lying on the table, comforted her. She took a deep breath, then two, then three. Her mind was clearing. She would take the cell phone with her and hunt for Rumpus and Hark. There was always the chance they'd had an unfortunate encounter with a pack of coyotes and she didn't need any more catastrophes.

Leaving the front door unlocked, she went out onto the patio and thought of the owl. Perhaps the owl *did* embody the spirit of La Llorona. Perhaps it was La Llorona who brought destruction and chaos to the inhabitants of this house. Carla had understood. Her fright was a warning to them all: the damned place was indeed haunted! Of course the tenants left! At the back of her mind Delia knew she was being ridiculous, but she decided she owed herself this indulgence of crazy thoughts.

Lights flashed outside the patio and Delia was amazed to see Jean-Paul being respectfully escorted back onto the portal by the same two police officers. Delia could hardly believe her eyes. She stood still for a moment, then ran to him, threw her arms around him and held him close.

"It is all right, *ma petite*," he whispered stroking her hair.

"We are sorry, Countess," the smaller policemen said to her officiously. "There was a case of mistaken identity." Oh, is that what it was: mistaken identity! A very stupid mistake! Delia thought the officer didn't sound very sorry. But he'd certainly changed his tune from the last time she'd heard him speak.

Jean-Paul released her from his arms and she stood facing the officer. Anger rose within her and she was ready to say something truly regrettable when Jean-Paul's voice broke in. He said quietly in French, "The governor of New Mexico telephoned the police station and ordered my release. Whatever you said to Victor, Delia, was certainly effective. They say the murder was actually caught on tape. There was a camera in the kitchen, hidden in the ceiling — in the vigas. The murderer was a slim, dark man; so the police assumed I was this man. But it must have been the boyfriend — whom they have not yet located. I gave them the name of Dolores and the matter is now out of our hands."

Once again, Delia was stunned. "A video? But who put a camera in the ceiling? How did the film get to the police so quickly?"

"Come out of the cold, my treasure. Let me clean up—shower, and then I will tell you what I know."

The police scurried away as if they themselves wished to be invisible. Delia supposed they should be at least credited for being embarrassed by jumping to wrong conclusions. As they were leaving, Rumpus and Hark came trotting through the patio gate. Rumpus growled at one of the cops and just managed to escape the man's answering kick.

Delia jumped, suddenly aware that her telephone was ringing. Perhaps it was the ambassador retuning her call.

"Hello?"

"Delia, dear, so glad to catch you. This is Molly. Such a splendid lunch. A very happy party! And, thank you both very much.

"But, Delia, I'm actually calling to find out if everything is all right. Ethan thinks he heard squad cars passing us—going up toward your house... We were wondering, is everything okay?"

No! Everything was not okay! Everything is completely crazy, a profound tragedy—the violent death of a young woman—had taken place, as well as the horrifying arrest of her beloved husband by a bunch of bullying goons... Hell no! Everything is not okay!

But did she want to get into this with Molly right now? Molly, whom she wasn't sure she completely trusted... No! No! Screw it!

Delia took a deep breath and sang in her sweetest, calmest voice, her brain racing just ahead of her words, "How kind of you to enquire, Molly. Yes, the police were here, but they'd made some sort of mistake, so they left. Actually, everything's fine. Thanks so much for checking on us." She felt like a fool, but she had to get rid of Molly.

Apparently, her lie was adequately convincing. Molly murmured something polite and hung up.

Shit! Delia thought. Was she going to have to deal with a call from Wilma, as well? No, probably not. She and Steve were no doubt relaxing in their bedroom-theater at the back of their house, where they probably wouldn't have heard the police sirens. She certainly hoped so. She was ready to dissolve on the floor in fragments. Coping with their neighbors' curiosity—no matter how well meant—was not what she needed right now.

She noticed, for the first time, that Jean-Paul had been standing at their bedroom door watching her handle Molly's call. His face wore an expression of astonishment and admiration.

Delia couldn't help winking at him and shrugging her shoulders.

19

"I need a whiskey," Jean-Paul said as he headed for the shower.

"Me, too," Delia replied. She strolled toward the kitchen but stopped when she saw Jean-Paul's coat lying forlornly on the dining table. How quickly situations turn, she thought, as she scooped it up and returned it to the hall closet before continuing to the kitchen, where she poured them each a double scotch without ice. She found a small pitcher and filled it with water, then proceeded back to the bathroom with the tray.

Jean-Paul was toweling off as she entered. She would have liked to plaster his body with kisses but decided the whiskey might do them both more good right now. She turned to the bathtub and began to strip off her clothes. The room was warm from the heat lamps and Jean-Paul's shower and there was evidently still plenty of hot water. As she sunk down into her bath, Jean-Paul pulled up the little chair, took a swig of his drink and carefully handed her the other glass.

"Do not let the glass break, my treasure. We do not need another catastrophe."

She nodded and sank back into the warm water. They drank in silence, each thinking their own thoughts until Delia said, "How could those clowns have taken you away like that and then just as suddenly brought you back? I was totally panicked. I didn't know where you were."

"*Eh, bien,* your call to Victor was effective. He wasted no time. He may have over-stated our situation—the police conclude I am a prince of importance most great and that their actions would cause an international incident of consequences most dire." For the first time, he smiled. "I never thought my uncle's title would be so helpful."

"I suppose we'll laugh about this one day..." She shook her head. "No, on second thought, I suspect we won't. That poor young girl with her whole life before her. Murdered. Dead. And why? Someone deranged came here. Who was it? That vicious boyfriend? Did they tell you anything?"

"Only that six months ago they arrest the boyfriend—Wayne Gomez, his name seems to be—on the charges of assault and battery. I understand he was on probation. He is a bad fruit."

"Seed? Maybe you mean seed?"

"*Oui.* A bad seed. They say only that 'his whereabouts are unknown'. Of course, he does not know he was caught on the video."

Delia sat up and placed her glass on the floor, then turned on the faucet and added more hot water. She began to wash herself vigorously, as if she could scrape away the horror of the last couple of hours.

"I wash your back, Délie." Jean-Paul took the cloth from her, soaped it and tenderly washed her back, calming her with his touch. She slid her body down under the water to rinse off and then rose out of the tub. He wrapped her in a big towel and kissed her, then handed her the gown and robe that hung on the door hook. While Delia brushed her teeth, Jean-Paul placed their empty glasses on the tray and took them to the kitchen.

Within minutes, they were settled comfortably together in their bed, the duvet drawn up to their shoulders. Delia repeated her question about the tape: "Who in the world put that camera in the kitchen ceiling?"

"I cannot find an answer. Only that a camera was lodged there...in the kitchen ceiling. Someone monitored it and called the police before we return. This man Wayne, he is dark and slim, so they arrest me. Those two cops, they did not know this Wayne guy. Before, he was picked up by the police in some place called Va-something...Va-lar-de—not Tesuque nor

155

Santa Fe. I think we passed thorough Valarde on our return from Taos."

Delia was picturing the map in the car and thought he probably meant Velarde, but then she began to laugh.

"What do you find amusing?" He was obviously slightly irritated.

"I'm probably drunk or I wouldn't see the humor in this. But you know, you've been rather peevish about being considered an 'Anglo' in New Mexico. But now you have been arrested for looking Hispanic. It's ironic. It's nutty, too."

Jean-Paul smiled. "I see the point. From now on I embrace 'Anglo'!" He sighed. "We must go to sleep."

"But, darling, what about the camera? Did Duthuit have it installed to catch the intruders? And who was monitoring it?"

"*Je ne sais pas.* If you think of it, this terrible night puts us no closer to understanding who the past intruders could be. It makes no sense that this Wayne guy haunt this house..."

"Unless his purpose was to terrorize Carla *and* Duthuit's tenants... But for what reason? Oh, we must go to sleep..."

Jean-Paul reached over and turned out the light. He wrapped his arms around his wife and snuggled close, hoping they would soon be asleep.

20

Of course, neither slept. They shifted positions and shifted again. Delia thought she heard moaning from the kitchen. No doubt La Llorona not only mourned for her children but for Carla as well. Or could it be the owl? But it sounded as if the moan came from the kitchen, not the patio. Maybe the bird was loose in the house.

Delia turned over again. Jean-Paul put his arm across her back. Delia thought she could hear the hounds snoring in the next room. One of them barked quietly in his sleep. Sleep. If only it would come. The image of Carla lying across the floor covered in blood, the sharp knife beside her, was painfully clear in Delia's mind. Now she was haunted by what she'd seen.

Jean-Paul moved his hand down her back. He squeezed her rump. "We must sleep," he whispered. But the way he caressed her was not conducive to sleep. His stroking became increasingly erotic; a soothing lovemaking ensued. Finally, they slept.

A pounding at the front door awakened them. Rumpus and Hark scrambled into the hall, barking in their loudest Basset voices.

"I will go," Jean-Paul murmured. He slipped out of bed, stumbled around for his dressing gown and slippers, and followed the sound of the dogs' baying to the hall.

"No. No. No!" Delia heard herself say. She turned to look at the clock. Only seven fifteen—this was too early for anyone to come calling. She pulled the duvet over her head. Why couldn't they have peace?

She heard voices in the hall but couldn't make out what was happening. Finally, Jean-Paul returned and sat down beside her on the bed. Rumpus and Hark followed him into the room. Evidently, they wanted to go out. "I will let them into the patio." Jean-Paul got up again with a sigh. When he returned, he said gently, "My treasure, it is those young people from across the road. They insist they must talk with us. I cannot understand the urgency, but they are upset. I told them we would come to the dining room in a few minutes."

"Everything has gotten so crazy," Delia said, desperate to snuggle back to sleep.

Jean-Paul leaned over and kissed her forehead, smoothing back her hair. "Yes, I agree—everything has become insane. Insane and tragic."

"Maybe we should leave," Delia suggested, pulling herself up and reaching for her robe.

Ten minutes later, they met their uninvited guests in the dining room. The sun had not yet risen, but Jack and Jill had managed to set the table for four, were brewing a pot of tea, and, as Delia and Jean-Paul entered, Jill set down a plate of scrambled eggs on toast in front of each person. The young people evidently knew their way around the kitchen and were attempting to make amends for their insistent interruption so early in the morning. Since Delia and Jean-Paul didn't drink tea nor eat eggs in the morning, they weren't overly thrilled at their guests' overture, but they struggled to be gracious.

"Thank you," Jean-Paul said. Delia could tell he was trying to muster a tone of cordiality. He was not entirely successful.

Delia toyed with the eggs on the end of her fork. She'd become used to their small French breakfast. Besides, she longed for their warm bed.

There was a moment of silence. Everyone looked down at their plates. Delia noted that the central heating had not yet come on. Damn these crazy kids. It was freezing.

Jack seemed to hesitate, then began, "We thought we needed to get over here and explain before anyone else got to you. Before people — the newspapers or the police — or just *people* started asking questions. A report of the murder is already in the local paper..."

Delia and Jean-Paul turned toward him. Jill poured her brother a cup of tea. Jack was a nervous eater. He held his plate up near his mouth, jabbed his fork into his eggs and shoveled them into his mouth as though he feared they'd escape.

Delia gazed from one to the other. They looked better this morning. Their days on the slopes had tanned their faces. They had left off their rings and Jack's dreadful red-tinted hair was lying flat against his head. They wore ordinary jeans, crew neck sweaters and dark quilted vests. Their innate beauty was more in evidence than at their last meeting. Obviously they were trying hard to behave constructively in a destructive situation.

Jack continued, "We have an explanation — a confession. It was we ..." Jill gave him a stern look. "It was I who planted the camera in the kitchen ceiling. On the day we came over to photograph the house."

"Why, may I ask?" Jean-Paul's voice was steely, his body rigid.

"It was a whim, sir," Jack shifted in his seat uncomfortably. "We happened to have some surveillance cameras and thought it might be interesting to watch what was happening over here. Not for any particular reason..." his voice trailed off.

Delia was furious—not only by the surveillance, but also by this morning's intrusion. What arrogance! Her mind was now fully awake and it leapt with unsavory implications. "And I suppose you also intended to lodge a camera in our bedroom as well—just on a whim, of course." Her voice was hard and sarcastic.

""Well," said Jill, apparently intending to be conciliatory, "but there wasn't the opportunity, because that's where you and I were sitting, so Jack couldn't..." She abruptly halted and looked towards her brother.

Delia and Jean-Paul glared at their uninvited guests, both struck dumb at the audacity of these two kids.

Jack straightened up and shoved his plate away. "Well, anyway... we saw the murder, you see. We saw it in progress. We'd gotten back from Taos late, the camera had been left running and we thought we'd take a look." He looked from Delia to Jean-Paul, who remained silent and stone-faced.

"We saw that boyfriend of Carla's arguing with her. She was washing pots and he grabbed her arm. There was no sound but it seemed he wanted her to leave with him and she was saying she couldn't leave 'til she finished cleaning up. Or something like that. Then he picked up the knife from the counter and began stabbing her."

Delia looked down at her lap. She didn't want to hear this. The narrative was too horrible. Jean-Paul was no longer a suspect and she wanted to withdraw from the whole situation.

Jack continued, "So we immediately phoned the police and told them what was happening—as it was happening, so to speak."

Jill interrupted. "That's how the police got here so quickly. We saw the cop arrest Mr. Duval, so we called again to say they'd gotten the wrong guy. Luckily they believed us. We told them where the camera was hidden, so after those two cops arrested Mr. Duval, that next group, the ones with the cameras, took our camera and video to use as evidence."

Jean-Paul looked at Delia but said nothing. Delia supposed he, too, wondered now whether it was the call from the French ambassador or

Jack's call to the police that had actually prompted his release.

"This certainly is an unusual set of circumstances," Delia said coldly. "Tell me, have either of you ever had a key to this house or come in when no one was here?"

"No, ma'am," Jack said. "We're not the type to break into people's homes." He seemed affronted at the suggestion, missing the irony of his remark.

Delia and Jean-Paul couldn't help laughing. These two young people seemed to think their behavior was entirely forgivable and had, in the long run, saved Delia and Jean-Paul a great deal of trouble. Which Delia supposed was true in one sense. But in another, it was clear that Jack and Jill were a couple of sociopaths.

"Please don't tell our mother and Steve," Jill said confidentially. "It'll upset them."

Aha, Delia thought. That's their worry. They hope their parents won't learn of their obnoxious behavior.

"Should they ask," Jack continued, shoving his chair back, "you could say you really don't know what happened. They're distracted by business at this point — they won't press you on it."

He and his sister began to clear away the plates and take them into the kitchen. Delia was tempted to tell them not to bother, but on second thought decided to let the little horrors finish what they'd started.

It occurred to her that when the killer was caught, there'd be a trial. She hoped with all her heart that she and Jean-Paul wouldn't be called to testify. The killer could, by now, be a long way off. It might take years to find him.

After the siblings' departure, Delia and Jean-Paul put on their warmest clothes and took the hounds out for an early walk. They wanted to clear their heads before any telephone calls.

The sun was rising behind the mountain. For a few moments the sky was golden all the way across to the west. The beauty of the landscape was enough to distract them as the Bassets sniffed their favorite spots in the arroyo.

By noon, Alice, and each of their new friends had called. They'd seen the report of the murder and Jean-Paul's false arrest in the Albuquerque paper. There were also several calls from the French embassy following up on last night's alarm. Delia and Jean-Paul learned that Victor had contacted the U.S. Secretary of State, who had a personal acquaintance with the New Mexico governor. Delia and Jean-Paul agreed that had been a great piece of luck.

They hoped their troubles were over. It seemed as if the changed locks had solved the problem of the break-ins. But they still hadn't solved the mystery of why the break-ins happened. They continued to suspect they were the result of something Duthuit had said or done—on purpose or inadvertently.

Kimber Garcia called to say Dolores would not be in to clean, but that she would send a substitute as soon as possible. Kimber gave them Dolores's address and they sent a bouquet of white roses to the grieving family. They also planned to attend Carla's funeral, which Kimber told them would take place in two days. When Molly called, she said she and Ethan would go with them. "Imagine being murdered because you wanted to finish cleaning up the kitchen," Molly said.

21

New Year's Eve Day—the day of Carla's funeral Mass at the Santuario de Guadalupe in Santa Fe, and the day before Jean-Paul was due to fly to France—had suddenly grown warm. The snow was melting everywhere, causing rivulets of water along the paved streets and slippery, splashing mud on the unpaved roads. Jean-Paul and Delia slid down the hill to pick up the Ridgeleys on their way to the church.

They drove in on Bishops Lodge Road, splashed by mud from every direction as other cars sped past. By the time they arrived at the church, there was already a large crowd and the parking lot was full, so they drove along the Alameda looking for a spot. Within a block, a guy pulled out and Jean-Paul was able to slip into his space. As they made their way back to the Santuario, the crowd continued to grow. Entire families, some with babies and young children, were coming to pay their last respects. Molly pointed out some of the attending Anglos, people who had hired some of Carla's family or who were part of the same congregation. Delia recognized no one from the pueblo, but she did see Kimber Garcia and Rose Martinez come in looking harassed. They, too, must have had trouble parking.

The church was completely packed. They couldn't see past the crowd and were forced to stand at the back. It seemed an old and interesting church — white adobe walls, huge beams and corbels and a wide Mexican-style alter — but the crowd obscured most of the interior.

"'Scuse me," said a girl about Carla's age who was attempting to squeeze in beside Delia. The girl had long dark hair, wore a green hoodie, jeans and purple, pink and silver running shoes. She looked as though she'd been crying and kept dabbing her eyes with a frayed tissue. Delia searched in her bag and handed the girl some fresh Kleenex. "Thanks," the girl said. "I knew this was going to happen. We all knew. And we told Carla to get away from that bastard Wayne before he killed her. She wouldn't listen..." The girl began to sob hysterically.

There didn't seem to be anyone with her, so Delia tried to calm her by asking a question. "Were you in school with Carla?"

"Yeah, from first to tenth."

"Well, then she was an old friend of yours. It's very hard to lose an old friend."

The girl gave Delia a long, appraising look. "Yeah, and she only dropped out because Wayne beat her up. She wouldn't come back while the bruises showed. Her gran told the school she was in a car accident, but she wasn't. And we knew, but we couldn't do anything. Wayne was rotten! We kept telling her, 'you gotta get away from that animal.' But she just laughed and said he loved her. Like...he just got a little upset

162

sometimes. She thought if she could keep him from drinking, everything would be fine. It was not gonna be fine! Wayne Gomez has been drinking since he was ten. Everyone in his family is a drunk. And she was so happy about being pregnant. Oh, shit!" The girl started to cry again.

Delia patted her arm as Mass began. The girl leaned against the wall and closed her eyes. She opened them within a moment and said, "Thanks, lady." As the service proceeded, the girl slid down the wall and sat with her head buried against her knees, her body racked with sobs. Delia was distressed for this mourning waif but could think of nothing to do for her except keep the people still pouring into the church from stepping on her. She wondered if the girl's family would come, but the grieving girl remained alone throughout the Mass. Then, just as the service ended, she rose and bolted out the door. Delia thought of her afterward and wondered if there had ever been anyone to comfort her.

In France, New Year's Eve is the most celebrated day of the holidays. And because France is eight hours ahead of New Mexico, Jean-Paul, upon returning from the funeral, immediately telephoned his daughter. Claire and André were about to leave for a party. Though their conversations were brief, there was a spirit-raising exchange of good wishes for the coming year. Jean-Paul's little granddaughters, Juliet and Sophie, had been allowed to stay up, so Jean-Paul and Delia each had amusing conversations with them, which temporarily dispelled their funereal gloom.

Later, Delia chatted with Jean-Paul as he prepared for his trip and the Bassets padded restlessly about the room. Packing always made Rumpus and Hark nervous. If their legs had been longer, they would have jumped onto the bed to lie upon the open suitcase. Delia, too, was uncomfortable, but she silently assured herself her lover would return soon and all would be right with the world again. They didn't talk about Carla's death or Jean-Paul's mistaken arrest, nor had they mentioned the tragedy to his children. After all, it was André who'd suggested they use this house for a holiday. No need to upset him unnecessarily.

They weren't particularly hungry, but because they had to arise at dawn the next morning to get to the airport, they decided to dine early.

Jean-Paul had a *demi-bouteille* of French champagne, which they drank before the fire in the sala. They ate hard-cooked egg slices on toast smeared with caviar. Delia had found some juicy Comice pears the day before, so they added them for dessert.

"What do you wish for the new year, my treasure?" Jean-Paul asked.

"You. Just you. All of you," Delia responded languidly. "And the joy of creating our new home in Maryland from that beautiful wreckage of the past. And you?"

"*Moi aussi*," Jean-Paul replied, fondling the back of her neck. "Let us leave the dishes. Come to the bed with me."

It was a very early New Year's Eve.

22

On New Year's Day, Delia drove Jean-Paul to the Albuquerque airport. She hated to see him go, but to accompany him was a needless expense. She believed their problems at the Duthuit house were over now and that all would be well in her husband's brief absence. She'd use the time to work on future gardening articles and think about some new projects for the coming year. Looking back later, she couldn't believe how wrong she'd been.

Since Rumpus and Hark were in the car, she dropped Jean-Paul off at the departure curb. "Good bye, my dearest treasure," he said, enfolding her in his arms. "I shall email you to report my progress and telephone if anything of interest takes place. Have a nice lunch with Cousin Alice and give her my greeting. And promise me, Délie, promise me, you will keep your little weapon close at all times."

"I promise. Don't worry. We'll stay in touch... oh, my darling, I'll miss you. I miss you already! Goodbye, my love!" She looked over her shoulder at the Bassets peering out the back window. "Doggies, say goodbye..." Hark and Rumpus wagged their tails and shifted their bodies, ready to join the humans in the next adventure.

Jean-Paul kissed her again and tapped on the car window to say goodbye to the hounds. And then, pulling his wheelie-bag behind him, he disappeared into the terminal. This was the moment Delia hated: he was gone. His trip would be a long one: Albuquerque, Houston, Washington, Paris, and then a drive to his château. He'd ensured her it wasn't as bad as it sounded because he'd stretch his legs between flights, and Air France offers exercises for the passengers on the movie screens. Nevertheless, from Delia's point of view, once he disappeared through the airport doors, he was thousands of miles away.

She went round to the driver's seat and threw off her coat into the passenger seat. The weather was still mild and Albuquerque was at least ten degrees warmer than Tesuque. As she reached into the glove compartment to get the directions to Alice's house, a pick-up truck shrouded in mud, honked furiously at her to get out of the unloading zone. How impatient people were. She considered throwing the guy a kiss — that always seemed to disarm folks — but not wanting to chance a conflict, she quickly pulled out into the traffic and headed north to Alice's house.

Her heart actually ached, missing Jean-Paul, feeling so alone. He probably wasn't even at the boarding gate yet, but he might as well be deep in the French countryside. They'd been together constantly during this trip; Delia felt suddenly cut adrift without him. She reminded herself that she'd spent several years alone after her first husband's death. She'd managed her widowhood by learning to be content and self-sufficient.

She noticed she was developing a scratchy throat. Damn. She could also feel pressure in her sinuses... oh well, at least if she came down with a cold, she wouldn't be disturbing Jean-Paul's sleep with sniffling and coughing. She hoped she could get over whatever this turned out to be before he got back.

The hounds peered out the windows with their skinny Basset tails waving in slow, contemplative fashion. When they arrived at Alice's drive, they immediately spied Zippy bounding from the garage to welcome them. They yipped with glee. Off the dogs went as soon as Delia released them from the car.

"Happy New Year!" Alice called to her from the garage. "We've got a very informal lunch today—not a proper Maryland holiday meal..."

After a welcoming hug, the cousins weaved their way through the crowded garage. Alice had everything ready, so they sat down together at the kitchen counter, devouring red chili enchiladas topped with a dollop of sour cream. The chili was so hot it brought tears to Delia's eyes. But she was sure she felt its nutrients zooming around in her body as she ate. She remembered Molly saying chili killed a cold or any respiratory problems because it was so full of vitamin C. That's what she needed.

Alice saw Delia eyeing the Coke cans she'd placed beside glasses of ice. "I know what you're thinking, Delia! Why on earth would two intelligent, grown women drink Coke with lunch! Right? Especially on New Year's day!"

Delia laughed. "Yeah. I don't think I've had a Coke since college. It's good though. I used to drink several every day in the summer at the beach. I thought I couldn't live without them."

But she had trouble pulling the lid off her can. Alice took it from her, yanked the pesky ring and poured the fizzing drink into Delia's glass. Delia noticed again how similar Alice's and her hands were. They had both been blessed with really beautiful hands, but even though Delia's hands had experienced years of gardening, Alice's were clearly stronger.

"Thanks, Alice. One thing I hate about the twenty-first century is how hard it is to get stuff open. All those wrappings are a waste and so tedious to deal with."

"How 'bout trying to open an aspirin bottle?" Alice laughed. "You need a sledge-hammer! What are the manufacturers thinking?"

"That they don't want to get sued by our litigious society," Delia said as she dried her enchilada-tears with her napkin.

Alice smiled, "This chili is awfully hot. The way to cope with spicy food is to have something sweet. Hence the Coke."

Delia took a big swig. "Oh, that is good! Chili and Coke! Got it! Another New Mexico lesson."

"Speaking of old stuff, I have a nice surprise for you. When we've finished, I'll get it for you."

"How nice! You know, Alice, it's really wonderful to reconnect with you after all these years." She patted her cousin's hand. "I'll be picking Jean-Paul up on Saturday—I hope—and we wondered whether we could come by and pick you up, too, and bring you up to Tesuque for a long weekend. I could drive you back on Tuesday. You don't have to teach classes on Monday, am I remembering that right?"

"Yes. That would be perfect—except I'll bring my own car. I've been dying to visit, but travel and Christmas got in the way." They heard a faint yip—Zippy's signal that she wanted to come in—so Alice went to the garage door to let in the doggie brigade. Alice had wisely set out a big pan of water, which the dogs headed for immediately. Delia apologized for the slurpy mess the hounds made on the floor, though she knew Alice didn't actually care.

After the two women cleared up the kitchen, they moved into the living room and settled on the sofa together. Alice handed Delia a slightly browned envelope. "I'm excavating the guest room—which I should have done long ago—and I found this in the drawer of the bedside table in the guest room."

Delia thought back to sleeping in that room when she and Jean-Paul first arrived in New Mexico—the night she found out about her dead twin. What a long time ago that seemed.

Examining the envelope, turning it over in her hand, Delia recognized her mother's handwriting. There was a three-cent stamp on the front, canceled by a postal circle: Frederick, Md. June 6, 19—the rest of the postmark was smudged. It was addressed to Alice's mother in Rochester, New York.

"Go ahead, open it, Delia. I think it'll make a difference to you."

Delia hesitated. She was afraid of what she'd find. The knowledge of her dead sister still upset her. This, she suspected, was a message from the past. She wasn't sure she was ready for it, but she willed herself to open the envelope. She took a deep breath and drew out a card.

On the front, in large, pink, cursive letters against a multi-colored floral background was printed: Happy Birthday, Sister! Inside was a note and a small black and white snapshot surrounded by a wide white margin with a crinkly edge. Delia looked at the photograph, which depicted a smiling blond girl in a sand pile waving a tiny shovel at the photographer. She knew it was herself. She turned the picture over and saw written in her mother's hand, "Our dear little Delia—age 3."

Then she read the note:
"Happy Birthday from the three of us. We hope you, Gavin and Alice will visit us soon. The little girls will have fun together! Delia is at an enchanting age! She's full of merriment and affection. There never was such a sunny child! We of course mourn the terrible loss of our Dorothy, but it occurs to us that Dorothy's spirit resides in Delia, who is our doubly glorious child! Every day she comes up with new loving ways and fills us with happiness and delight. You can see from the picture how precious she is! Oh! We are lucky, lucky people! Have fun on your birthday! Hugs and lots of love from us all. XXXXXXOOOOOO!!!!!!!!!!!! P.S. Come visit before the summer is over!"

Delia stared at the card in her hand. Her first thought was how much her mother had liked exclamation points. (She suddenly remembered that when she'd first learned to read, she'd called them 'excited marks'.)

The implication of the letter began to sink in: she *had* been enough for her parents. They had loved her, had taken delight in her and were comforted by her existence. They weren't depressed or resentful, as she'd feared. She needn't feel guilty for her own survival.

The reason why they'd never told her of Dorothy's death still escaped her. But suddenly it didn't matter. Maybe they truly didn't think of it. But, clearly, they were the happy little family she'd originally believed them to be. It was all right.

Delia's relief was enormous. Until this moment, when she let go of the emotional burden she'd been carrying, she hadn't realized just how onerous it had been. Alice had delivered her. She'd given her a great gift: the knowledge of her sister's existence and death, as well as the means with which she could accept it.

Alice remained silent. And then she reached out and put her arms around Delia. They continued to sit together until Hark came along and bumped against Delia's knee. She disentangled herself from her cousin and laughed with relief and gratitude.

"I've felt so sorry, Delia, that I broke the news of Dorothy's existence so unthinkingly. Of course, I'd assumed you knew. And when I realized you didn't, I felt totally inadequate to relieve your bewilderment and suffering. You've always been such a sensitive soul. I remember when I read nursery rhymes to you — when you were a tiny girl — you wept over the little pigs having their house blown down by the wolf... When sad things happened, your heart would break. So when I found this letter, well, I think it might have been as great a relief for me as it is for you... I knew it would provide the reassurance you needed that you hadn't misunderstood the childhood happiness you'd remembered."

"Thank you, Alice. I could dance a jig!"

23

Delia and Alice spent a happy afternoon together. As the shadows outside lengthened, Delia started back to Tesuque. The setting sun was still warm, and when she, Rumpus and Hark arrived at the top of La Bajada Hill, the enormous sky stretched into a cloudless sapphire blue.

She drove into Santa Fe by way of Old Pecos Trail, admiring the snow-covered mountains and feeling relieved that the roads were no longer icy or wet. In the last twenty-four hours the temperature had risen twenty degrees and evaporated yesterday's mucky mess. 'The January thaw', people called it. The snow was lovely, but the drier conditions made it easier to get around.

She waved at Ethan as she passed the entrance of his driveway. She noted a pile of mail clutched in his mittenless hand. He must have walked down to the post office. Delia felt rather good about being exactly where she was, heading to a lovely house with her steadfast hounds. And she noticed her cold symptoms had disappeared.

She parked the car in the garage and left the patio door open for the dogs, who were inclined to nosy around for a while after their hour's journey. The house doors appeared secure; she opened the front with her new key and locked it behind her even though she would have to open it again when the hounds came looking for supper.

Her cell phone rang. She rummaged in her bag and quickly pulled it out before the call went to voicemail. It was Jean-Paul.

"Hello, my treasure. All is well?"

"Indeed! I had a lovely time with Alice this afternoon and yes, she'll come for a visit next weekend. She found an old letter from my mother to her mother, which has given me new insights into my parents' attitude toward Dorothy's death. I'm very relieved. I'll tell you more about it when you return."

"How glad I am for you, Délie. I know your heart was heavy."

"No more. Don't worry... I'm peaceful now. So, my love, where are you?'

"Already I am in Washington. There must have been a tail wind. We arrive ahead of schedule, so I have extra time to talk with you before the Paris flight is called. There are many French people here at the gate."

"You must enjoy hearing your own language."

"*Ah, oui, c'est vrai.* But most amazing! You will not believe with whom I make the acquaintance in the lounge of departure!"

"Oh, I know! Michelle Obama!" Delia remembered the comical

guessing game they had played over his chance meeting with Jane Fonda at DeVargas Mall.

"I shall not keep you in suspense, Délie. But you will be surprised. Guillaume Duthuit!"

"No! How did you recognize each other? You've never met."

"*Vraiment, chérie.* By chance we took seats in the lounge and fell into conversation. He is returning to France from the recital in Mexico City. I tell him you and I take the winter vacation in Santa Fe in the house of a singer. Perhaps, since he, too, is a man of music, he might know M'sieur Guillaume Duthuit. His reply, '*Je suis Guillaume Duthuit!*'"

"How amazing, Jean-Paul! Do you have the impression he's a difficult man who set up all this trouble?"

"*Pas de tout!* He is no longer beside me so I may speak freely. He departed to seek a drink. Délie, he is charming. Large and handsome with a speaking voice of beauty most notable. We must attend a performance. I have no doubt he is magnificent."

"So you like him!"

"*Bien sûr.* And you, too, my darling, will be enchanted. We have arranged to shift the seating of the plane so that we may ride together. He also is in the class of business. Will that not be a pleasure?"

"Darling, I'm so glad! That flight can be tedious. You've never flown to France from so far west. What a piece of luck!"

"He possesses the *appartement* in Paris and also an ancient house in Burgundy with a vineyard. He knows of our family and tells me he once met my uncle. The world, is it not small?"

"As we age, we gain more connections."

"And we speak also of the vexation of the ghost in his house. I gather he is a practicing Catholic and knows the priest at Cristo Rey Church. He considers requesting that the priest perform an exorcism. He is concerned most deeply for the trouble we experience and the death of poor Carla. His patience, it is tried, and he suspects ours is as well... Oh, but the plane is announced. My dearest precious one, I will apprise you of my safe arrival. We will speak again soon.

"*Oh, attends*...there is one more coincidence! I saw those kids, Jack and Jill, in the line of the ticket counter. They fly to Chicago and then to their universities. You will not be further molested by their antics."

"Well, good riddance to them! Although I suppose they did, in fact, save us a great deal of trouble in the long run..." Delia didn't want to recall that dreadful night of Jean-Paul's arrest. "I love you, Jean-Paul."

"And I you. We will not be apart long. Goodbye, my treasure."

Delia turned off her phone, hung up her coat, went into the kitchen and turned on the radio. It was tuned to Radio France, which kept her feeling connected to Jean-Paul. She felt remarkably peaceful despite his absence. Alice's enchilada had cured her sore throat. The letter from her mother was in her purse — she treasured it as a talisman of release — and now she had already had a call from Jean-Paul with such interesting news. Imagine running into their mysterious landlord in Dallas!

She was tying on her apron with the idea of preparing a light supper when the music from Radio France broke off. In that moment of silence Delia heard the moaning of La Llorona, louder than ever, as though she were right there in the kitchen with her.

24

Since La Llorona's calls were now so distinct, Delia decided to investigate. She stood listening then moved silently to the laundry room, convinced the groans were emanating from there. She distinctly heard a woman's mournful wail. Yes. La Llorona was very near. She tiptoed toward the door, which she knew was locked. But to her surprise, when she put her hand on the doorknob, it turned and opened.

The sound grew louder, but the space beyond was pitch black. She noted a light switch on the laundry room wall. Hoping it was the right one, she flicked it on. Yes! There was a dusty bulb in a socket just inside the doorway. And revealed in the uncertain light was a steep, narrow staircase against an unplastered adobe wall. The stairs, barely a foot across, had no railing. Peering down, Delia saw a narrow platform beside a dark chasm of rapidly flowing water. She stood listening, holding her breath. Was there really a woman trapped down there? No. She exhaled with the realization that it was probably the passage of water that caused the beseeching groans.

She continued to stand in the doorway, taking in her unexpected surroundings. She realized this underground flow was part of the acequia irrigation system on the property. Because it flowed from the direction of the patio, she surmised the well in the patio must be positioned directly above the acequia.

From where Delia stood the roar of water was disturbingly loud. Outside, the snow continued to melt rapidly. The sudden thaw increased the volume of mountain run-off that now rushed through the acequia. That was the sound that had caught her attention.

But how curious that the door was unlocked. Delia was sure that until now the door had been locked. Perhaps Kimber was aware that the sudden thaw might cause damage to the property and had sent someone to check. And they'd forgotten to secure the door when they left.

But, no, Kimber didn't have the new key and Delia had definitely left the house locked. The moaning was now so insistent that Delia decided she must investigate further. She wanted to make sure it was only water — and not someone trapped and distressed.

The discovery of her mother's letter had brought such relief she wondered if she was entering a phase of reassurance. She often sensed that segments of her life were informed by theme: everything would go beautifully, or one vexation after another would have to be dealt with. Now, she surmised, might be her time of resolution: she'd been so reassured by the discovery of her mother's letter and her expression of abiding love. And perhaps, too, Jean-Paul might find Jacques's legal problems easily solved. He'd already cleared up the mystery of Guillaume

Duthuit's character when he discovered Guillaume was not the sort of man to make enemies.

And now... this house. A mystery would be solved. The haunting moans were only the sound of flowing water, increased during above-freezing temperatures, decreased during a hard freeze. That would explain their intermittence.

With one hand against the wall for balance, Delia carefully descended the narrow steps to the wooden platform beside the water. How many people, she wondered, knew of this basement acequia? Delia understood how La Llorona became associated with the moaning water. Carla, an impressionable teenager, and others like her, would understandably be frightened and incorporate the resident owl into the myth of La Llorona. It was magical thinking on a communal level. But why the break-ins? Even in times of drought, if neighbors needed water, they could draw it from the patio well, assuming the acequia hadn't run dry. The groaning was explained but not the break-ins.

Delia continued to make her way cautiously along the adjacent platform by the yellowish light of the bulb above. She peered into the shadows under the stairs to make sure no one was there. She called out, "Anyone here? Hello? Hello?" No answer. Just the roar of the rushing water.

Suddenly, to Delia's horror, the light flicked off and the door at the top of the stairs slammed shut. The basement was pitch-black. She felt for a wooden stair beam and held on, not daring to take a step forward.

How the hell had that happened? Certainly a draft could slam the door but not switch off the light. And, she remembered, the switch was on the inside of the laundry room.

There was somebody up there! And it was a human somebody — not a ghost. She thought she heard footsteps from above, but because of the sound of the rushing water, she couldn't be sure.

Now she thought she heard barking... By the way, where were Rumpus and Hark? She'd locked the front door when she'd come in, but had she left the patio gate open? Probably. Yes, that was definitely the sound of Bassets baying. They were there. Something was very wrong.

They wouldn't howl simply from hunger. Something—someone was disturbing them.

It dawned on her that she was trapped. She was trapped in a place where no one would find her. Sweat broke out all over her body. She began to panic. She'd disappear. Maybe some day her skeleton might be found. They'd say it was the bones of La Llorona.

And Jean-Paul. Poor, wonderful man! What would he think? That she had deserted him? No, he'd know she'd never leave him. But he might never find her! Could she last until his return? Three days at least? And how would he know where to look? Maybe he'd think to contact Guillaume, who would tell him to look down here. But he'd suffer horribly before he found her, and who knew what condition she'd be in by then?

No! she told herself. No! She couldn't allow him to suffer like that. And she was in no way ready for the end of her life! She laughed grimly to herself. So much for her sense of resolution. Questions loomed large and fearful.

What about the dogs? Standing in the pitch dark, she strained again to hear above the rushing water. She definitely heard them barking. She pictured them inside the patio, warning of an intruder. But could they get out again? Had she actually propped open the patio gate? Would they eventually wander around the neighborhood if she didn't return? Would someone find them and understand something was wrong?

Think. She commanded herself to calm down and seek possibilities. Take a deep breath, she told herself. The air smelled dank and moldy—not like anything she'd encountered so far in New Mexico. And the darkness was so complete... even now, with her eyes adjusting slightly to the total blackness all around her, she could not trust herself to climb the narrow stairs.

There had to be a way out. She was careful to remember which way she was facing. It wouldn't do to become disoriented. She could hear the water racing to her left. She mustn't veer towards it and fall in.

Then it occurred to her the water knew the way out. Did she dare slip into it and let it take her down stream—so to speak—where it would flow at some point out into the open? The water must flow into the orchard to the south of the house. She and Jean-Paul had never walked there because they'd beaten a convenient snow path through the orchard west of the house. They'd noticed the irrigation ditches but hadn't investigated. And those ditches, she thought, had been dry. She strained to picture them. There may have been a water gate closing them off from an acequia to the south orchard. And that ditch, she thought, was covered in snow and ice so that she could only imagine that water flowed downhill beneath it. Yes, there was always a little water in the arroyo where they walked, some of which must come from this acequia running under the house. But all of it was a confused muddle in her mind. She couldn't picture the actual situation.

She decided slipping into the water was too chancy. The opening might be too small to swim through and she'd freeze in the icy snowmelt even if there were an adequate opening. And of course, when the acequia broke out into the downward slanting ground, there might be an unmovable grate. She'd still be trapped.

What a fool she'd been to come down here! Why hadn't she at least brought a flashlight? Curiosity killed the cat, she remembered, and laughed ruefully in the darkness.

Still keeping a hand on the stair support, she slowly turned around. Now the rushing water was to her right. Her eyes were finally adjusting to the inky dark. She began to make out shapes. And then, like the advent of a miracle, a silvery spotlight appeared. Her prison was becoming illuminated. Was someone coming toward her with a flashlight? Was it friend or foe? For a moment she visualized the Baby Jesus in a pair of new Walmart shoes from the Chimayo Chapel altar.

"Help! Help!" she cried. "Help, I'm trapped. Look down here!"

But no one answered. No one was there. So where was the light coming from so suddenly? She stared, trying to find its source.

Then she knew. It was the moon. The light of the moon shone down through the patio well! It would be overhead only a short time as it traveled through the night sky.

She must act quickly.

With great care she turned back around and began to creep up the stairs, her left hand against the rough adobe wall of the house. The staircase was so narrow that one misstep would send her tumbling over the side, most certainly to her death. But she couldn't take her time. She must move with as much urgency as she dared. The moon would quickly slip across the sky and she'd be left again in inky darkness.

Her hope now was that the door was still unlocked. Obviously shut but not locked. Slowly, laboriously she made her way up. And then she was there.

Above the sound of the acequia, she could now hear hysterical barking. Somehow the Bassets had gotten inside the house. And there was somebody or something disturbing them. A raccoon? A coyote? Or a hostile human.

She put her hand on the knob, but it would not turn. Oh no! The door had locked when it slammed or someone on the other side had deliberately locked it.

A sob rose in Delia's throat. Panic gripped her once again. The moonlight would grow dimmer and she'd be stuck in this dungeon. She had to think. She knew she didn't have the strength or body mass to break through the door. And besides, because of the abrupt drop beyond the narrow platform, she couldn't back up to get a running start.

Think! Think! she commanded herself. Your life depends on it!

Her cell phone! Could she have put it in her pocket? What had she done with it after taking Jean-Paul's call?

She remembered she'd put on her apron which had a wide pocket across the front. She was still wearing it. She felt along the front of her body.

Careful to remain standing still, she slipped her hand into the pocket and felt something hard. Cold and hard. No, it wasn't the phone, it was the Beretta! She'd absentmindedly stuck it there to fulfill her promise to Jean-Paul to keep her weapon near.

Oh, glory! She might manage to copy the guys in the TV westerns and shoot her way through the door. If the waning light would only hold. She needed to hit the lock squarely to get it to shatter. How many shots did she have? She was pretty sure the gun was loaded.

She ran her hand over the safety. Detective Scott back in Washington had admonished her to always keep her weapon loaded with the safety on or in an emergency it would do no good. So, yes, her plan might work. Good ol' Detective Scott. The memory of his homely freckled face and intelligent grey eyes swam before her — a sustaining image.

She reminded herself that she had only a few feet of platform on which to stand. There was no railing, even here by the door. Luckily, her weapon was so small she needn't fear a disabling kick. Her little gun wouldn't cause her to pitch over backward.

She carefully drew it from the pocket. It wouldn't do to drop it. Even if it didn't fall into the rushing water, it would be difficult to find in the waning light, and perhaps the sky wouldn't be clear again for a long time. She couldn't remember the weather forecast. No... it was now or never.

And just like that, the moon moved off. Or a cloud obscured it. Its light was extinguished. Darkness closed in. She hadn't expected it to happen so fast. Well, at least she'd made it up to the door. She'd clearly seen the lock before her only a moment ago and held an image of it in her mind's eye. But could she shoot the lock in the pitch dark? Would the shot ricochet and injure her? How many bullets did she have in the chamber? She must hurry!

She cocked the gun and felt for the trigger. With her left hand she felt for the lock where it protruded on this side of the door. The trick was to aim the gun properly with her right hand without shooting her left.

And if, as she suspected, the dogs were just on the other side of the door, she'd have to slant her aim upwards, so that if the bullet pierced the door, it wouldn't hit one of the animals. Shit! How was she going to manage that? She had no choice but to do her best.

Slowly, cautiously, she placed the barrel against her left hand, which lay over what she now thought was the lock. She removed her left hand, while stepping back only a few inches, pulled back the gun as far as she dared and fired.

25

There was a spark and an explosive pop, a clattering and a nasty smell. Delia stepped forward in the now total darkness and tentatively shoved against the door. It fell open.

Her eyes at first focused on the lighted kitchen beyond. The laundry room was dim. There was an odd odor mixed with that of the gun-power. Rumpus and Hark stood silhouetted against the light, barking fiercely at something to her left. Their teeth were bared and the hair on their backs stood stiff. They had something trapped.

Delia now saw puddles of blood on the floor. And glass. Shards of jagged glass lay in the blood. No, not blood. Something paler.

What the hell was going on?

Delia instinctively jumped behind the hounds to face the enemy, her weapon still drawn. Rumpus and Hark paid no attention to her, but held their ground, barking, barking. And then she perceived the outline of a man. He threatened them with something sharp and shiny. A broken wine bottle. That was red wine on the floor, not blood. He brandished the jagged glass at the incensed dogs — and now, at her.

"Call off those dogs!" her enemy thundered.

For a split second she thought it was Jean-Paul's new friend, Slim Fellows. What was he doing here? And why hadn't she ever suspected him of being connected with the break-ins? He was an old-timer in this area — no doubt he possessed a lot of secrets and perhaps had made enemies. And he had those tiny eyes. Delia never trusted people with tiny eyes.

Parallel to this jumble of thoughts was the suspicion she might be going crazy. Perhaps the nightmare events were causing her to lose her mind. But, no. It was Steve Kovic!

He shifted to his right, blocked on his left by the hot water heater. The dogs grew more frenzied. She and they shifted with him; they remained facing him. It was a weird, macabre dance and Delia ended up with her back against the kitchen light. He may not have been able to see her weapon, but he had to know she was armed because she'd shot through the lock.

"Call off those dogs!" he repeated, thrusting the jagged bottle towards them and further slipping to his right, his back now before the open cellar door.

Delia's weapon gave her power. And the incensed dogs tipped the balance further in her favor.

Time stood still—dogs growling, adversaries glaring. Then Steve lunged toward her and the dogs sprang at his legs. He howled in pain and fell backwards through the open door, scrambling and finally tumbling off the platform, screaming as he fell.

There was a sickening thud. Then silence, except for the moan of the water.

"Good god," Delia murmured, shaking not from fear, but an all-encompassing fury. Her dogs stood before her, their hackles still up but their tails wagging slightly. They suddenly brushed past her and sat side-by-side on the kitchen floor, looking at her expectantly. She turned, snapped on the basement light and looked down over the acequia. Steve lay crumpled beside the rushing water, his neck snapped—his head in an impossible position—a part of the lethal wine bottle still clutched in his fist.

Clearly, he was dead, but Delia wasn't about to go down to check. Impulsively, she grabbed a broom and furiously swept the broken glass and puddles of wine toward the basement door. A torn part of a label told her Steve's weapon was one of Jean-Paul's bottles of French wine. In her rage, she swept the mess over the side of the narrow platform and watched it fall down onto the narrow platform below. Quickly, she switched off the light and slammed the door shut. She realized her finger prints were on the light and doorknob, but there was no point trying to wipe them off since they were all over the inside wall as well. Besides, she'd done nothing illegal; the man had fallen to his own death, even if it was connected to her killer dogs and her weapon.

"Well, that's how that turned out," she said philosophically to the dogs, now lying with their muzzles on their paws, watching her. Surely, praise was in order. "Good, good, Rumpus. Good, good, Hark." She bent down to pat their heads and they instantly rose, rubbing themselves against her legs. Oh, how she loved her funny animals! They were—yes, indeed—they were such good, good dogs! "Whatever would I do without you?"

Clearly they were happy for the praise, but now they were even more intent on eating supper. As they headed briskly back to the brightly lit kitchen, Delia realized neither she nor her animals had even had their dinners! She followed their wagging tails, patting her apron pocket to be sure her beautiful Beretta was back where it belonged. But had she replaced the safety? She checked. Yes, she had. Thank goodness for good habits.

So how on earth did everyone get in? Had Eloy kept a set of keys, after all?

The answer was right there in front of her. The trapdoor beneath the kitchen sink was wide open. Of course! She needn't have dragged the trash bags out the kitchen door. The area under the sink was conveniently open to the trash storage area in the patio. That's how the mouse she'd found on their first afternoon in the house had entered. That's how the intruder had always got in! In was just a matter of bending down and crawling through. Then the intruder opened the doors and windows from the inside. And the intruder had always been Steve Kovic!

Delia was calming down now and she felt herself regaining focus. She first tenderly examined her dogs for cuts and bruises. They liked that. She thought they were okay. She took their bowls from the cupboard and distributed their food. As she placed the bowls near the breakfast nook, she remembered the first time she and Jean-Paul returned to the invaded house. The doors and windows had been wide open and the lights and furnace had been blazing. They'd been at the Kovics' party.

She remembered, too, how Wilma had greeted them at the door and apologized for Steve's temporary absence. "He went down to the village to get some booze," or words to that effect. The point was: he wasn't at the party. And she and Jean-Paul were away from the house so he could easily enter — with or without a key — and spook them or any other tenants on their return. Delia realized there were never any break-ins when he was out of town.

The dogs rushed happily to their suppers, but Delia's thoughts continued elsewhere. Things were falling into place. Steve must have been the villain all along. But why? What earthly reason would he have to prevent Guillaume Duthuit from keeping his tenants? Unless he had a personal vendetta against him...

But now that Jean-Paul, who was an excellent judge of character, had met Guillaume and found him simpatico, Kovic's mischief didn't make sense. There was a puzzle-piece missing.

Also there was the matter of the dead man lying unreported in the basement. Well, fuck him. If she chose not to report the mishap (she couldn't bring herself to think of it as a tragedy), it would be a long, long time before the body was discovered.

But she couldn't think what to do next. She suddenly felt removed and uncaring about the entire train of events and experienced an odd distance from recent reality. She was aware only of fatigue and hunger. She supposed she was in shock. Well, she'd fix some supper and think about it after she'd eaten. She did decide, however, to light a fire in the bedroom and eat her supper off a tray in there. Yes, she'd start the fire now so the room would be cozy when her dinner was ready. She liked the idea of putting distance between herself and the corpse. She would figure out what to do later. Rumpus and Hark had already trotted off to their beds. And soon she'd be headed to bed, too.

26

elia sat before the bedroom fire slowly eating her omelet. The eggs and mushrooms were fresh and the red peppers sweet and flavorful. Jean-Paul always said it took only a little thought to transform the drab to the delicious. The omelet tasted luscious. She willed herself to relax despite her mind slipping back to the traumatic events. It probably wasn't right to leave a dead man undiscovered in her landlord's basement. It was also probably illegal to let a fatal accident go unreported. On the other hand, if she called the police, she'd be in for endless questions and perhaps even a lengthy procedure or trial; although, she couldn't see how anyone might think she were the killer. Still, she wasn't happy about taking a chance on getting charged for murder and maybe even convicted. That would be worse than dying alone in the dark basement beside the icy acequia. Her mind wouldn't stop racing; she supposed she could always plead self-defense... Yes, maybe she should make a call.

But she was so tired and whom should she call? She didn't think she'd met any lawyers in New Mexico. She tried to remember the guests at Steve and Wilma's party. No lawyers that she could remember. The Ridgeleys or cousin Alice probably had a lawyer who could advise her. Or, she could call one of several attorneys she knew in Baltimore...

But she was pretty sure she already knew what they'd say: report the death to the police immediately. And the police would ask her why she'd waited to call. She was in shock, she'd say. Even now, as she tried to relax before the fire, she wasn't sure she was thinking rationally. It'd been a long day. She concluded she couldn't make a decision that night.

As she gathered up the dishes her cell phone rang. She set down the tray on the ottoman and walked rapidly into the hall to get the phone. It was past nine o'clock and she couldn't imagine who'd be calling now. Jean-Paul wouldn't have arrived in Paris yet. Perhaps it was Wilma to ask if she'd seen her husband. Then what would she say? "Oh, yeah, sorry, Wilma. He did stop by before supper, but unfortunately, like Humpty-

Dumpty, he had a great fall and, well, I'm afraid he's now lying dead beside the secret acequia. Sorry about that."

No, that would never do. She checked the number of the incoming call. It seemed familiar, but she wasn't sure. She recognized a Washington, D.C. area code. The French ambassador perhaps...

She took a deep breath and answered.

"Hello," said a familiar man's voice. "Hello? Mrs. H? Detective Scott, here."

Detective Scott of the D.C.P.D. was one of the few people who still called her Mrs. H, which referred to her first husband's last name, Hager.

"Hello, yes. It's me. How are you? I'm extremely glad to hear your voice!"

"Mrs. H, I've got disturbing news. You and Mr. Duval are in grave danger."

Delia almost responded by saying giddily, 'So what else is new?' but she bit her tongue and waited.

"You still there, Mrs. H?"

"Yes, yes. Is there a problem?"

"'Fraid so. Remember those photos you sent from your phone? Well, we forwarded them to the F.B.I. who has informed us that the weapon—it's a Makarov pistol—is common in Eastern Europe. I've never seen one before. But I'm calling because the documents you photographed belong to a gang of dangerous international criminals. Serbs. International jewel thieves. Very clever and very dangerous. Two women—one probably American, the FBI thinks, and a man by the name of Stefan Stojkovic.

"It seems they're in your immediate vicinity, Mrs. H. They're killers. You and your husband need to evacuate the premises immediately."

Delia stifled a giggle, then gulped as the news sank in. Maybe Wilma and the silent sister-in-law were the women to whom Scott referred. Could that be possible? After what had happened that evening, she suspected it was.

"Detective, I'm here alone. Well, sort of alone. Jean-Paul left for France this afternoon. The man whom I think you're referring to, who goes by the name of Steve Kovic..."

184

"That's him," Scott broke in.

"Scott, he's here. He had an accident, I'm afraid. In fact, I was just trying to figure out what to do about it when you called."

"An accident? What kind of accident?"

"He fell down the cellar steps and it looks like he broke his neck. He's lying dead in the basement, and somehow, well, somehow, I haven't gotten around to calling anyone. I couldn't quite figure out what to do..."

"You're there alone?"

"Right."

"And no one knows about his death?"

"Right again."

"Trust you to facilitate an investigation, Mrs. H!"

"What?"

"And you think this guy is someone called Steve Kovic?"

"That's what he told us his name is. He's got a European accent... I mean had, and told us he is—was—French, but Jean-Paul said no, he wasn't French. European, though, no doubt. Not South American or New Zealand or anything like that." She thought she might be babbling and stopped.

"Mrs. H, you've got to get out of there. How soon can you leave?"

"Well, I'll have to get the dogs and pack a few things. I haven't got very much. We're just here for a month or so. And Jean-Paul took most of what he had to France. His laptop and cell phone and warm clothes. I guess I could be out of here in ten or maybe fifteen minutes."

"Go, Mrs. H! Go! Get out now! You still got that cousin in Albuquerque? Mrs. Alice Spencer, I think you said her name was... Can you get to her house?"

"Yes, yes, I'm sure I can. I was just there this afternoon."

"Okay. Get the dogs, pack and go. I've got your plate number." He read it off to her.

"Right. It's Jean-Paul's new car."

"Okay. I'm looking at the map now on the Internet. Yeah. Go. Get out onto the highway and go straight south on Interstate Twenty-five. You'll pick up a tail. Make sure the officer sees where you turn off. I'll notify your cousin that you're coming and arrange for another officer to meet you there. Don't call anyone. Just go. Now. Go!"

"Okay. What about my husband? He's aboard an Air France flight for Paris. I can't remember the number off hand, but I've got it written down."

"Don't worry, Mrs. H. We'll check the passenger lists and someone will meet him at the airport. You got my number in case you need it?"

"Yes, Scott, I do. Thank you. I'll go now."

"And be sure you take your weapon."

"Okay." She felt in her apron pocket. It was still there. She supposed the fact that she was still wearing her apron indicated how disoriented she was. It also occurred to her she'd forgotten to pour herself a glass of wine. She couldn't remember when she'd last had dinner without wine. But it was a good thing she didn't have to drive back to Albuquerque having consumed alcohol, even if it were only one glass.

<h1 style="text-align:center">27</h1>

Delia left the dishes unwashed, pulled a screen over the bedroom fireplace, grabbed her wheelie-bag, stuffed it with clothes and her laptop, checked to make sure she had her weapon and cell phone, and, after a quick look through Jean-Paul's bureau and desk, called the hounds and jumped into the car. She wondered what to do about the new house key. Perhaps she'd leave it with the Ridgeleys, but then she remembered time was of the essence.

The clear night sky was now so bright she could almost have driven by moon and starlight. She saw the Land Rover and Audi were parked in the Kovics'—or Stojkovics' driveway, the Audi parked heading out, and she hoped neither Wilma nor Monika noticed her driving past.

She rolled through the stop sign at the bottom of the road. She knew the pueblo police hid their cars in the bushes and would suddenly roar out to entrap speeders, but she was scared and wanted to get onto the highway fast. She didn't care if the pueblo police did pursue her. Actually that might be protection as long as they didn't try to detain her or shoot at her.

She checked her rear-view mirror. No one was behind her.

Delia was an excellent driver. When she drove her own BMW she knew exactly how it would react and what it was capable of. But now she was driving Jean-Paul's new Subaru—a very different entity. She'd helped drive it across country, but that was what she considered "stupid driving." You drove in a straight line with the cruise control on. All you have to do is be mindful of signs and other drivers and signal your lane changes. But now she was driving as fast as she dared on a small, neglected country road, and until she got to the highway it was going to be tricky. She felt the car slip a bit as she accelerated and turned beyond the stop sign. Ice must have formed—ice she couldn't see. The snow had melted in the thaw but now the dashboard thermometer read 29 degrees. If she weren't careful, she could go into a spin and get herself into more trouble. She accelerated as fast as she dared, gripping the steering wheel while straining her eyes.

She was exhausted. Her eyes burned and her neck ached. She hoped she wouldn't get one of her infrequent but debilitating headaches. She couldn't even remember the beginning of the day... this New Year's Day seemed to have lasted forever. The early-morning trip to the airport, the lunch with Alice, the rollercoaster ride of emotions, all culminating with the terror of being locked beside the acequia and then the threat of Steve moving toward her with that broken bottle... the dogs coming to her rescue... and finally the call from Scott telling her to evacuate—it was a nightmare. But one she was living, not dreaming.

And where was Jean-Paul? When would he hear she was in danger? What exactly would the French police tell him? Did he have Scott's number or e-mail address so he could get accurate information? What on earth would he think?

Really, it was all too much. She thought she might be safe for the moment, but how long would that last?

She glanced frequently into the rear-view mirror. Except for the sky's light, the road was dark. And then she thought she saw the silver Audi come round the curve. It, too, was moving fast. Too fast! It would rear end her.

It was hard to identify the driver because what she was seeing in her rearview mirror was essentially headlights. She slowed and then sped up. The car remained close behind her, seemed to be adjusting its speed with hers. She was getting spooked, wanting to shake that car and find the promised trooper, who at the moment was still nowhere in sight.

Then the trailing car began to pass. Delia feared it would force her off the road or maybe the driver would shoot out her tires. She swore under her breath and decided to pull out to the middle of the road even if it meant getting crashed into by the car behind. She'd take the chance and hope the collision — if it happened — wouldn't be so severe as to keep her from moving forward.

She swerved abruptly to the middle of the road. The driver hit the brakes and sat on the horn. Delia accelerated again. The speed-limit sign she passed said 25 mph; she was doing 61. The dogs were getting thrown from side to side. They probably thought they were having nightmares. She wondered if that other car would now deliberately ram her. It probably would if it caught her.

She braked abruptly at the on ramp and then sped on to the highway, barely missing a collision with a pick-up truck. The driver honked furiously and changed lanes — which, she thought angrily, he should have done in the first place. Surely he could see her coming. It seemed that the driver behind her, sensing the eminent collision with the pick-up, had braked to avoid a pile-up. Delia saw her chance and pulled rapidly into the passing lane. As she sped past the pick-up, the driver honked at her and shook his fist like a madman, probably thinking she was a drunk driver. Hopefully, he'd call the police. Where the hell was the promised cop? "Never around when you want them," she growled between her teeth. She was now traveling at 88 miles per hour. Luckily there was little traffic on the highway. But if she hit an ice patch, she'd be a goner. In the mirror she thought she saw the threatening car gaining on her again.

She realized she was shaking. She was not only shocked and frightened but furious. Nasty people were screwing up her life. She was sick of the drama. She wasn't interested in them or their motives. She wanted a nice holiday in New Mexico and not other people's craziness. Other people's pathological agendas.

Rumpus and Hark were now in heraldic mode, sitting up straight and still, side-by-side on the back seat, looking blasé almost. Perhaps she should have put hats on them in an attempt to give the impression that there were two men in the back seat. But two men with long Basset ears? Oh, damn—she'd forgotten to bring the wide-brimmed hat Alice had given her. Jean-Paul's, she remembered, was still in the back of the car where he'd left it when she'd dropped him off at the airport. Oh, well, Alice knew Guillaume, and if she and Jean-Paul didn't return to Tesuque, he could return it to her—along with whatever else she'd left...

Her thoughts were wandering while her speedometer read 101. Whew! She didn't think she'd ever driven so fast. She felt almost giddy. But she snapped her attention back to the rearview mirror; she had to outrun the Audi until the police spotted her. Where the hell were they? Maybe she could pull off the road and call 911. But could she evade the pursuer? She could have phoned directly from Jean-Paul's new car, but she hadn't had occasion yet to learn how to do it. Certainly she couldn't reach in her bag and use her phone at this speed.

She sped by four more cars. She wondered if someone would throw a wheel rim at her. The Audi—for now she was sure it was Monika in her silver Audi who pursued her—had come up behind her. Suddenly—from where, she couldn't figure—four squad cars appeared on the road, sirens squawking and lights rotating. One moved in front of her and one beside her. They began slowing down, forcing her to diminish her speed. Help at last!

She started to brake but the cops beside her signaled for her to continue driving. So she proceeded on, now at the legal speed of 75 mph.

She strained to see what had become of the Audi. It looked as if the other two police cars had forced it off the road. But traffic was now moving normally behind her and she soon lost sight of them. And before she knew it, she was atop La Bajada Hill and ready to ease up on the gas for the steep descent. She wondered if the troopers cared if she broke the speed limit. Since they were staying with her, she really had nothing more to do than keep pace with them.

As she neared Albuquerque, the traffic grew heavier. The dashboard clock said nine thirty. Wow, she'd made good time. But she was down to less than a quarter tank of gas. She'd forgotten to fill up when she'd returned to Santa Fe. Since this was Jean-Paul's Subaru, she was not familiar with how much leeway the dashboard reading allowed her. She'd just have to hope for the best. At least the police would help her out if she did end up running out of gas.

Rumpus and Hark were still sitting up, taking it all in. They knew something was amiss.

Delia gave her police tail plenty of warning before she turned off the highway onto the road to Alice's house. There were no lights on this road, and she and the troopers were the only traffic. The sky was still bright, but clouds were forming in the southwest, making her visibility less clear.

There was another squad car parked in Alice's driveway and Delia came to a halt next to it. As she got out of the car, feeling stiff and shaky, she was surrounded by four officers and Alice. Feeling suddenly weak, she leaned against the car, breathing rapidly, her heart pounding. At least she'd made it this far—she felt safe at last. Rumpus and Hark were still in the car, peering out impatiently. Without a word, Alice let the hounds out, put an arm around her cousin and walked Delia into the house, the troopers following silently behind. Delia had only a vague realization of entering through Alice's front door, the interior house lights shining warm and welcoming.

The rest of the night was a blur. Two troopers left after they'd received word that Wilma had been arrested at her house. They told Delia and Alice she'd resisted arrest and the police had to chase her through the piñon trees. Picturing that scene, Delia began to laugh hysterically, but when she saw the expression on Alice's sensible face, she managed to quiet herself.

Monika had indeed been the driver of the Audi, the cops said. She admitted she'd seen Delia's car pass and, since Steve hadn't returned on schedule, she realized something unforeseen had happened and that Delia now had more information than was good for them. Fortunately, Monika had jumped into her own car so quickly, she'd forgotten her weapon. Realizing she couldn't shoot Delia, she determined to drive her into a fatal accident.

At this point, it appeared that the "persons of interest" were either dead or in police custody. No doubt others of the gang were still at large in Europe, especially in Serbia, but the troopers deemed Delia safe. Nevertheless, the cops who'd followed her from Santa Fe had orders to guard the house throughout the night. Delia had forgotten to grab the hounds' beds, but Alice pulled out an old blanket for them, and the sympathetic young trooper suggested it might be a good idea for the Bassets to sleep beside Delia in her room, to act as an extra alarm. Perhaps he thought Delia, and now Alice, might still be in danger.

Questions continued to buzz through Delia's mind. "How large is this Serbian gang?" she suddenly asked. The troopers didn't know. It occurred to her that the local police would not yet know many details of the recent events. She'd have to save her questions for Scott.

Alice was clearly weary and ready for bed. She asked if Delia would like her to sleep in the other guest bed, but Delia felt the dogs plus the troopers outside offered adequate protection. Besides, she needed to be alone with her thoughts. She just wished Scott and Jean-Paul would call. She longed for more information but didn't want to disturb them in the night.

She needed to get a better grip on what had happened. But she couldn't keep her eyes open. Within moments of lying down, Delia fell asleep with her clothes on, although she had managed to remove her apron with its weapon-filled pocket. She laughed at herself when she realized she'd driven all the way from Tesuque to Albuquerque with her apron on.

At four in the morning she awoke from deep sleep, went into the bathroom, changed into her nightgown and got back into bed. The next moment — or so it seemed — her cell phone rang. It was Jean-Paul. Scott's messenger had contacted him when he'd arrived in Paris, but Jean-Paul waited until he calculated it was morning in New Mexico before calling Delia. The troopers had relayed the message that she and the dogs were safe at Alice's house and that Steve had fallen in Guillaume's house and died.

Delia, fuzzy with sleep, didn't try to fill him in on the details, just reassured him that essentially all was well. She knew she was over-stating the case, bolstering herself as well as her husband from the terror of her ordeal, but it seemed the right thing to do. They were far away from each other and the opportunities for misunderstanding and anxiety were great.

Within the next few days, however, events moved quickly. Detective Scott called several times with updates, including more about the arrest of Wilma Snyder and the pale-faced Monika. Steve's body had been removed from the acequia; and Guillaume Duthuit had also been brought into the picture. Jean-Paul invited Guillaume for lunch at his château, compared notes with him and gave him the new set of keys.

Sooner than Delia expected, Jean-Paul called to say he was returning. Speaking in French, he told Delia, "It is now clear that the young man, Jacques, was not involved with the troublemakers. He finally confessed that he'd been out with his girl, who on that particular night had been forbidden by her father to leave the house. Jacques had persuaded her to sneak out and, rather than allow her to get in trouble with her fierce father, had gone to jail and remained silent. But, then, one of the troublemakers told his lawyer that Jacques had not been with them."

"What a relief! I've been worrying about Lili and Lucien! They must have known in their hearts that Jacques was incapable of committing arson. It made absolutely no sense. But do you now feel your trip has been for naught?"

"No, my treasure. It gave me a chance to check on everything, to assure Lili and Lucien that I shall always support them — after all, they have worked all their lives for our family — and to meet the charming

Guillaume Duthuit. He sends his greetings to you and deep appreciation for all you have done. You cleared up the mystery for him and he is most grateful.

"But have you more news of the Stojkovic gang? Incidentally, Guillaume says he has read about them in the French papers. They recently hit a Parisian jeweler, killing two clerks and one of the customers and stealing thousands of euros' worth of gems."

"Yes, darling, I do know about that tragedy in Paris. Scott has called several times and I'm beginning to piece together the big picture—so to speak. I'll tell you about it when you return. When do you think you'll fly back?"

"*Demain*, Délie! I'll see you tomorrow night, if you don't mind coming to the airport to fetch me. I'm longing to be with you! The bed here is too wide and much too cold without you."

"Oh, Jean-Paul! I'm so glad! I was afraid it'd be another week. I really need you. I miss you terribly."

"We shall be reunited tomorrow night. The connecting plane from Dallas will arrive in Albuquerque at seven forty-one."

"I'll be there, my love."

28

Delia and Jean-Paul were ready to head back to Maryland by the second week of January, but Alice prevailed upon them to remain with her through the weekend. She decided to roast a turkey with green chili and yams, to go along with a couple of bottles of French wines Jean-Paul had bought in the duty free shop in Paris. She also invited Ethan and Molly to join them for their farewell lunch that Saturday. The Ridgeleys eagerly accepted the invitation — they were anxious to learn first-hand what had actually happened to the Duvals in their neighbor's house. Not to mention the inside information on the Kovics.

The sky was overcast and the temperature barely above freezing. But snow wasn't predicted until after midnight, so Ethan and Molly didn't have to hurry back to Tesuque. They sat around Alice's dining table until late in the afternoon, everyone contributing questions and opinions until a full picture of the past weeks' terrifying events emerged. Everyone sought a sense of closure.

Molly began by saying, "Ethan and I visited Dolores on Tuesday. She's naturally very cut up about Carla, but her grandson, Juan, had time off for the Christmas holiday and was staying with her. So were several other relatives. The local Hispanics have a sustaining sense of family. We should have known she wouldn't be alone."

"Have they caught that Gomez guy?" Jean-Paul asked.

Ethan said he thought Gomez was still on the run. "I understand he was spotted in a supermarket in T or C, but managed once again to elude capture."

"What on earth is T or C?" asked Delia.

Alice chuckled. "It's a town in southern New Mexico, named Truth or Consequences after that old TV program that was a radio show first. The town was originally called Hot Springs — there's a spa there, but then in 1950, the emcee — oh darn, what was his name..." She clicked her fingers as if she could conjure him up to join them.

"Ralph Edwards," Molly shouted.

"Right! So Ralph Edwards announced on the radio that he would air the program from the first town that changed its name to Truth or Consequences. Hot Springs won!"

Jean-Paul rolled his eyes and poured more wine for everyone. "I think we passed through that place on our way here."

"No doubt," replied Ethan. "Anyway...that Wayne Gomez is a dangerous fellow. I hope they catch him before he harms someone else. He's got a long record of violent crime. It's a wonder he was still at large at the time Carla was going around with him."

194

"Do you know if it's true that Carla was pregnant?" Delia asked. That's what a girl at the funeral Mass thought..."

"I'm afraid so," Molly replied. "Dolores is inconsolable over that. She believes Gomez committed a double murder."

Delia wondered if the discussion of Carla's tragic death wasn't enough misery for the day. Perhaps they might avoid the details of Steve's death and Wilma and Monika's arrest. She hadn't yet talked much about all of that to Jean-Paul, but Ethan naturally brought it up. "Delia, will you please shed more light on what happened? All we know is what we read in the paper: that Steve's body was removed from Guillaume's house... from the basement, the paper said."

"Let's move to the fire in the living room," Alice suggested. "I'll do the dessert dishes later."

There was much scraping of chairs and resettling as Jean-Paul put another log on the fire. It was more of that sweet-smelling piñon wood. Delia knew there was a lot about New Mexico she was going to miss.

She also admitted to herself that she'd been totally wrong in her suspicion of the Ridgeleys — which she'd half-known all along didn't make sense. She was glad she'd never mentioned it even to Jean-Paul. Clearly, Ethan and Molly were among the kindest and most knowledgeable people they knew. She looked forward to a continuation of their friendship and, through them, learning more about the southwest.

The three dogs were stretched out, warming themselves beside the fire, and the humans were now all comfortably seated and waiting for her to begin. She could see from their expressions they were avid for answers.

"Well, apparently, Steve, Wilma and that sister-in-law, Monika, who really is Steve's sister-in-law but is actually Albanian — they had all eluded capture for a long time. My friend in Maryland, Detective Scott, says the FBI and the CIA have had an eye on them for years. But they couldn't amass enough evidence. This lethal little gang was canny. They cleverly covered their tracks.

"You may remember that Wilma told us Steve and Monika had gone to a jewelry show in Las Vegas. That was a lie. They flew to Paris, where they robbed a high-end jewelry store, killing three people in cold blood—two clerks and a customer who happened to be there. Jean-Paul and I saw the jewelry store surveillance tape, and you would not believe what Monika looked like! Beautifully dressed and made up, she looked like the typical privileged customer. That mousy, dowdy persona she presented to us was her disguise in reverse!

"I'd seen boxes of wigs in a closet at Wilma's house and mistakenly assumed they were Wilma's. I'd figured Wilma must have had cancer, undergone chemo, and used the wigs until her hair grew back. I was way off! The wigs were Monika's to use during one of their heists."

"Clever," Ethan commented.

"But was Wilma in on all this?" Molly asked.

"Apparently so. She has several art galleries in various places that were used to launder the jewelry profits. I was told her galleries were an integral part of the operation." Delia turned to look up at Jean-Paul. "Darling, do you remember when we first arrived at their party that night, Wilma told us that Steve had gone down to the village to get more gin? He was gone all right! But I've figured out that he went up to Guillaume's house to open the windows and doors and turn on all the lights! To spook us when we returned—to continue his campaign against Guillaume. Then when he returned to his party, Rumpus and Hark followed him. He couldn't leave the house open without them getting out. But he rightly suspected we wouldn't figure it out. That's why the hounds were waiting for us when we left the party."

"Very sinister," Jean-Paul responded. He moved forward, reached for the coffee pot on the table in front of the couch and filled Delia's empty cup. "So what about the young people? Did they know?"

"According to Scott they did not," said Delia.

"Gosh, I wonder what'll happen to them now?" Molly's gray-blue eyes looked troubled. "Unlike Steve and Monika, their mother may not be a murderer, but she's certainly an accomplice. She'll go to jail."

"She is there already," Jean-Paul said grimly. "Unless by now she makes the bail..."

"I *knew* those Kovics were on the make!" Molly said with a degree of passion Delia hadn't seen in her before. "That house is absurdly grandiose! Wilma never stepped out of her house without looking like a fashion model or an actor in a play. And I never knew her to be on time for anything—she always swanned in late to call attention to herself. So tiresome! And her relentless promotion of that gallery, connecting with everyone of consequence and insinuating herself onto boards. She absolutely lived for the spotlight! And did she ever want to infiltrate the opera! Which didn't work..." She shook her head for emphasis. "I tried to be a good neighbor... tried to be charitable. But I was foolish. Even though I considered her and Steve crude, never in my wildest dreams did it occur to me they were criminals!" She ran out of steam and took a deep breath, finishing with a rueful laugh. "But they did give awfully good parties. Were excellent hosts. And I have to admit that, despite Wilma's exasperating faults, I kind of liked her.

"But isn't it ironic that her kids installed the surveillance camera? That's actually exactly what Guillaume needed. What if they'd seen their own stepfather running around the house creating chaos? What do you suppose they'd have done?"

"There is no way to know," Jean-Paul said, thoughtfully shaking his head. "Guillaume, he mention to me, when we meet in the airport, that if Délie and I did not solve the mystery of the breaking ins, he would install a system of surveillance as last resort. But of course, the management would have to turn it off when he had tenants, so it might not have caught the culprit."

Ethan smiled ruefully in agreement and asked, "So what happened to the jewels they stole?"

Delia replied, "They were smuggled to Albania where they were re-cut and re-set. Monika was in on that operation, too. Apparently she's an absolute genius when it comes to gems. It was her family who reformatted—if you will—the stolen jewels. Then they were smuggled back to Steve's legitimate jewelry outlets and sold for enormous sums."

She went on to explain how she had managed to take photographs of odd documents in Cyrillic and a strange-looking pistol in Steve's desk one day while Wilma was on the phone instead of drinking coffee with her.

And even though she didn't know whether the pictures were important or not, she'd sent them to Detective Scott, who forwarded them to the FBI. Apparently that was the evidence they lacked to close in on Steve and Monika. The documents were plans and negotiations for another jewelry heist and possibly more killings.

"But what I do not understand is why Steve threatened you, darling." Jean-Paul put his arm across Delia's shoulder. "Why did he trap you in that place most horrible? And when that did not succeed, what had he in mind that brought the dogs to attack?"

Hark, upon hearing the word 'dogs', got up and shoved his way against Jean-Paul's legs. He turned his big head and sad eyes upon his master and let out a long doggie sigh. Everyone laughed.

Delia thought it would be the better part of discretion not to reveal that during Steve's final moments she was holding a gun on him. She decided to skip that little detail. She'd already told Jean-Paul because she'd wanted him to know she'd followed his advice about keeping her weapon near. Now she ran her hands through her short wavy hair and leaned back against Jean-Paul's arm. "I can't be sure what Steve had in mind — he clearly wanted me out of the picture. But after giving it a lot of thought, I believe he was convinced I knew too much — even though I didn't. Detective Scott says Wilma told the police she'd seen me photographing his documents and gun. And she told Steve what I'd done when he and Monika returned from France. So that's what set him against me. But the irony is that I didn't know what I was photographing! Somehow, it just seemed the right thing to do."

Her audience remained riveted as she sipped some coffee before continuing. "Steve couldn't figure out what I knew — who I was working for or what I'd done with my information. But he suspected me and decided to get me out of the way." Delia shivered. "I don't really like to think about it."

"Oh course, my treasure. You must try, if you can, to put it out of your mind." He kissed her on the forehead and drew her close.

"But what I still don't understand," Molly broke in unhappily, "was why Steve bothered Guillaume's tenants. What was the purpose of creating all that chaos? Guillaume hadn't done anything to Steve, had he?"

"No," Delia acknowledged. "But Steve wanted Guillaume's property."

"*Ah, oui*," Jean-Paul added emphatically. "In France Guillaume told me Steve had made offers most numerous for the property — increasingly large offers. But Guillaume, he did not wish to sell. He loves the house and wants to use it when he is there. In addition, he considers the property an investment of excellence. He is determined to retain it."

"So why," Alice asked, "didn't Steve simply accept that? He already has — had a big house across the road."

Delia patted Jean-Paul's knee, which Hark took as a sign of affection for himself. He licked the back of Delia's hand as it continued to rest on Jean-Paul's leg. She hardly noticed her hound's behavior as she continued in a clipped voice. "Steve wanted what he wanted. And here's the crux of the matter: Guillaume told Jean-Paul that Steve tried to buy the water rights from him, but Guillaume had been advised of their value and had already bought them himself at the time of his original house purchase. Because Guillaume runs a commercial orchard, which he's hired Joseph to tend, the water rights remain legally with the property. And here's another thing I figured out from what Gillian and Jonathan told me: Steve had land, but the water on his property is scarce. As everyone knows, water in New Mexico is more precious than gold. And Guillaume possesses many acre-feet of water — which is probably why that beautiful house was built there in the first place. Steve wanted the land, but he needed the water rights to develop it."

Delia paused, looked around at her cousin and her dear new friends, and said in a lighter tone, "Everyone marvels at how large and lush the trees are on Guillaume's property — those big cottonwoods in front of the house, for instance. I also noticed how the Kovic land, which I'd have thought would be damper since it's lower and closer to the river, has only small piñon and juniper trees. Trees that need far less water than Guillaume's cottonwoods, apricot and apple trees. Now we know the reason. No acequia runs through Steve's property. Many years ago the water from the mountain run-off was diverted to the property above — to Guillaume's. The running water probably always gave off that strange groaning sound, so the property had a haunted reputation that Steve exploited."

Delia paused as another realization slipped into place. "Jack and Jill told me Steve developed resorts in various parts of the world. He has one in Trinidad — I think they said — and one in South Africa. Like Wilma's art galleries, these resorts are not only moneymakers but also effective ways of laundering the large ill-gotten gains from all those jewelry robberies. Steve, Wilma and Monika prospered big time! I bet Steve wanted to develop one of those large resorts on Guillaume's land. But he needed the water rights to do it."

Ethan clapped his gnarly old hands. "So Steve made it difficult for Guillaume to keep a tenant in hopes that he'd get fed up and sell out!"

As Delia nodded, Molly shrieked, "Our peace and quiet would have been gone forever! If we thought the Kovics' house building was misery, think what it would be like if they'd built thirty houses!" She shivered.

Alice added, "And think what it would have done to that beautiful land — that 'strokeable terrain' as the poet William Gates wrote. Many sections of foothills would have been destroyed had Steve gotten his way!"

Epilogue

Alice had gone into her study to do some work. Delia and Jean-Paul were enjoying a late breakfast before starting their long drive back East. They planned to head south, pick up Interstate 10 and stop off with a university colleague of Jean-Paul's in St. Mary Parish, Louisiana, then continue on through the South until they got to Interstate 95 and head north to Maryland. That way they hoped to avoid any heavy winter weather. But a dusting of snow had fallen the night before and now, with the temperatures still below freezing, the roads were slick. They decided to wait for a rise in temperature.

Jean-Paul was meticulously cutting grapefruit sections and suddenly laughed.

"What is it?" Delia was sure there wasn't anything funny about the grapefruit—despite its suggestive French name, *pamplemousse*.

"I was thinking how funny it would be to see dapper Steve crawl from that patio into the kitchen." Jean-Paul laughed again. "Arriving from under the kitchen sink. Or even funnier, departing under the kitchen sink!"

Delia giggled. She pictured Steve in his tailored suit, his soft felt hat and expensive gloves. It would be like Henry James, whose outfits Steve's resembled, taking up plumbing.

Jean-Paul placed the sectioned grapefruit on the kitchen counter and slid onto the stool beside Delia. She knew that if he'd fixed grapefruit for breakfast—along with their customary croissants and café au lait—it was because he dreaded the lack of fresh food during the next few days of their road trip.

"The basement key," he said after tasting the fruit and declaring it delicious, "Guillaume told me, it was meant to hang beside the doorway. But it was never there since we took possession of that house, *n'est-ce pas?*"

"No, that door was always locked. I assumed it wasn't meant for the tenants, so I never asked about it. But Steve had taken the key. The cops found it in his pocket.

"I guess I would have called Kimber if I'd realized that was actually where that moaning came from. It usually seemed as if it were from the patio."

"*Probablement* the sounds we heard were actually from the well under which the water flowed. But we never guessed it was the flow of water. It didn't sound like water. I suspect the sound was distorted by the surrounding masonry — or adobe. It was an echo we heard. But I understand why Carla became frightened."

"It was spooky. The greater the volume of water, the louder the noise." Delia was squeezing their remaining grapefruit juice into little glasses. "You know I ruined the lock on the basement door when I shot it. Kimber had to get Eloy in to replace the whole mechanism."

Jean-Paul tenderly closed his hand over Delia's wrist. "My treasure, tell me, when you aimed your little weapon at Steve, before the dogs attacked, do you suppose you would have shot him?"

Delia leaned down and kissed his fingers curled around her wrist. She thought for a moment, resting her head against his arm. "I've wondered about that. Clearly he intended harm to the hounds and me — he was threatening us with jagged glass. Yes, I think if he hadn't stepped back to avoid the rush of the dogs, I'd have shot him. Maybe not to kill. I'd have aimed at his shoulder or his knees. But, yes, I would have shot him. He wasn't going to take that weapon away from me! That would have been my death warrant."

They sat in silence. Delia passed Jean-Paul the raspberry jam for his croissant.

"We have many adventures, *n'est-ce pas?*"

"Some are wonderful and some not... What have you liked best about our stay in New Mexico, darling?"

"*Je pense*... the sky. The grand sky — and all the cloud shadows — the stars and moon so huge and brilliant. And you? What did you like best, *mon ange?*"

"Hmm. Let me think... The day at the pueblo, probably. Such an embracing sense of community. That's rare in this country. The dancing was so moving. And the peacefulness of the people gathering for lunch — that sense of fulfillment... I loved that."

What she didn't say was how much she enjoyed hearing Jean-Paul pronounce the word 'arroyo' with his French R.

When the sun had burned through the ice, Alice emerged from her study to bid her guests goodbye.

"You must be our first guest, Alice, when our new house is built," Jean-Paul declared.

Delia agreed. "Yes, please come! And of course Zippy is invited, too." She hugged her cousin, hoping to convey how grateful she was for everything Alice had given her during the past month. "You never made it to Tesuque. But what a wonderful hostess, cousin and friend you are, Alice! You will remain a special part of our life."

Alice promised they'd stay in touch and when their house was finished she'd visit with great pleasure. Zippy stood beside her outside the open front door as she waved them off.

Rumpus and Hark peered back through the rear window as Delia and Jean-Paul waved out their windows until their hostesses were no longer in sight.

It wasn't long before they'd joined the traffic on the highway heading south.

"Oh look, darling! Look at that old truck ahead. The one loaded down with wood. Isn't that the same one we've been seeing — the one with no license plate?"

Suggested Reading

All Trails Lead to Santa Fe: An Anthology Commemorating the 400th Anniversary of the Founding of Santa Fe, New Mexico, in 1610. Santa Fe: Sunstone Press, 2010.

Austin, Mary Hunter. *Earth Horizon.* Facsimile of 1932 edition. Santa Fe: Sunstone Press, 2007.

— — —. *Land of Little Rain.* Facsimile of 1904 edition. Santa Fe: Sunstone Press, 2007.

Bullock, Alice. *Discover Santa Fe.* Santa Fe: Rydal Press, distributed by Sunstone Press, 1973.

— — —. *Living Legends of the Santa Fe Country: A Pictorial Guidebook.* Santa Fe: Sunstone Press, 1978.

Dean, Rol, ed. *Santa Fe, Its 400th Year: Exploring the Past, Defining the Future.* Santa Fe: Sunstone Press, 2010.

Cather, Willa. *Death Comes For The Archbishop.* New York: Vintage Books, 1990.

Dittert, Alfred E. and Plog, Fred. *Generations In Clay.* Flagstaff: Northland Press, 1980.

deBuys, William and Harris, Alex. *River Of Traps.* Albuquerque: University of New Mexico Press, 1990.

Gates, William. *House Born Of Mud.* Santa Fe: Sunstone Press, 2010.

Hoefer, Jacqueline. *A More Abundant Life.* Santa Fe: Sunstone Press, 2003.

Hillerman, Tony. *The Great Taos Bank Robbery.* Albuquerque: University of New Mexico Press, 1973.

La Farge, John Pen. *Turn Left At The Sleeping Dog*. Albuquerque: University of New Mexico Press, 2001.

La Farge, Oliver. *Behind the Mountains*. Santa Fe: Sunstone Press, 2008.

— — —. *The Enemy Gods*. Santa Fe: Sunstone Press, 2010

— — —. *The Man with the Calabash Pipe: Some Observations*. Santa Fe: Sunstone Press, 2011.

— — —. *The Mother Ditch, La Acequia Madre*. Spanish translation by Pedro Ribera Ortega. Santa Fe: Sunstone Press, 1983.

— — —. *A Pause in the Desert*. Santa Fe: Sunstone Press, 2009

LeBlanc, Sydney. *Secret Gardens of Santa Fe*. New York: Rizzoli International Publications, Inc., 1997.

Mather, Christine and Woods, Sharon. *Santa Fe Style*. New York: Rizzoli International Publications, Inc., 1986.

Nichols, John. *The Milagro Beanfield War*. New York: Henry Holt And Company, 1974.

Ortega, Pedro Ribera. *Christmas in Old Santa Fe*. 2nd ed. Santa Fe: Sunstone Press, 1973.

Pacheco, Allan. *Ghosts-Murder-Mayhem, A Chronicle of Santa Fe: Lies, Legends, Facts, Tall Tales, and Useless Information*. Santa Fe: Sunstone Press, 2004.

Skolnick, Arnold. *Paintings Of The Southwest*. New York: Clarkson Potter/ Publishers, 1994.

West, Elizabeth, ed. *Santa Fe, 400 Years, 400 Questions*. Santa Fe: Sunstone Press, 2012.

Readers Guide

1. Delia and Jean-Paul sense their house is haunted. Have you ever experienced a ghostly presence? Under what circumstances might that occur?

2. On their drive to Santa Fe, the visitors are threatened by road rage. How would you respond? Do you consider the West more violent than other parts of the U.S.? Why? Why not?

3. What upset Delia most upon learning of her dead sister? Have you ever discovered a family secret had been kept from you? Explain.

4. What is Jean-Paul's reaction when Alice classifies him as "Anglo"? Why? Does his attitude change?

5. What's your opinion of Delia's idea that because New Mexico's three predominant cultures keep their identities, yet live together relatively harmoniously, they offer a solution to global conflict? Is this a transferable vision to the Middle East or Africa? Why? Why not?

6. Is cultural harmony the book's primary focus or do you perceive other more significant themes? Be specific.

7. Why is Delia startled when first encountering Jack and Jill? Did her expectation rest on a stereotype? Are stereotypes useful? Are they cruel? Why? Why not?

8. Water is a focus of *Ghost Tears*. Identify other non-human "actors." How do they impact Delia and Jean-Paul's adventures?

9. Why, after Delia's terrifying encounter with a killer, does she refrain from getting help? Is she confused? Is she in shock? Is she immobilized by fury? Explain.

10. Delia's visit to Wilma is interrupted by phone calls. How do the calls affect the plot? If someone you're with has an eye on their phone, does it alter the quality of your conversation? Explain.

CPSIA information can be obtained
at www.ICGtesting.com
Printed in the USA
FSOW02n0219140616
21487FS